GHOSTED

AT

Christmas

www.penguin.co.uk

GHOSTED

AT

Christmas

HOLLY WHITMORE

PENGUIN BOOKS

TRANSWORLD PUBLISHERS

UK | USA | Canada | Ireland | Australia
India | New Zealand | South Africa

Transworld is part of the Penguin Random House group of companies
whose addresses can be found at global.penguinrandomhouse.com.

Penguin Random House UK, One Embassy Gardens,
8 Viaduct Gardens, London SW11 7BW

penguin.co.uk

Penguin
Random House
UK

First published in Great Britain in 2025 by Penguin Books
an imprint of Transworld Publishers

001

Typeset in 11/14pt Giovanni Std by Six Red Marbles UK, Thetford, Norfolk
Printed and bound in Great Britain by Clays Ltd, Elcograf S.p.A.

The authorized representative in the EEA is Penguin Random House Ireland,
Morrison Chambers, 32 Nassau Street, Dublin D02 YH68.

A CIP catalogue record for this book is available from the British Library.

ISBN: 9781804997574

Penguin Random House is committed to a sustainable future
for our business, our readers and our planet. This book is made
from Forest Stewardship Council® certified paper.

MIX
Paper | Supporting
responsible forestry
FSC® C018179

GHOSTED

AT

Christmas

1

MIA

'This cannot be happening.' Mia has been looking up at the departures board for the last seven minutes, as if looking for longer will somehow change the reality that's staring her straight in the face. 'They can't *all* be cancelled, can they?'

A dreadlocked backpacker with cloudy blue eyes pushes his way through the crowd, and Mia creeps back to avoid being stepped on by his size thirteen feet. His colourful trousers billow vibrantly around him, the pinks and yellows in stark contrast with the more predictable grey or black wool coats of the other passengers pressing around them. The backpacker lets out an impressive groan filled with despair as he squints up at the board.

Leaning on the handle of her rolling suitcase, Mia peers hopefully at the bold yellow lettering once more. The board delivers the same unflinching result. CANCELLED. She tugs her phone out of her pocket, careful not to drop her mitten on the polished floor. Swiping through the unlock pattern, Mia's hopes are further dashed. No new messages.

Phone and mitten safely returned to her pocket, she sighs, tilting her head even further to soak up the soaring ironwork above. Normally, Mia loves the Victorian architecture of Paddington station. Being in the station was a peaceful kind of chaos – with all those people coming and going around her – that helped her feel centred.

She'd become a regular – of sorts – over the years. The coffee-shop baristas knew her by name, and she'd even had a preferred stall in the massive ladies' bathroom. (The one on the right at the end, thank you very much.) The station had truly been a refuge for Mia from her over-stimulating and disorganized life.

But today, the mood is quite different. Even with the cheerful Christmas decorations strung up between the ironwork, the whole train station is immersed in pervasive depression. Travellers all around Mia are muttering, glaring at the boards full of cancelled trains, staring at their phones with equal amounts of frustration. A TV drones on to the right of the departures board, the weather channel briskly updating what Mia already knows. Due to heavy snow, all trains out of Paddington have been cancelled throughout the weekend.

'Mum's going to be so mad,' she mutters, gripping her suitcase and working to navigate the press of the crowd. 'I hope the buses are still running.' It crosses her mind that she could probably rent a car, if the rental companies have any left. But that would cost a fortune, and her snow driving skills aren't exactly top notch. So, bus ride it is.

The dreadlocked traveller groans beside her again. 'Thought I'd treat myself to a train ride today, instead of the bus. These legs don't take kindly to being pretzelled into those little seats.'

Mia's not sure why this man is talking to her. And – oof. To each their own, of course, but the smell of weed and body odour wafting off him is . . . powerful. She gives him a polite but wan smile and moves past him, resisting the urge to pull out her phone once more. She *just* checked her messages. She is *not* desperate.

After a few minutes of navigating the overly crowded concourse, Mia reaches the ticket counter. She forces what she hopes is a friendly smile, because this is bound to be a rough day for the poor employee, and secures a ticket on the rail replacement service to Worcester, silently thanking the powers that be when the dreadlocked traveller secures his own ticket to Bath. Small miracles, she won't have to hold her breath for the entire five-hour bus ride. Having to take a bus at all is injury enough today.

Speaking of injury, her obliques scream at her as she reaches back for her suitcase. Damn Lucy and her insistence that hot yoga is the answer to the world's problems. This is what happens when you take life advice from your best friend. A buildup of lactic acid.

'Happy travels,' the backpacker chirps. Mia shakes her head, mildly annoyed by his good mood, no doubt the result of the marijuana. Sally Wadsworth, the most adventurous of her colleagues at the hospital gift shop, convinced her to try weed two years ago at a Friday night book club get-together. Though Mia had voiced her concerns about the after-effects, she was still a little disappointed to find out she was one of the unlucky ones who experienced neither the mind-numbing relaxation of marijuana, nor the gripping anxiety of others' experiences. She simply felt . . . nothing. The next morning, upon recounting her experience in the book club's group chat, Sally had declared Mia 'too emotionally guarded' to receive any benefit from the drug. Which . . . whatever. Having emotions was overrated.

Mia plops down on to a hard metal chair, wishing the forty-five minutes until her bus's departure would just magically dissipate. There's a family seated nearby, and their two young kids are sharing a set of earbuds to watch a film. Curious, Mia shifts close enough to see what they're watching, and chuckles to herself as she recognizes the opening scenes of *A Christmas Carol*. She and Charlie loved that film when they were little. Who doesn't love a little ghosty goodness at Christmastime? Mia moves back to her spot and pulls out her phone (to check the time, nothing else, she insists to herself) only to wince at how few minutes have passed. Shoving back up out of her seat, she heads to the public toilets. Might as well empty her bladder since there won't be opportunity on the bus.

Standing in front of the sink, Mia scrutinizes her freshly shaped eyebrows, partially hidden under her fringe. Her complexion, although appearing slightly sallow under the fluorescent lights, is clear and fresh, thank God. None of those annoying stress-induced pimples she used to get.

An elderly woman in a plush turtleneck takes the sink beside her. 'Love your lipstick, dearie.'

'Thanks,' Mia returns, with a genuine smile. 'If I have to suffer the bus, at least I can console myself with the knowledge that my lips will look good for the whole trip.'

The woman smiles, laugh lines appearing in her cheeks. 'That's the spirit.' She shrugs into her heavy overcoat with a sigh. 'Looks like I'll be missing my niece's ballet performance tonight. She'll be terribly disappointed. She is the sugar plum fairy, you know. The most important role in the whole production!'

'How awful,' Mia commiserates. 'Is this storm going to ruin everyone's plans?'

'I imagine so.' The woman dries her lined hands with a paper towel and tosses it into the bin. 'What plans did you have?'

Mia double-checks her cat eye in the mirror and wipes away a teensy smudge. There; perfect. 'My mum's annual neighbourhood Christmas party, which is always a good time. Although I imagine she'll be less disappointed than your niece about my lateness.'

The woman clucks her tongue in sympathy. 'It really is a shame. Nothing can be done about it, though, I suppose!'

Mia adopts her best tragic expression, and says, 'Think of the children! They shouldn't have to suffer!'

The woman laughs and pats her on the arm. 'You're funny. Keep up the good spirits. I'm sure your mum will understand. And you'll still have a lovely holiday together.'

Mia sends the woman a genuine smile and gathers her things. They exit the toilets together and the woman gives her another friendly smile before heading to the opposite corner of the station. Mia makes her way outside, where the bus is waiting by the kerb, billowing exhaust into the cold air. She hunches against the swirling snow as she loads her suitcase into the luggage hold, cursing Lucy all over again for her sore muscles. Clambering aboard, she finds an empty row of seats and tucks in beside the window. There's a smudge on the glass where a previous passenger's oily head left a mark, and she wipes it off with her sleeve, tamping down her annoyance. Hopefully the bus won't be too crowded and she'll have both seats to herself.

While she waits for the other passengers to board, she fires off a text to Lucy.

All trains cancelled. Guess who gets to sit on a mouldering bus for untold hours?

Lucy, God bless her, is absolutely addicted to her phone. Which means she immediately texts back. *You lucky duck. Try not to contract chlamydia.*

Thanks to you every muscle in my body is sore. Why did I let you talk me into that class? By the time I get off this bus, I probably won't be able to walk.

She can practically hear Lucy's cackle. *Guess you'll just have to find a gentleman who will carry your bags for you. Shouldn't be hard in Worcester. I hear they're a wholesome bunch.*

Mia rummages in her handbag for her headphones and straightens up, only to feel the telltale catch of her hair pulling on something. After the disgruntled few seconds it takes to disentangle herself, she notices the glob of chewing gum on the back of the seat in front of her.

'Ew. So gross. So, so gross.' She crosses her arms over her chest and calms her breathing. This isn't so bad. She'll enjoy the trip, she decides – *mind over matter!* It will be nice to see the snowy countryside slip by through the windows from the warmth of her seat. Some of the houses will have their Christmas lights up. It will all feel quite cosy, and she has a great playlist queued up. And who knows, this might be her one chance to relax in the quiet for a few hours before all the hustle and bustle at her parents' house.

The Robinson Christmas parties are legendary. The tradition pre-dates her parents, includes the entire neighbourhood, and often ends up in the local paper. Even after the Robinsons moved to London over a decade ago, they continued the festivities, travelling back year after year to the family home – dubbed Willowby Manor by some long-gone relative. Before they retired and moved back to the manor, Mia's mum and dad would take an extra week off work to prepare for the party, and Aunt Gertie hadn't missed one in fifty years. Even as an adult, Mia looked forward to the event all year.

Mia's phone vibrates, and her spirits soar. She can't help it. This must be James, *finally* texting her back! She fumbles to pull the device from her pocket and hurriedly unlocks it.

Mum wants to know where you are. Party starts in 45 minutes.

Damn. It's from Charlie. Her brother is eleven months

older than her, a fact that their mother loves to tell anyone and everyone. *'Irish twins those two! Got into so much trouble. I couldn't sit down for more than a minute for years!'*

Mia ignores the text and swipes back to the home screen. Tapping her finger against the side of the phone, she holds out for another ten seconds and then opens the thread with James. Her last message, sent five days ago, is still unread. The upbeat, no-pressure message taunts her.

Hey! Last night was so great. Want to get together sometime this weekend?

Lifting her chin, Mia draws in a deep breath and stows the phone back in her pocket. She will *not* check again until she reaches Worcester. She will *not* allow herself to obsess over unread messages. Second-guessing her decisions. Especially the most pertinent one that she has a sneaking suspicion has led to this sudden silence. Instead, she is determined to enjoy this trip. To *relax*. And when she gets off the bus in Worcester, James will surely have sent a text explaining his silence.

The bus is set to depart in five minutes. The seat next to Mia remains untaken, and she takes the liberty of scooting her handbag over into the empty space beside her. The driver fiddles with things in the front and the engine roars to life. Mia breathes a sigh of relief. Finally, they can be on their way.

One straggling passenger hauls herself up into the bus and makes her way down the aisle in search of a seat. Mia turns towards the window, hoping the woman will get the hint. There are still plenty of other places left.

But today is not going Mia's way, a fact she silently

laments as the woman sets herself down in the seat beside her, pointedly nudging Mia's handbag back into its proper space.

'Glory,' the woman pants. 'Thought I was 'bout to miss the bus. And wouldn't that have been a shame?'

'A crying shame,' Mia agrees. She *won't* cry. She's not the crying sort. But if she were, she imagines it would be a sort of relief to simply crumple into tears at the way life has been treating her for the last week, especially when she is trying *so* very hard to stay positive and strong and—

'I'm Trudy. What's your name, love?'

'Mia,' she offers reluctantly, hoping these introductions aren't the beginning of a five-hour-long conversation.

'Mia! One of my kittens was Mia. Loved that little tabby. She'd sit on my lap at meals and eat real human food! Have you ever heard of a cat that liked carrots?' She shakes her head and – are those tears sparking in her eyes? 'She lived to be fourteen years old, if you can imagine that.'

'Impressive,' Mia murmurs, taking note of the copious amount of cat hairs sprinkling Trudy's tweed coat.

"Course, her memory lives on.' Trudy sniffs and dabs at her eye. 'She birthed six different litters throughout her lifetime. My little black one, Mischief, is her grandson.'

'How many cats do you have?' Mia asks, almost afraid of the answer.

Trudy laughs as the driver eases the bus into the traffic. Finally, they are on their way. 'Oh, not too many. Last I checked there were eight of them.'

Mia hopes her expression is still pleasantly neutral. It would be rude to let her jaw drop. 'That's . . . a lot of cats.'

'Do you think so?' Trudy laughs again. The sound is a little bit like a wheeze. 'I like them better than my children, really. And I live in a rambling old house that's practically enormous. Plenty of room for all of us.'

'Do you own the house, then?' Mia says, looking out the window as if for an escape. The landscape is almost entirely obscured by falling snow. So much for getting lost in the view. Her nose is starting to tickle – maybe from the cat dander? Between the window and her chatty seatmate, she's starting to feel decidedly trapped.

'Yes, I bought the place in the early aughts. Been fixing it up to suit my tastes ever since. I don't suppose you want to see some pics?' She reaches a hand into her pocket, contorting so her body presses briefly against Mia, then pulls out a large phone in a faux fur case. 'I'm quite proud of the before and afters.'

'Why not,' Mia says, with as much enthusiasm as she can muster. Which isn't much. She leans towards Trudy, mindful of the cat hair covering her coat, and resigns herself to what lies in store for the next five hours.

Five hours turned into six, what with the traffic and the weather. Mia has never been so ready to disembark, and she gathers her things, mildly impressed that Trudy *still* has anecdotes about her cats to share. Mia thought she'd surely run out around the three-hour mark as Trudy had fallen silent for, by Mia's count, thirty-seven seconds. Until she'd visibly brightened and said, 'Ah! But I haven't told you about the twins' antics from last year!' and carried on for another three hours.

'Nice chatting with you,' Mia tells Trudy as they make their way down the aisle. And, to her surprise, she means it. The constant conversation has held her anxiety at bay, and she hasn't thought of James or checked her phone once.

'Oh, you too! Don't forget to look me up next time you're in Westminster!' Trudy hauls a dilapidated suitcase out of the bowels of the bus, and waves a jolly goodbye as she crosses the car park. Mia follows suit, locating her suitcase and pulling it free from the melee with a hearty yank. She staunchly ignores the answering twinge in her abs.

As her patent leather boots sink into the slush that's built up in the car park, she winces against the cold, pausing to wrap her scarf more tightly so that she can tuck her chin into its warm folds. Finding a somewhat sheltered corner, she pulls out her phone and dials her parents' landline.

It rings and rings. 'Come on . . .' Mia mutters. But there's no answer.

A call to Charlie produces the same result. Of course, the Christmas festivities are in full swing by now, and it's likely that everyone is too busy partaking in holiday cheer to answer their phones. Well, good for them. Mia imagines them all merrily ensconced out of the cold, drinking hot toddies and wearing their thick Christmas jumpers. The thought makes her inexplicably angry.

She wades over to an alarmingly scarce line of taxis, struggling to drag her rolling suitcase behind her. The taxi driver cracks his window and Mia gasps out her parents' address.

'That'll be a hundred and twenty pounds, luv.' He glances her over. 'A fair price for how bad the roads are tonight.'

A hundred and twenty pounds! That's highway robbery. She should have rented that car in London – although they probably would have gouged her even more. And chances are she would currently be stuck in a ditch, freezing to death. Mia sucks in yet another calming breath. It's not lost on her that she's been doing a lot of those today. Of course she'd prefer it if her family picked her up and she didn't have to shell out, but what choice does she have? 'Can I put my suitcase in the boot?'

The cabbie nods a yes and presses a button, and as it pops open he mentions, with just a touch of glee, 'It'll be another five pounds for the boot, luv.'

'Of course it will,' Mia mutters, dragging the suitcase around the back and hefting it into the boot. 'For five pounds you could at least help load it.' But he seems more than content to wait within the comforting warmth of his car. She trudges around to the rear door and lets herself in, batting the snow from her head and shoulders. 'All right, let's get on with it then.'

The interior of the taxi is stiflingly hot. Mia opens her jacket, fingers brushing over the knitted design of her favourite Christmas jumper, which she proudly whips out on 1 December and wears all month long. Her dedication to the jumper is arguably a testament to how much she usually loves the festive season.

But this year, with her phone still proclaiming its

demoralizing lack of notifications, the trek up here as miserable as it could be *and* the sinking realization that things have gone very, very south with James? There's nothing happy about this Christmas. The festivities she would normally take pleasure in now seem like they're rubbing these miseries in her face. As if the world is saying, *Everyone else's lives are happily working out. What about yours?*

'What about mine,' Mia grumbles. Indeed.

After a harrowing forty-minute ride over ice and snow, the cabbie dumps her at the bottom of the steep drive up to her family home. 'Drive's too slick to make it up, luv.' Mia bites her tongue, hard, and pays him his fee. She's tempted – *very* tempted – to skip the tip, since this chap has already made more than his fair share off her, but forces herself to pull out another five pounds. It is Christmas, after all. She can't avoid a tiny bit of snark, though, in her over-the-top cheery, 'Thanks for a *lovely* ride.' She receives a mere grunt in response. Not even a thanks for the tip. Just pops the boot and inclines his head as if to say 'off with you then'.

Tramping out into the snow once *again*, Mia drags her suitcase behind her as she starts up the drive. Her boots slip on the gravel over and over. At least the cabbie wasn't exaggerating. She grumbles and pants, wrestling her suitcase – *why* did she pack so many clothes? – handbag sliding down her arm, toes frozen solid. The hundred metres or so up to the house seem like an eternity, and Mia realizes three things as she struggles.

One: the sight of Willowby Manor has never felt more

comforting. The house has been in her family for generations and feels as timeless as the landscape it resides in, with its many gables and peaks outlined in warm white lights, the ancient stone reassuringly solid against the falling snow, the golden blocks of window light spilling out on to the pristine landscape. The sprawling estate holds so many lovely memories for Mia, including sledging down this steeply pitched drive as children. Tonight, despite the challenging travel, the weather and the way the world at large seems to be fighting her personally, she's never been happier to be home.

Two: never let Lucy talk her into joining a hot yoga class again. She knows that a single girl of her age has to make some effort to stay in shape, sure. But with her calves screaming at her as she lugs her suitcase up the drive, Mia decides that the world doles out torture enough on its own. There's no need to go seeking it out by subjecting her abdominals to the horrors of yoga again.

Hunching against the howling wind, Mia finishes up her mental checklist as she takes the last few steps towards the house. Sadly, her final realization is the one responsible for the tears lurking under the surface all day. As she plods around to the back door, not yet ready to face the masses of revellers inside, Mia accepts that James is never going to respond. She slept with him last Friday, and apparently that's all he wanted. A week has gone by, and his silence is crystal clear.

Three: Mia's been ghosted. At Christmas.

2

MIA

Muttering all kinds of grumpy threats towards James, the snow, the English railway system and humanity in general, Mia fumbles with the door handle. This one always sticks, and no matter how many times Mia's mum has nagged him about it, her dad's never quite got around to addressing it. In fairness, her mum's to-do lists for her dad while they're at the manor are always a mile long, and the back door is rarely used. Its location allows for a quick route to the gardener's cottage, but that's the only outbuilding on this side. Everything else is off to the south, and more readily accessed from the side patio. This little entrance is sheltered and protected, but mostly forgotten about. Which is exactly why Mia has chosen it.

She thumps her weight against the door, but it still doesn't budge. Fiddling with the latch, she tries again. It's not locked, but the weather has probably made it stick again. Pounding on the door with a mittened fist, Mia

15

slams her weight into it once more, yelling out a disgruntled, 'Come *on*!'

Mercifully, the door swings open, but between the sudden give of the door and the weight of the suitcase pushing her off balance, Mia half stumbles, half falls into the house. She's not yet able to find her bearings before someone has caught her by the upper arms, steadying her so she doesn't wipe out on the slate floor.

'Easy there!'

Her hair has fallen forward, filling her mouth, which keeps her from vocalizing the plethora of swear words that have rushed to the forefront of her mind. She's immensely grateful to whoever has kept her from sprawling across the hall floor, and she fumbles to push her hair back to thank her rescuer.

While her vision clears, she is momentarily distracted by the fact that the house smells *incredible*, a combination of gingerbread, cinnamon and citrus that's utterly mouthwatering. There's also a shocking amount of noisy conversation resounding throughout the house. Mum must have upped the guest list this year. But after a few moments taking in the sounds and smells, Mia finally realizes who her rescuer is.

Samuel Williams.

The last person she ever expected to see here.

'Mia?'

She's too stunned to answer. What is *he* doing here? *Why* is he here? Mia has the almost uncontrollable urge to look around for hidden cameras. This has to be a prank. In fact, this whole day has to have been a setup.

'Charlie said we were expecting you hours ago. Frankly, I was getting a little worried, but you know how your brother is. He said you probably just took a later train or something, and not to stress about it. But the storm looked so bad and—'

'Trains were all cancelled,' Mia mumbles, still trying to orient herself. She pulls her suitcase all the way into the house, and Sam closes the door, shutting out the howling wind.

'Cancelled? So, what did you do? Rent a car?' Sam's peering down at her as she shrugs out of her soaked coat and sheds her mittens. Mia lets them all fall to the ground in a heap. She'll deal with them later.

Squaring her shoulders, she looks up at Sam. His face is just like she remembers, only, he's grown even more attractive. How disgusting. He's maybe an inch or two taller than the last time she saw him, and she resents the fact that she has to look up to see his face, even in her heeled boots. His haircut is more stylish now, showing off the shining head of thick brown hair she used to fawn over. Brown eyes accentuated by clear-framed glasses, giving him a vibe that can only be described as 'hot academic'. Not that Mia is into that look. But Sam's eyes have always been so expressive, and right now they're brimming with concern. For . . . her? This does not affect her in any way, whatsoever.

'Here, let me grab that for you.' Sam's words come out all in a jumble, and he reaches for the handle of her rolling suitcase. 'I imagine you're in the usual room upstairs?'

He turns away, presumably headed for the back

staircase. Mia toes off her soaked boots and follows him numbly, noting how broad his back is and how his waist tapers so perfectly – probably all taut muscle under that shirt. Ugh. Her mind is spinning, careening between noting every attractive detail of the man walking in front of her, and cataloguing the unfairness of the situation.

Why is Sam *here*? Why hasn't he become even a little bit ugly over the last six years? Like not even a misplaced mole or a crooked tooth or *anything*. Did Charlie bring him? He *knows* how she feels about Sam. He was *there*, for crying out loud.

Rage bubbles up in Mia's chest. On top of all the other shit she's had to put up with today, is she supposed to just roll with the fact that Sam Williams is here, in her family home, for their Christmas party? Will everything she was looking forward to be ruined?

'You know what? No.' Mia reaches out and grabs Sam by the elbow, yanking him into the kitchen. Surprised, Sam releases the suitcase and lets her drag him along. He's wearing some fantastic cologne that tickles her nose. It's woodsy with a bit of spice, and is frankly swoonworthy, but Mia is determined not to swoon. She pulls Sam over to the expansive island, also ignoring the feel of his muscled arm beneath her grip. Does he still play tennis? Can you even *be* this in shape from playing tennis? Leaving Sam standing on one side of the island, she crosses over to the other, and immediately feels better with the space between them. This distance is safer. She will remain in control of all her faculties this way.

'So, this is clearly a prank, correct?'

Sam's face fills with confusion. 'Sorry?'

Mia didn't remember him being hard of hearing, but a lot can happen to a person in six years. She speaks slower this time, enunciating every word. 'Why-are-you-at-my-house. At. Christmas?'

'Ah. Charlie invited me.'

Mia folds her arms, giving him her best glare. 'And he did this at gunpoint? While you were tied up in a chair? Tilted over boiling lava? So, you had no choice but to say yes?'

Sam grins. 'I've always loved your sense of humour.'

'No.' Mia shakes her head. 'Don't do that.'

Sam leans on the counter, shoulders bunching attractively beneath his thin cardigan. He doesn't seem fazed at all by her barrage of questions. 'You look amazing, Mia. The last few years have been good to you.'

She nearly lets the smile produced by his compliment sneak out, but snatches it back at the last second. Schooling her expression, she stabs the counter with her finger. 'You didn't answer my question.'

The corner of Sam's mouth hitches up in that little smirk that she had swooned over for years. 'I needed to get out of the city for a bit. Work's been terribly stressful lately. I was talking to Charlie, and he invited me to join in for your mum's party. You know, change of pace, get into the festive spirit, shed some stress. So . . . I did.' He reaches up and rubs the back of his neck.

'And you didn't think for a second that I might not *want* you here?'

'I, erm . . .' He gives a foolish little smile. 'I mean, so

19

much time has gone by, Mia, I . . . I figured it was time to let bygones be bygones?'

'Bygones?' She lets out an exasperated breath. 'Who talks like that? This isn't a Regency novel, Sam. This is my life. I thought I was pretty clear the last time we spoke.'

Sorrow clouds Sam's expression. 'It was an honest mistake, Mia.'

She shakes her head again. 'An honest mistake is when you accidentally let yourself into someone else's car, because it's the same make and model. What happened between you and me? That was life-altering.'

Sam opens his mouth, and then closes it. He takes a step, as if he's going to move around the island, and Mia scrambles backwards, not bothering to look over her shoulder.

'Ow! Darling, you simply have to watch where you're going.'

'Mum!' Mia spins around to see her mum walking through the kitchen door and pulls her into a hug, heaving a sigh of relief. 'So, so sorry. I'm all clumsy from being so absolutely exhausted. Getting here was a complete *nightmare*!'

'Yes, what took you so long? We expected you hours ago. Aunt Gertie had to make the shepherd's pie, and her palate isn't what it used to be. And then poor Sam has been so worried about you, even though Charlie kept assuring him you were fine. Why didn't you take the earlier train like I told you?'

Poor *Sam*?

'Lucy did a hot yoga class . . .' Mia begins, as Sam

straightens up and runs a hand through his hair. He glances towards the doorway, like he's not sure whether to stay or to leave. Mia is very tempted to make that decision for him – he can leave now, in fact, with his cardigan and his hot muscled academic nonsense—

'And I needed your help with the cutout biscuits – something about them didn't turn out quite right. You know you have the magic touch, dear.'

'Mum, I'm here now. And I can help with whatever you need.'

'Well, now's not the time to be stuck in the kitchen. I just came in myself to refill the mulled wine. Sam, be a dear and refill this, would you?'

'Of course, Penny.' Sam crosses over to take the empty glass pitcher from her hands, giving her a wink. 'Anything for the beautiful hostess.' Penny giggles, patting her coiffed bob, held in place by a pearlescent headband. It coordinates perfectly with her sparkly black cardigan layered over a cream silk top with embroidered Christmas trees all over it. Her slacks are neatly pressed as well – Mum finds wrinkles offensive. Both the facial and the clothing varieties. She claims her smooth forehead is the result of her 'facial yoga', but Mia knows it's her supersecret Botox appointments. She hasn't dared to admit to her mother that she's been on to her for years.

'Oh, you're incorrigible. Mia, how lovely is it that Sam could be here? Charlie called me up last weekend and asked if he could come, and of course I said yes! The more the merrier, I always say! Oh, don't fill the jug too high, dear. Mr Thrumble has a touch of Parkinson's, although he swears he's as steady as ever, but I can't have my lovely Christmas linens paying the price, now, can I?'

Penny darts over to where Sam is ladling mulled wine from a saucepan into the jug, giving him second by second directions. Mia should really offer to cut up more oranges, but Penny is commandeering all of Sam's attention, and they seem to have forgotten her presence. Seeing her chance, Mia slips back towards the stairwell, hefting up her suitcase and lugging it upstairs. The case bumps along behind her on the corridor runner as she passes the first few gleaming wooden doors until she reaches her bedroom.

After manoeuvring the suitcase inside, she closes the door and leans against it. The room is comforting, hardly changed since her childhood days. Her mum had swapped out the curtains a few years ago, but the rug and the blanket on her bed are still the same. As are the shelves lined with tiny glass figurines that Mia collected over the years. Setting her toiletry case on the wooden dresser, she moves to stand in front of the shelves, tracing a tiny glass dolphin she received on her tenth birthday. Mum must do the dusting regularly – there isn't a speck to be found. Turning to face the room again, Mia tries to collect herself. She needs a fresh change of clothes, a quick brush through of her hair, something warm for her damp feet. And it wouldn't hurt to locate her missing Christmas spirit while she's at it.

Rummaging through her suitcase, she pulls out a shimmery red jumpsuit. She'd been excited to see James's reaction to this outfit – the fabric practically begs to be

touched. Mia pushes away the sharp pang of disappointment that comes with the thought of James and continues
hunting through her bag until she finds the pair of Christmas socks that she purchased on impulse last week. They
are sprinkled with reindeer, all of which have tiny red
pom-pom noses. They'll be hidden by the legs of her
jumpsuit, but work perfectly as the private pick-me-up
she needs. She'll change, freshen up and enjoy the rest of
the party. She can just pretend Sam's not there! There are
plenty of other people to talk to, neighbourhood gossip
to catch up on – ignoring him won't be that hard. And
once her stomach stops grumbling and she's downed a
cocktail or two, everything will feel better. Christmassy.

Mia shuts her bedroom door behind her and moves
towards the front staircase. Her hands are free – it was
a conscious decision to leave her phone and her disap-
pointments in her room. The landing is still devoid of
Christmas cheer as the second tree hasn't made its way
up yet. But when Mia rounds the corner, she soaks in
the familiar festive sight. Mum has the banister decked
out like always, the intricately carved wooden staircase
dripping with a thick garland that's studded with warm
white lights, taffeta bows and shining Christmas ornaments. The grandfather clock at the base of the stairs is
also draped in ribbon, poinsettias and ornament baubles, and the hall tree has been outfitted with a tartan
tote stuffed full of fresh evergreens.

But the tree in the front room, situated directly in
front of the large bay window and flanked by dramatic
silk drapes, is the real showstopper. Mia winds her way

through the press of guests, pausing to admire its lush beauty. This is the one consistent battle her dad always wins. Every year, Mum tries to convince him to buy a pre-lit, artificial tree. But Martin Robinson is a Christmas purist. Come hell or high water, the tree is fresh cut, way too big for the space and absolutely dripping in lights and ornaments. Her father spends all year deciding on a theme and this year's is – apparently – peppermints and elves.

'*Mia bella!* There you are!' Her father ducks around a cluster of neighbourhood widows and sweeps Mia up into a smothering hug. 'I was getting worried.'

'Trains were all cancelled,' Mia says into his wool cardigan. Her dad always smells exactly the same, dresses the same and loves the same. She breathes in the familiarity and safety of his embrace, and then leans back to give him a quick peck on the cheek. 'Missed you, Daddy.'

He grins down at her, peering through his dated glasses. He hasn't updated them for decades. He's gone on record saying they're 'too comfortable to replace'.

'I love your tree this year.'

Martin brightens visibly and takes Mia by the elbow, steering her to the side of the tree. 'I came across this mischievous-looking elf at a car boot sale last summer. And that got the old wheels turning, you know? But elves alone weren't enough, and there is a staggering amount of them that just look far too evil. Not Christmas appropriate. So, I added in the peppermints in all sizes. See the big ones? Can you guess what they're made out of?'

Mia scrutinizes the tree, which is absolutely dripping

in festivity. She's always loved this tradition of her dad's. The year he came up with the steam train theme is still one of her fondest childhood memories. Somehow, he'd fashioned a track that wound its way around the entire tree, and the train had darted in and out of the branches all season long. It had been absolutely magical. 'Dad, I'm not sure.' She leans into one of the giant peppermints and traces her finger gently over the surface. 'Wait, did you paint Frisbees?'

'That's my girl!' Martin scoops her up in a hug, lifting until her feet leave the floor. 'You always were my brightest child.'

'I take exception to that.' Charlie pulls Mia in for a side hug, having emerged from the crowd, his phone pressed to his ear. 'Yeah, hang on one sec, babe. Mia's finally here.'

'Important business call?' Mia teases her brother.

He gives her a playful shove. 'No, dummy. It's Molly. She couldn't make it up for the party.' He holds out the phone. 'Say hi to Molly, everyone.'

Mia and Martin crowd in close, calling out a cheery hello to Charlie's girlfriend, though it's too loud to hear if Molly responds. Charlie melts back into the throng of guests, the phone still glued to his ear. 'Mrs Wilkins brought those little mince pies, and they're some of the best I've ever had. You wouldn't believe the flavour packed into those suckers. I asked what's in there and she told me it's a secret! But I think maybe she uses cardamom . . .' Charlie's voice trails off as he turns the corner, and Mia's attention returns to the tree, laughter still bubbling out of her. Her dad squeezes her around the shoulders and then moves away to greet another guest.

She's warm from her head to her toes, and so relieved to finally be here with her family. Even the excessive noise isn't bothering her right now. This is going to be a good visit.

'Your dad really outdid himself with this tree,' a voice says at her shoulder.

And just like that, all the good feelings sour. Right. Sam is still here. And her strategy of ignoring him won't exactly work if he's following her around.

'So glad we have the approval of the tree decorating expert,' she shoots back.

Sam chuckles. He's standing so close to her she can feel the heat of his body against her back, causing her to edge away.

'I'm just saying. It's a beautiful tree.'

Mia turns to face him. 'Beautiful seems a little blasé for you. Don't you mean "spectacular"? "Grandiose"? "Magnificent"?'

Chastened, Sam clams up. Mia shoots him a sarcastic smile and moves away, suddenly thankful for the press of neighbours. She weaves her way around the clusters of people, heading for the dining table sagging beneath the enormous amount of food. Yes, food! She is starving. Grabbing one of Mum's juniper berry festive plates, she leans in to load it up. Spotting one of the mince pies Charlie was raving about, she adds that, but not before sniffing it. Hmmm, yes ... cardamom ... and maybe ginger? Next, she swipes a wedge of pomegranate and some pungent cheeses – the bluer the better, as far as she's concerned. A variety of biscuits and a couple of tiny pigs in blankets round out her selections. Mia finds a relatively quiet corner and digs in, hoping the party food will boost her spirits.

It's apparently not meant to be. The food fills her up, but every time Mia scans the room, her eyes seem to land on Sam, like he's positioning himself in her line of sight on purpose. Burning resentment churns in her chest, ruining what little happiness could be left in this terrible day. How dare he come here, and violate the sanctity of her family home? How dare he even show his face here, after what he did to her?

She moves to the bar, still ruminating. Her bitterness over the trajectory of her day is growing, and she bypasses the sugary cocktail offerings in favour of a stiff drink. She pours a finger of brandy, then adds another when Sam moves into her line of vision once more.

Her eyes stay trained on him. Maybe if she stares at him hard enough, she can burn two holes straight through him. He's bent slightly at the waist, to better hear Mrs What's-her-face, nodding, giving the chatty woman his full attention, which means Mia can both stew and stare to her heart's content. She sips the brandy, watching as Sam throws back his head and laughs at something his companion says. He's laughing? Of course he is. He preys on the innocent and unsuspecting, and apparently doesn't have an ounce of remorse about it.

And that whole ruse he put on to her family about being so worried about her? *Poor Sam was so worried about you* . . . It's so *two-faced*! He's got them all fooled, though she can't blame them, because his act really is flawless. He seems kind. And friendly. And sincere. But she knows better.

At least he's only here tonight. Like her annoying travel, this is a temporary blip in what can still be a magical Christmas.

The grandfather clock in the hall chimes cheerily, calling out half past ten. Mia downs the rest of her glass, places it in the bar sink and threads her way back through the crowd. The party will start wrapping up soon. Everyone will leave, including Sam. Mia will get a good night's sleep and come down in the morning and help with the cleanup. Offer to do some cooking – and perhaps some holiday baking too. And then, finally, she'll be able to start enjoying her Christmas holiday.

3

MIA

A tiny beam of sunlight has slipped through the clouds, as well as the sheer curtains at the window. The beam lands on Mia's face, bathing her in light. This isn't the worst way to wake up. Her room smells faintly of the furniture polish Penny has preferred for the last twenty years, the duvet is warm and soft against her skin, and despite the harrowing events of the day before, Mia is grateful to finally feel rested and refreshed as she sits up.

Mia stretches, feeling the workout she gave her calves through all that snow yesterday along with the residual yoga after-effects. They're not too sore, though, just a little tight. A hot shower should melt away those aches and pains. A shower, some food, conversation with her family, and she'll be set to rights. She needs to find Aunt Gertie too – there were so many people last night that Mia never crossed paths with her.

She slides from the bed, curling her toes into the thick rose rug at her bedside and gathering her hair up into a messy topknot. She was too tired to do anything with her hair last night, and now several long strands are plastered to the side of her cheek. Was she *drooling* overnight? She shudders slightly. Hopefully it's just a bit damp upstairs.

Mia's stomach lets out an impressive growl, and she amends her plan. Food, then shower and a cute outfit, along with time with her family. But food has become imperative. Shoving her feet into her favourite fuzzy slippers – the ones that look like oversized plushy feet stuffed into tiny flip-flops – she pads over to the dresser.

The wooden dresser, inherited from her grandmother, glows beautifully. Mia has always loved the curved drawers, and the elegantly swooping arms on top that hold the mirror in place. When she was gifted the piece as a child, she'd felt so grown-up. She'd gently opened each and every drawer, and her delight had increased when she'd discovered the fabric-covered jewellery box in the top left drawer.

Grandma Joan had given her several beautiful pieces – all costume jewellery, of course, but Mia had loved the mixture of corals and daffodil yellow beads and heavy bangle bracelets. Her absolute favourite were the earrings Gran had included. Easing open the drawer, Mia lifts the padded case out on to the top surface of the dresser. The brass clasp on the box has tarnished a little over the years, but it swings open smoothly. Mia's gaze falls to the lone earring nestled in the silk compartment.

The earrings had been a present from her Grandpa Morris to her grandmother on their honeymoon in Iceland. Grandma Joan was a gifted storyteller and had told

Mia about the trip countless times, painting pictures of reindeer, volcanic pools and the majesty of the aurora borealis with her words. And every story had ended with Gran opening up the expansive jewellery box. She'd gently lift out the gorgeous set of earrings, her wrinkled cheeks stretching into a smile as she showed Mia.

The gold screw back held a large amber stone that seemed to shine from within, set alongside beautifully cut emeralds and sapphires that evoked the northern lights. The artisan had crafted delicate strands of twisted gold that fanned out from the expertly set gems, and Mia had always thought they were the most beautifully made pieces she'd ever seen. Grandma Joan wore them for holidays and special days like her wedding anniversary, and after Grandpa Morris had passed away, she'd worn them even more often.

Mia had been incredibly touched when Grandma Joan had given the earrings to her on her sixteenth birthday. They were so sentimental, and she'd always taken great care with them. Tracing a finger over the lone earring, a twinge of sadness settled over her. She'd been devastated when one of the earrings had gone missing almost ten years ago. For days, she'd searched high and low, retracing her steps, wracking her brain trying to imagine where the piece might have disappeared to. And in the years since, she'd spent an inordinate amount of time rifling through piles of antique jewellery at flea markets and antique shops, all in the hope of discovering a match for the lonely earring.

Closing the lid, Mia pushes away the sadness that

comes from thinking about the lost earring. She can always keep looking for a replacement. Plus, she enjoys her typical Sunday morning routine of rooting through musty stalls, chatting with the vendors and searching for treasure. In fact, her ridiculous slippers had been a flea market find.

Flipping open her toiletry case, Mia smooths on some face cream, pushing away the stiff hair that is still glued to her cheek. Then she fishes out a pair of under-eye patches purported to be made with real gold, patting them gently in place. Lucy proclaimed them to be a total scam, but Mia swears they are helping with her perpetual dark circles. She gazes at herself in the mirror, amused at the picture she strikes. Weird gold blobby half-moons stuck to the skin under her eyes. Crusty hair sticking out to the side, fringe looking positively possessed. Faded Christmas pyjamas and fluffy slippers. Oh well. The only ones who will see her like this are her family. It's not like she is trying to impress anyone. A silver lining, perhaps, to the dark fact that James isn't going to be texting her any time soon. Mia quietly lets herself out of her room and creeps down the stairs into the kitchen.

She is craving comfort food, so she rummages in the fridge for a bit of inspiration until she locates cheese, eggs and potatoes. She rinses and chops the potatoes into cubes, then throws them on to an oiled tray. She gives them a liberal coating of salt, pepper and the smoked paprika she finds in Penny's spice cabinet, then pops the tray into the oven before setting a timer and whisking the eggs. Her mouth is already watering, and she can feel her nerves settling down. This trip may not have started out as satisfyingly as she'd hoped, but things are looking up. Perhaps after this meal, and a nice long shower, Mia can finagle a ride into town. She can buy a coffee and drown out her troubles with a little retail therapy.

'Ah, there you are. Morning, dearie.' Aunt Gertie's quavering voice interrupts Mia's daydream.

Mia pauses in her preparations to give her great-aunt a hug. 'Good morning. I missed you last night!'

'Ah.' Aunt Gertie waves a gnarled hand decked out in several rings. She's wearing loads of jewellery like always, which makes a gentle tinkle as she totters along. Aunt Gertie is nearly a hundred years old, and still has a style that Mia envies. Today her bony frame is swathed in a brightly coloured silky kaftan. 'I was tired, so I nicked a plate of food and went to my room right after dark. Your mother wore me out with all her stressing about the party preparations.'

'Aww. You're always the life of the party. We missed you.'

'Pfft. No need to lie, darling. I'm sure no one else even noticed I was gone.'

Aunt Gertie lives in a small flat in town, though Mia has a feeling that she would prefer to still live out her days here at the manor. Her aunt had been convinced by Mia's parents to move closer into town where friends could keep an eye on her.

'You want some coffee?' Mia hides her smile as she knows what her aunt's response will be.

Aunt Gertie makes a disgusted sound. 'Not even in the slightest. I don't know how you tolerate that horribleness.

I'll just make myself some tea to drink in the sunroom.' She fills the kettle and sets out her teacup and saucer – the same one she's used for as long as Mia can remember. She pops a teabag into the cup.

Mia's phone lights up with a message from Lucy, and Aunt Gertie grunts disapprovingly.

'Wretched things, these mobile phones. Make you accessible to everyone, everywhere, all day long. A person can barely get any peace and quiet any more. You know, when I went on safari in Africa, I was gone for three months. Never made a single phone call, and didn't even send a letter home. Best three months of my life.' She pours the hot water into her cup, her hands shaking slightly. Mia sets aside her whisk and leans against the counter. She loves Aunt Gertie's stories. 'I had a torrid affair with our guide while I was there. He was a beautiful man, taller than the doorways and thighs like tree trunks. The positions he could hold . . . Oh, he was gorgeous. I wish you could have seen him, dearie. I nearly stayed in Kenya for him.' She stirs in a spoonful of sugar and takes a sip. 'Mmm, perfect. But he still visits me in my dreams.' She grins up at Mia. 'Best part, he hasn't aged a day!' And with that, Aunt Gertie totters from the room, humming softly to herself.

Mia returns to her cooking, chuckling over yet another of Aunt Gertie's outrageous stories. She's bent over the counter, grating the cheese while humming a Christmas carol, when someone clears their throat behind her.

'Coffee is made,' she says without turning around. 'Don't mind me in the way.' She could move, of course, but she wasn't the one who chose to place the coffee maker directly by the hob.

Whoever's joined her in the kitchen leans in behind her to grab the coffee carafe, and she's surrounded by the scent of woodsy cinnamon and spice. She breathes in appreciatively, then frowns. That's not her dad's scent, and Charlie never wears cologne. Until now, apparently. Maybe it was a gift from the new girlfriend.

'Sleep OK?' she asks, never taking her eyes from the cheese in front of her.

'Well enough,' comes the answer. The voice makes her freeze.

No. *It can't be* . . .

She sets the block of cheese down and spins to face the voice's owner.

Sam stands just inches away from her, transferring steaming coffee into a heavy-bottomed mug. He finishes his pour and glances up at her, a sleepy smile creeping over his face. Up close, she can see the rich colour of his eyes more clearly. 'Morning, Mia.'

She has lost the power of speech. Her mind races along, struggling to process that Sam Williams is once again standing in her kitchen. The sunlight is pouring through the windows at the back of the breakfast nook, the nearly cooked potatoes are filling the room with their earthy fragrance and Mia's tongue is stuck to the roof of her mouth.

Damn it. Her one constant, her true companion, is her razor-sharp wit. Why is it deserting her now? Perhaps because Sam *flipping* Williams is standing mere inches

35

away from her, smelling like an enchanted forest. His feet are bare, peeking out from beneath royal blue pyjama bottoms. Mia swallows a groan. She's a sucker for a man in pyjama bottoms. And, there's a little more exposed skin at his throat, where his dressing gown gapes slightly open. Her eyes want to stay on that smooth vee of skin for days. Sam shoots her a more alert smile and then tilts his head back to down a gulp of black coffee.

Mia is not ogling. She is simply watching the way his throat works as he swallows. Sam has great skin. Barely a pore in sight. Her fingers could simply glide across that smooth expanse, exploring to their hearts' content. Mia is horrified at the effort it takes to restrain that impulse.

He shouldn't be here. She hates him, will continue to hate him until her dying breath. It's the least he deserves. But she's not blind. And immunity to Sam's charms has never been a strength of hers.

And if he's going to invade the sacred space of her family home at Christmas – before she's even *eaten* – then the man deserves to be objectified. He's pretty. Too pretty. And while that may have caused her heartache years ago, it's old news. Today's Mia is strong. Confident. In control of her future. Comforted by her ability to successfully relegate Sam to a simple sex symbol, Mia turns back to her pile of cheese and scoops it into the waiting bowl, sneaking a few pinches into her mouth. 'Care to fill me in on why you are still here, Sam?' She pauses for effect. 'A bit too much of Mum's mulled wine, perhaps, to drive home?'

Mia's pleased by how normal and at ease she sounds.

Well done, she thinks to herself as she waits for Sam to answer. After all, there must be a reasonable explanation for his presence, and drinking too much is an obvious choice. Or the snowstorm – yes, that's it! The storm delayed his departure and he'll be on his way first thing this morning, once he drinks his obligatory coffee. Of *course* he can take a moment to have his coffee before he gets on his way – Mia isn't a *monster*. She breathes a sigh of relief as she pours the eggs into the heated pan. They sizzle merrily, and her heart rate returns to normal.

'Your brother invited me to stay until Boxing Day,' Sam replies. His voice has just the faintest touch of gravel in it, which definitely does *not* make her stomach clench in appreciation, but does make her take a second longer to process Sam's words.

'Sorry, Charlie did *what*?'

Sam shoots her a rueful look, as if he was expecting this kind of response. 'I had hoped he would talk to you about it, but I guess that was wishful thinking. Charlie invited me to spend the week with you all. So, I wouldn't be alone for Christmas.'

'The party,' Mia spouts out. 'You said last night that he invited you to Mum's party—'

Sam winces. 'And the rest of the week. Yeah, I suppose I didn't have a chance to get to that part.'

Mia leans against the stove for moral support. 'You have your own family, Sam.'

'True,' he responds, before downing another gulp of coffee. 'But they decided to go on a cruise for two weeks.

A whole Mediterranean adventure kind of thing. And I couldn't get the time off, so I wasn't able to go with them.'

'You could have joined in part way,' Mia says pointedly. She stabs at the air with her spatula for emphasis. 'Don't cruises let people off at ports? Couldn't you have boarded, in, I don't know . . . Venice? Barcelona? Athens?' She clamps her lips tight before she reels off a dozen other Mediterranean cities.

Sam smiles sadly. It's that crooked one and it tugs at her heart. 'That's what my sister said. And I could have, I guess. But I suppose the idea of joining halfway felt a little pathetic, somehow? So, I told her I had my own plans. And I'd see them for New Year.' He gives a sheepish shrug. 'If I'm honest, I guess I was hurt that they made a plan for Christmas without asking whether I could make it. So, I opted out entirely.'

Mia is appalled by a sudden and unwanted stab of empathy.

She does *not* feel bad for him. Fine, maybe she does. A little. How awful would it be if her family left her high and dry, especially during *Christmas*? She shoves away the twinge of sympathy and tries to focus.

Sam sets the mug down on the counter and leans one hip against the edge. 'Plus, I thought maybe we could work through some—'

The timer goes off, interrupting whatever he was going to say. Mia has a pretty good suspicion, though, and her heart starts pounding as she leans over to pull the potatoes from the oven. She does *not* want to go there. The past is just that, the past. She will focus on the present, and she will be her best self. Today's Mia can even be impressively polite. 'Grab two plates, will you?'

The plates materialize next to her, and she spoons steaming potatoes on to each one. Then she adds cheesy eggs and a quick sprinkle of parsley. Turning around, she presents the dish to Sam, who's suddenly looking ravenous.

He takes the offered plate, gratitude brimming in his expressive eyes. Mia shakes her head sternly as she heads towards the breakfast nook. 'Don't get any ideas. Your family ditched you for Christmas, which is a travesty. But you and me – this doesn't change anything.'

Sam pads after her, taking the seat across from her. The sunlight highlights the stubble dusted across his firm jaw, and Mia scowls down at her plate. She. Is. Immune. They sit in relatively comfortable silence while they eat. Once his plate is clear, Sam utters a satisfied groan and leans back, appreciation lighting his gaze. 'Those are some spectacular slippers,' he comments. He reaches into the fruit bowl in the middle of the table and pulls out a banana, peeling it deftly.

Mia wiggles the foot crossed over her knee. 'Aren't they? They're one of my latest finds. I had a heck of a time deciding between these and the T. rex ones.'

'Why not both?' Sam asks around a mouthful of banana, which makes her laugh.

'I nearly did,' she admits. 'But my flat is small, and I have to save room for the next treasure, you know?'

He nods enthusiastically and Mia feels an unexpected sense of camaraderie. This feels nice, like perhaps having

Sam here all week won't be the worst thing in the world. After all, their history happened six years ago. Mia was an entirely different person then. She's grown. Matured. Definitely developed more of a compassionate side. Maybe it *is* time to let things go. But then Sam's eyes flick up to her face, and he seems to cover a grin before asking, 'And, ah, the commas under your eyes? Are those also found treasures?'

Mortified, Mia's hands fly up to her face. She's completely forgotten about the under-eye patches. Her hand brushes the crunchy strands of hair, and she's surprised that her face doesn't burst into literal flames. Faded jammies, crazy hair, her face in a state. Here she's been, ogling Sam, feeding him and *relaxing*, and all the while she's a hot mess. Nothing *here* to ogle. Embarrassment reigns, a feeling that is horrifyingly familiar in Sam's presence.

With a scoff, Mia shoves to her feet. 'Glad to have been a source of amusement once again. You must really be enjoying this.'

'Mia, wait.'

But she doesn't wait. Instead, she flees up to the sanctuary of her room, where she scoops up a change of clothes and takes refuge in the bathroom. As she steps under the scalding spray of the shower, she mutters curses against Sam Williams. And Charlie, while she's at it. Might as well curse James too. And actually? Mia decides to just add the entire male gender to the list.

4

MIA

Freshly showered, Mia shuts off the taps and fumbles for a dry towel. She somehow managed to get shampoo in her eye, and now she's fumbling through everything half blind. Pushing back the shower curtain, Mia steps over the edge of the clawfoot tub. It's a manoeuvre she's navigated hundreds of times, and yet she still wobbles as she sets one bare foot down on the tiled floor. The Robinson family home has loads of charm and history, but Mia is briefly homesick for the modern flat she shares with Lucy with its walk-in shower and temperature regulator. She hasn't missed doing this awkward dance every time she needs to shower.

Wrapping the towel under her arms, Mia wipes the fogged-over mirror and squints at her reflection. The gold-infused eye patches did their job at least – her dark circles have been erased. Mia quickly brushes her teeth and runs another towel through her hair. The rest of her toilette will happen in her room. Old habits die hard, and Mia is eternally aware of the fact that there is only one bath-room on this floor. Six bedrooms, one bathroom. Leave it to her ancestors to plan poorly for the future plumbing requirements of this house.

The ceramic doorknob is cool on her palm as she twists the door open. Her eye smarts again, and she squints her eyelids shut tight, trying to blink away the pain. She could navigate this corridor in her sleep, but she doesn't account for the unexpected obstacle in her way.

'Ow! What the—?' Mia stumbles backwards.

'Mia! Aaggh!!'

Mia pries her eyes open enough to see her brother hop-ping indignantly on one foot, rubbing his shoulder with one arm, his phone tucked between his cheek and the other shoulder. Is he hurt? Serves the traitor right.

'Let me call you back,' Charlie mutters. He stuffs the phone into his trouser pocket and shakes his head. 'Ouch. That's gonna bruise. Mia, why don't you watch where you're going?'

'I hope you do bruise,' Mia hisses, clutching her towel tighter. 'I hope it bruises enough that it hurts every time you breathe.'

Charlie's eyes widen comically. 'O ... K. Is there a reason for all this misdirected anger? Or am I supposed to just roll with it?'

'How could you?' Mia snaps, folding her arms across her chest.

Charlie's expression morphs from pained to bewil-dered. 'I'm gonna need more to go on here. How could I ... occupy space on the landing?'

Mia smacks him on the arm. 'No, idiot. How could you invite *him*? *Here?*'

At first, he simply looks bewildered. But Mia sees the exact moment he catches on. He takes on an annoyingly kind, paternalistic expression that she'd like to punch off his face.

'Mia Tia, come on,' he says, as if he can just jolly her right along. Also, he knows *exactly* how much she despises that nickname. 'We're all grown-ups here. It's not that big a deal.'

His brush-off hurts more than she expected. 'Charlie. You were there. I was humiliated!'

'It's been years! Don't you think it's been long enough for you to—'

'I could be decaying in my grave and it still wouldn't be long enough.'

Her brother rolls his eyes. 'Grow up, Mia.'

Heat fills her face. 'Let me hear you say that *one more time*—'

'Hey, Charlie, your mum said to ask you where the spare toothbrushes are?' Sam's rich voice travels down the corridor and Mia freezes mid-sentence. 'I seem to have forgotten mine.'

And it's all too much. Sam, intruding in her home. Charlie, being so obtuse, making it seem like she should just get *past* it? As if *she's* the problem?

She shoves past Charlie, hurrying down the corridor just short of a gallop. She will not run into Sam wearing nothing but a towel. Somehow, at some point, Mia will find a way to exact her revenge, but this is not that moment. Bursting into her room, she slams the door behind her and hurriedly dresses in her light pink 'Merry Everything' sweatshirt and a clean pair of jeans. She shoves her feet into battered duck boots and throws her hair up into a ponytail.

After determining the coast is clear, Mia slips down the back stairs and lets herself out into the garden. She just needs to clear her head. Maybe she'll call Lucy to have a nice little bitch session. She'll vent about James, and the trip out here, and the unwanted house guest. Once she's paced the length of the property and cried about it all to Lucy, she'll feel better.

Rounding the house, Mia is hit with an icy blast of wind. The resulting shiver goes all the way down to her bones. It's one of those horrible days where the snow feels like it's pelting tiny arrows at her skin. Mia hunches inward, desperate to find shelter. Given the awful outdoor conditions, and the fact that the house is out of the running, she has no choice but to head for the gardener's cottage at the back of the property.

Penny has been hounding Martin for years to finish fixing up the cottage so they can rent it out as a holiday house. Penny has waxed eloquent on more than one occasion that the untold masses of London would give their left arm for a weekend in this part of the country. As Mia approaches, she grudgingly admits her mum might be right. The cottage practically oozes country appeal and the promise of refuge. Her eye catches on the charmingly uneven roofline as she reaches the sage green door with the antique brass knob, the colour perfectly coordinated with the warm tones of the stone. The cottage seems right at home within the landscape, especially covered in snow. Mia rummages in the flowerpots at the base of the dormant climbing rose until she locates the spare key.

Letting herself inside, she stomps the snow from her boots. After toeing them off, she sighs appreciatively at the warmth inside the little cottage. The crackle of a fire beckons her through the whitewashed kitchen, with its collection of pottery teapots in the deep windowsills and the mismatched chairs set around the rough-hewn table. She pads across pleasingly clean slate floors, and ducks through the low doorway into the front room.

This room has always been a favourite. There's a thick, faded rug covering most of the wide floorboards. An inglenook is carved from the same stone as the exterior walls, its brown tones homey and comforting. Inside, a wood stove burns merrily, radiating heat throughout the room. Wood is stacked all around the stove, with smaller kindling tucked at the ready just to the side. The mismatched furniture screams comfort. Mia knows from experience how perfect the sofa is for a long reading session, but she settles on the wingback that faces the window to call Lucy. She'll have a great view but she won't have to freeze her arse off. Pulling her phone from her pocket, Mia presses the call button, taking the last two steps towards the chair. As she moves around to the front of the chair, her phone beeps in her ear. Pulling it away from her face, she grimaces as the call fails to go through.

'Ugh. Well, isn't that just the bitter icing on the cake of disappointment. Of course I can't make the call. Of course!' She flops down into the chair with exaggerated motions. 'Because with my luck – AGGHH!'

Heart pounding, Mia belatedly registers the fact that another human is occupying the cottage. And this chair, more specifically. She's just landed in the lap of a man who is rather bony and pointy. An argyle sweater-wearing man who looks just as surprised to see her as she is him. Mia shoots up out of his lap in surprise.

'What the hell?'

'You can see me?'

'Well, of course, I'm not blind!'

'No, I can see that, but . . . you can *see me*?'

'I mean, I really hope I am not hallucinating. Wouldn't that be the perfect development in this already abysmal weekend?'

It occurs to Mia that they could continue this way for quite some time. After all, the man's presence is entirely unexpected, but then again, Mia realizes she probably shouldn't have assumed she was alone once she saw the fire roaring in the hearth. Is this a friend of the family? Yet another unexpected guest? Or has her mother already begun to rent the cottage out?

'Sorry, let me try this again,' says Mia. 'Who are you?'

The cottage guest now looks completely at a loss for words. He pushes to his feet, all tall and lean, more gangly limbs than svelte runner. His face has the not-unpleasant lines of someone in their late thirties and there's a smattering of early grey mixed through his dirty brown hair.

Mia is no hairdresser, but she suspects the man has low-lights added to the mix as well, and the overall effect is quite dashing.

'Sorry I sat on you,' she apologizes. 'I just didn't expect anyone to be in here. Mum said the cottage wasn't ready for guests yet.'

The man smooths down his multicoloured sweater and combs his hair back from his eyes. They are deep set, but brightened by the endearingly confused expression he's currently wearing. 'Yes, well, this is all a bit of a shock, isn't it?' His voice is raspy, as if it's been unused for quite some time.

Mia sticks out her hand. 'I'm Mia Robinson. Sorry to have intruded on your quiet morning.'

The man huffs out a laugh. 'That's quite a lot of sorrys. And, I have to confess it's been a little longer than a morning?' The man seems to be searching for words, but Mia has the distinct impression that he's not as surprised to see her as she is him. 'So, you must be – oh, apologies. I'm John.' He extends his hand, the fingers long and graceful, a small gold ring on his little finger. They exchange a firm handshake, and then John slides his hand into the pocket of his perfectly pressed and pleated trousers. 'I'm the gardener for this estate.'

Mia frowns. 'Mum didn't say anything about hiring a gardener.'

John's expression is wry. 'Yes, well, truth be told, I was hired about forty years ago.'

No way can this be true. The mental maths of his age doesn't work, for one. Furthermore, she would have noticed when she was a little girl if someone lived in the cottage . . .

Mia can feel her eyebrows creeping up her forehead. A million sarcastic responses leap to her tongue, but she manages to hold them back. For a moment, at least, and she settles on, 'What does a gardener do during the winter?'

John laughs. The sound is pleasant and rich, but not deeply masculine like Sam's. No, *why* is she thinking of Sam again? She shoves him back out of her mind. 'Well, to be honest, I haven't done any work for the last three decades or so.'

'Come again?'

'Well, you see, there was a bit of an accident here on the property and I was quite injured—'

Mia rolls her eyes. 'If you're planning to sue my parents, I think the statute of limitations ran out after the first two decades.'

'Oh dear,' he says, his forehead wrinkling. 'I would never—'

'Do you rent this place, then? Or—'

'No, no – you see – well, it's rather a long story, but—'

As he fumbles through his words, now Mia sees what she's dealing with – an opportunist. A mooch, who's apparently been taking advantage of her family for years. How has she never heard of him before? With the exception of her Botox appointments, her mother can't keep things private to save her life – surely she would have vented to Mia at some point about their long-lingering 'gardener'? Clearly the man is lying, though shame on him for thinking he can get away with it.

'Your skin is surprisingly good for someone so old,' she says, not bothering to keep the accusatory tone from her voice. Did he get Botox with her mother? Secret Botox buddies?

John's hand instinctively goes to his face and he seems inordinately pleased by this compliment. '. . . thank you?'

'So, you stay here for free,' says Mia, determined to get to the bottom of this. 'And my parents haven't asked you to leave?'

'I don't cause any trouble,' he says defensively. 'And, well . . . you see, my injury – it—' He scratches his head, an expression of distress again wrinkling his brow, but Mia will not be softened by his act. She sees no evidence of any injury in the way he's moving, and if he thinks he can just stay here for ever, unchallenged, because her parents are too good-hearted to confront him, he's got another thing coming. She gestures towards the door. 'Listen, erm . . . *John*.' If that was even his name. 'I don't mean to be rude' – she did – 'but you might want to just move along. You know, find your own place to live. Basically, get a life.'

She's not sure what she was expecting, but it certainly isn't the dejected way that John flops back down into the wingback.

'Get a life?' He lets out a small, bitter laugh. 'I would if I could, believe me! In fact, there's nothing I'd like more than to "move along".' His long fingers make air quotes. 'Alas, I am stuck here. For ever, it would seem.' John turns to face Mia more fully. 'You see, my dear, I am a ghost.'

49

5

JOHN

It's hard not to wince when one has just announced one's status as a ghost. John barely reins in the subconscious body movement. Instead, he fidgets a coin between two fingers inside his pocket. Lately he's been practising rolling it across his knuckles, a silly, useless trick, but it's not like he's short on time these days. He could probably master a few card tricks too, if he worked at it enough.

Not that there would be anyone to perform the card tricks for.

'Really funny, mister,' Mia scowls at him. 'I don't believe in ghosts.'

'Well, believe it or not, that is, in fact, what I am.'

'Prove it.'

Something about her tone galls him. The unbridled audacity to put the onus on him to prove he's a ghost? After all this time, someone can see him, and they don't believe he's real? The nerve.

'Listen, Miss Robinson. I've been peacefully tucked

away in this cottage, bothering no one, for thirty years. I don't make the lights flicker; I don't howl in the corridors. To the best of my knowledge, no one has seen me floating across the grounds in the dead of night. I'm more of a morning person, truth be told.'

'If you were actually a ghost, one of us would have run into you before now. There would be stories of the manor being haunted. I think you're just a squatter. In fact, I'm going to call the police.'

This makes John laugh. He can only imagine – the police responding to the call, barging in here and seeing Mia talking to an empty room. Maybe they'd humour her for a while, though, young and pretty as she is. She wears her hair in a stylish cut, with a fringe that just brushes her eyebrows and draws attention to her large, expressive brown eyes. She's got great curves too, and John knows – well, *knew* – plenty of guys who would have fallen all over themselves to get her number. Not him, of course, girls have never really caught his eye, but that's beside the point.

'Why are you laughing? I swear, I'll call them right now,' Mia reaffirms, visibly frustrated by how unbothered John is by her threats.

'Go right ahead and call the police, darling. I imagine you'll encounter stranger folks than I once they haul you away to the looney bin.'

'The looney bin? No one says that any more. It's offensive to people with mental health struggles.' Mia grimaces, then strides angrily across the room to stare at the fire. 'If you're a ghost, how did you lay this fire?'

John runs a hand through his hair. He's inordinately

pleased to still have his thick head of hair. There are some benefits to passing away so young, and his body keeping the appearance of his thirty-six-year-old self is one of them. 'I'm no expert on ghost lore, but there are apparently different kinds of ghosts. Some cannot interact with the physical world any more. Some display unusual powers. Some possess telekinesis.' He shrugs.

Mia half turns and shoots him a glare. 'So, make that table float then.'

John rolls his eyes. 'I'm not that kind of ghost, I'm afraid. How about, instead, I do something a little less clichéd. See that wireless speaker the builders left in here after the renovations?'

Mia's gaze follows his finger to the black dot on the nearby table. It chirps to life, and streams of warm Christmas music flow from the surface.

Mia shakes her head. 'Could be voice activated.'

'But I didn't actually say—' John cuts himself off with a sigh, realising there's no use arguing the point. Instead, he places his palm on the plaster wall, sending a surge through to the electrical cables. The overhead lights flicker ominously, which makes Mia crack a smile.

'Now that's just faulty old wiring,' she says.

There's nothing to it. He's going to have to man up and prove it in the most undeniable way. John grits his teeth and faces Mia fully. 'Well, you've left me no choice. But this better convince you, doubting Thomasina. Because, I assure you, it is my least favourite thing to do. And if I throw up, it will be your fault.' With that, he takes a deep breath, and steps through the closed bay window into the outdoors. The wind tugs at his sweater, and he forces himself to stand still long enough for a light dusting of snowflakes to gather on his shoulders. Then he sucks in another breath and plunges back inside.

Mia gapes at him. John shudders, stamping his feet clean of the snow clinging to his brown leather boots. He presses a hand to his middle and groans. 'I'll have indigestion for the rest of the day, so I hope that's finally convinced you. Walking through walls always rearranges my insides in the most unpleasant way. The only thing worse than that is passing through a living human.'

Her mouth is still hanging open. He brushes the snow-flakes from his shoulders and shakes his head like a dog, then carefully arranges his hair back into place. 'Well, I'm glad that's settled. So, Mia Robinson. Why don't you tell me what terrible events drove you down here to my door-step? You seemed rather at the end of your rope when you arrived at the manor last night.'

Mia twists her fingers in the hem of her sweatshirt. She looks to the spot outside that John had just occupied, and then back to where he stands in front of her. She seems to debate for another few seconds and then shrugs. 'Yeah, it was kind of a miserable day. Well, week, actually. I was trying to call my friend Lucy out here, but there's no signal, because this whole place is positively medieval. So, who else am I going to talk to? Mum?' Mia makes a buzzer sound. 'Fat chance of that. She'll just tell me how wonderful *Sam* is. Charlie is blissfully unaware of anything twenty-three hours a day, and my dad, I love him to death, but he's probably absorbed in the latest predictions about the cricket season. And I can't *believe* James hasn't responded, but what can you expect from a guy who apparently was only after one thing?' She shakes her head and straightens her shoulders. 'You know what? It doesn't matter. It's fine. I'm fine.'

John brushes the last of the snowflakes off his sweater and gestures towards the low-slung sofa that practically screams cosy. 'Yeah, you definitely seem fine.'

'Good. Because I totally am.'

John laughs again, and Mia flops down beside him. 'I'm not fine. I'm furious. For starters, I spent all week perfecting the window display in the hospital gift shop I work in, just for some little demon – maybe seven, eight years old, old enough to behave himself, you know? – to fly into the shop and destroy the whole thing. It literally took me *hours* to fix.

'And my mum has been pestering me to come up all week, but it's like, I have a life, you know? I deserve some quiet and relaxation in my own home. Plus, Charlie's here, and his girlfriend is coming up at some point and me and my brother get along well enough, but not when we live in the same house, if you know what I mean. And then, *then!* Charlie has the unmitigated gall to invite Sam Williams to spend the week up here.'

'Which is a bad thing, evidently,' John says, loving the play by play he's getting from Mia. Dear heavens, how he's missed this – interaction, conversation! All of it! He could do this for hours. Days. Years! Of course, he mustn't act *too* enthusiastic. He doesn't want to scare Mia off.

'The worst. I haven't even spoken with Sam since – well,

it doesn't matter. I certainly haven't thought about him in years. But Charlie knows that the *last* person I would want to spend Christmas with is Sam, and he invited him anyway! I mean, that's a betrayal of the highest order.

'I could have been rummaging through the West Abbey flea market today. It's one of the best fleas of the year, but I can never go, because Mum always wants me up here *"with the family"*. And you're probably like, hey, Mia, aren't you an adult? Which I totally am, but some fights are not worth it. Although I'm giving serious consideration to having it out with James.'

John leans back against the corduroy scatter cushions and lifts one hand. 'All right. Let me see if I've got this.' He ticks off his fingers one by one. 'You had a shit week at work, which is understandable. No one wants to be working the week before Christmas. The whole week should be a national holiday.' Mia smiles but doesn't interrupt. 'Your mum smothers you, which you find annoying. Also understandable, although I'm sure it comes from a good place. I'm guessing your dad is lovely but never crosses your mum, which you also find annoying. You braved the great snowy apocalypse and your brother Charlie brought your nemesis here for the week. Have I covered it all?'

Mia's smile nearly turns into a chuckle. 'Almost. You missed the flea market, and James ghosting me.'

'I'm sorry, he did what?'

Mia raises an eyebrow. 'He ghosted me? Oh, sorry, I forgot you won't understand modern dating since you've *been* a ghost for the last thirty years.' Her tone is sarcastic enough that John debates if he should be taking offence, but he doesn't want to ruffle her feathers any further and risk her leaving. 'Ghosting is what you say when someone stops communicating with you with no explanation. It's very rude.'

'Well, of course it is, but why call that *ghosting*?' John looks marginally horrified.

Mia's expression becomes even more condescending. 'So, as an *actual ghost*, you have to understand the term, right? Surely there are people you suddenly stopped communicating with because you were . . .' She trails off, gesturing in John's general direction.

'Yes, but *I* didn't have any choice in the matter,' John objects. 'This James person just up and decided not to talk to you any more, without giving any sort of explanation as to why.'

'Oh, I know why,' Mia grinds out. 'I just don't want to admit it. I cooked the man the best meal of his life and then afterwards . . . well, let's just say he didn't leave disappointed that night.' Mia's words are belligerent, but there's a slight vulnerability shining in her eyes.

John slowly nods. 'Ah. So, you finally slept with your boyfriend after—'

'Two months.'

'Two months. Wow, really? Well done. That's some impressively delayed self-gratification. And now he's not returning your calls.'

'My texts. People text now, John. Calls are exclusively to make doctor's appointments.'

'Right, right, of course I've seen everyone with their

pocket phones . . . But the point is, you're wondering why, exactly, he's gone silent.'

'Why he's ghosted me. Yes.'

John shakes his head, an amused smile stretching his cheeks. 'No, I really don't care for that phrase. It's quite offensive actually. But the answer is obvious. He stopped talking to you because he's a dick.'

Mia's eyes widen. For a moment, John thinks she might laugh, but then her face twists and she drops her gaze. 'I guess that's just the kind of man I attract, the ones I think are into me, but turns out are just using me. I'm not sure what that says about me. That I'm ridiculously naive?'

John shakes his head. 'Everyone wants a happily ever after. You can't fault yourself for that.'

Mia looks out the window. 'Maybe. But you know what, John? I'm tired of all this. I can't believe I got dumped right before Christmas. Do you know how hard I had to work to try the whole dating thing again?' She shrugs her shoulders. 'I know better than to get my hopes up.'

She's had a tough go of it, that's abundantly clear. John begins to wonder whether there's something he can do to make things a little better for Mia while she's at the manor. Of course, she's only here for Christmas and will leave soon after, but he is finding it incredibly refreshing to talk to another human being. And now he thinks about it, maybe helping her could do him some good too. Even if he can't let himself get used to her company, why not enjoy it while he's got it?

'OK, so here's what I propose, Mia. You deserve to have something go your way. Go back to the big house and grab your things. Take over the cottage while you're here – it's really quite lovely, and it will give you some space.' His heart – or what *feels* like his heart, since his real one stopped years ago of course – sets to pounding. He's issued this invitation to Mia lightly, casually, but he finds he's quite desperate to get her here, to be involved in her life, to hear more about these shenanigans with her family and this Sam character and that – not 'ghoster' – non-*responder*. To his surprise, he finds that he somehow, suddenly, inexplicably . . . *cares*.

Mia snorts. 'So generous of you. Where will you go then? No offence, but bunking with a ghost was not on my holiday to-do list.'

John grins back at her. He's going to play it cool. He can't let her know how desperate he is for the company, or he'll just scare her off. 'I'll wander around the big house when you want your privacy. Don't worry. I know how to make myself scarce.'

'You can go to the big house?' Mia says, narrowing her eyes. 'I mean, you're not . . . bound here to the cottage? So to speak?'

'I'm actually able to move about the entire property,' he says. 'And the big house is large enough there will be a quiet corner or two for me to linger. I might listen to your Aunt Gertie's ramblings – did you know she's quite fond of ghosts? It's always very entertaining to hear her opinions on the spirit world. Maybe I'll even try my hand at traditional haunting, perhaps it will be fun. And, when you need to vent a bit, blow off some steam, I'll be here to listen!'

It's this vision of getting to hear more about Mia's life that exerts the strongest pull on John. Listening to her just now, all her mundane troubles, he felt like he did as a child, looking in the window of a toy shop at Christmas, palms pressed against the cold glass, his breath making a circle of fog. Gazing upon the marvellous things that maybe he couldn't have, but he was glad to know existed.

Heavens, how he misses *living*.

'Wait, Aunt Gertie believes in ghosts?'

'Yes, I'm afraid she wasn't left much choice thanks to Mags' antics.'

'Sorry, who?'

'Oh, of course, she pre-dates you. Mags was the old cook at the manor in the eighteen hundreds, died in some awful kitchen accident and was stuck on the property for nearly two centuries. She was here when I arrived and helped to ease me into the whole "being a ghost" thing, for which I will always be grateful.' John smiles fondly to himself before going on, 'Mags was more prone to some light haunting than I am, occasional shattered crockery or wailing in the corridors, that sort of thing. It never seemed to put off your dear Aunt Gertie, though. She took it remarkably well, all things considered.'

'Sounds like Gertie,' Mia responds with a chuckle, before turning to John with a confused look. 'Wait, if Mags is *actually* haunting the house, how come I've never seen it?'

John hesitates, an unexpected lump rising in his throat. 'Well, Mags isn't exactly around any more. She passed over soon after I arrived. She was my only company in the last thirty years, and I must admit, I miss her quite a lot . . .' He casts his eyes skywards for a moment, before gruffly clearing his throat. 'I do find comfort in the fact that her legacy lives on in Gertie's ramblings, though. Helps to ease an old ghost's heart.' John pauses for a moment to gather himself, before clapping his hands suddenly and saying with a bright smile, 'Anyway, back to the matter at hand!'

Mia jumps, startled by the abrupt change in mood. 'Sorry, what matter? Gertie's opinions on the spirit world?'

'No, no, my dear, your move down to the cottage!' John laughs as Mia rolls her eyes. 'Tell you what, why don't I sweeten the deal by gathering your things and bringing them down here myself? Don't worry, no one will see a disembodied suitcase floating around. I'm pretty good at skulking. Call it an art I've perfected over the last three decades.'

'I don't know,' says Mia. 'I mean, I'm in my childhood bedroom. Yes, it's a bit crowded, but . . .'

Think, think, John tells himself. Suddenly it hits him.

'One bathroom,' he says, in a final, desperate attempt. 'One bathroom, six bedrooms. You can't tell me you enjoy sharing with that many people. Wouldn't it be better to have an entire bathroom to yourself?'

'Mmmm,' murmurs Mia. 'The toilet per capita ratio is rather lower than it should be . . .' Her eyes glimmer, a smile teasing her lips into a little curve, and he's pretty sure that was the winning stroke.

John stands, preparing to head out. Mia holds up her hand. 'Wait. John, be honest with me.'

Uh-oh. A sick feeling burbles in his already-disturbed stomach. Is she going to ask how he died or why he hasn't moved on?

Mia blinks at him with her big eyes. 'Just be honest. Are you going to possess me in my sleep?'

John lets out a relieved laugh. 'Of course not, Mia.' He leans down, hands on his hips. 'I wouldn't do it while you were sleeping. I'd do it while you were awake, so you could be properly mortified.'

Mia nods, apparently satisfied by this answer. 'Perfect. Your dark humour is really a breath of fresh air, John.'

A surge of joy fills his chest. He mock salutes her and heads towards the back door.

'Wait, what are you doing? Why not take the shortest way?' She points out the window towards the big house.

'Because my indigestion is just starting to settle down, no thanks to you.' He ducks out the door, Mia's laughter trailing after him. As he makes his way up towards the big house, he can't help but wonder why she's able to interact with him. It's startling, after years just sitting around here, invisible to everyone who's occupied the estate. He hasn't laughed this much since those pleasant evenings so long ago with Alastair. But he won't think about that now – no point in dredging up old, painful memories. Better to stay focused on the present, and the tiny Christmas miracle the universe has sent his way – someone to talk to.

6

MIA

Mia's tucked into a mountain of pillows on the feather bed in the gardener's cottage, scrolling through her camera roll, her Sad Girl playlist playing quietly through the speaker. It felt extra indulgent to slip into bed once John brought her luggage, and she has zero regrets so far. It had been quite amusing watching John painstakingly move her luggage a few feet at a time, disguised in a bin bag in an attempt to draw less attention.

Now, the cottage is feeling like a downy fortress of solitude, and the quiet and space from the big house are giving her the courage to do a little mental decluttering. Even though she's just been here for a couple of hours, she's already convinced that moving down here for the week was absolutely the right move, and true to his promise to give her privacy when she wanted it, there hasn't been a peep from John since he brought down her things. Having a bathroom to herself is also rather glorious.

Looking over the few pictures she'd taken of her and

James, Mia can't help the sadness creeping in. The Mia in these photos is so full of hope. Little did she know how quickly their relationship was going to crash and burn. There's the one from the night they met – standing together at Sally's Halloween party. James is looking at the camera, his dazzling grin and warm eyes sparkling, but Mia is looking up at him with a wide smile. She'd been particularly drawn to James's confidence that night, seemingly able to dazzle anyone he spoke to. Whenever she had thought back on that night, it had made her feel like she'd chosen well – someone smart and articulate.

Then the selfie shortly afterwards in the park that – despite the ghosting – she still loves. The trees are dressed in autumn colours and her outfit that day had been the epitome of cosy girl. James had worn a huge, chunky knit jumper that Mia had desperately wanted to steal from him, and the light had been so beautiful all afternoon. It had been James's suggestion to meet up and cycle through the park, and by the end of the day, Mia had been over the moon. She'd texted Lucy that night – *I think he's a keeper!*

She scrutinizes the next picture, taken outside a cinema in front of a mural she'd always admired. James's arm is wrapped around her shoulders, and they're both smiling at the camera. They'd asked an older man to take it, and the gentleman had commented on what a cute couple they made. Mia studies James's body language. Were there clues, even then, that she'd missed? Something that foretold he was only in it for a good time, and then he'd move on without another word? Mia huffs out a frustrated sigh.

She's overanalysing all of this. Lucy is always telling her to accept what the universe brings her way and hold everything loosely. But Mia can't stop herself from looking at the photo more closely. Their bodies are pressed together in that comfortable and casual way of two people who find the other attractive and interesting. And the goodbye kiss that night had been full of passion . . .

The next song on her Sad Girl playlist starts, and Mia wavers in her determination not to cry over James. She still feels firmly that he's not worth her tears, but the disappointment is burning through her. She'd finally psyched herself up enough to take a chance on love again, and look at where it's landed her. She should have stuck with her tried and true first dates only approach. She's never caught feelings after one of those.

Mia swipes a few stray tears from her cheeks and tosses her phone on to the duvet. She looks around the room, anxious for a distraction. The bed is decadent – plush linens and a softly tarnished brass bed frame pushed up against a rustic stone wall. The other walls in the room are plaster and have recently been painted a soothing sage green that makes the rich wood tones of the dresser and washstand glow, and someone has decked the room out with sprigs of fresh evergreen. The subtle scent fills the air and she breathes it in, letting it soothe her ragged nerves as she gazes out of the window. But just as she feels herself growing calmer, her eyes snag on a decidedly Penny-looking figure, trudging through the snow, clearly headed for the gardener's cottage.

'Oh, Mum, what are you doing?' Mia mutters. Not

wanting to be caught in bed, she launches herself up and grabs her jumper from the hook on the back of the door, winding a scarf around her neck and pulling on her mittens as she heads down the stairs. She's just reached the landing when Penny wrestles open the front door.

'Yoo hoo! Mia darling? Are you in here? Oh, there's a fire! How lovely.'

Mia rounds the corner. 'Hey, Mum. I'm here.'

'Oh, there you are!' Penny stands in front of the fire, blowing on her fists and stamping her feet. 'I've been looking for you everywhere. Your room is empty!'

'Yes, we moved – well, I moved – my stuff earlier this morning. There's just a bit more quiet and relaxation down here.'

'But I'd prefer everyone to be together—' Penny begins, her eyebrows knitting together across her forehead.

'It's so nice over here, and I haven't been inside in ages,' Mia hurries to interrupt. 'You and Dad have done such a beautiful job restoring the cottage.' Mia gestures towards the toile print curtains. 'Did you sew these yourself?'

Penny smiles, smoothing her hair as she walks towards the window. 'No, I hired a girl in the village. It really is coming along, isn't it? Your father had the stone repointed this summer, and it made *such* a difference. The cottage was so terribly draughty before, you know.'

With the renovations her parents have overseen, the cottage is now the perfect little getaway spot. Romantic, even. Despite herself, Mia is hit with another wave of disappointment. She *really* wishes James were here.

'Well, the cottage is just so cosy now,' Mia says, shaking

off her disappointment and donning a bright smile. The trick to Penny was to keep her distracted, and when necessary, ply her with a glass of white wine. Penny always had ideas of how things should go, and she could be impressively stubborn. But Mia had discovered years ago that she was easily swayed to another's opinion as long as she was buttered up with a few well-worded compliments. 'I'm sure the cottage will be a smashing success. You really have an eye for these things, Mum.'

Penny beams, her eyes crinkling up. Her mascara is just a little bit clumpy, and her blush is too strongly applied. But that's how Mia's mum has always preferred her makeup. And in a world where Mia can't even count on a man to return her texts, she finds that continuity comforting.

Mia's stomach rumbles impressively, and Penny chuckles. 'Oh dear. Someone's hungry. Oh, and that's why I was looking for you!' Her sweet, high voice echoes slightly. 'I wanted you to make one of your soups for lunch today. Something warm and delicious that will feed a crowd.'

Mia raises an eyebrow. 'A crowd? Please tell me you haven't planned another party.'

Penny pats her on the shoulder, and then tugs her towards the door. 'Of course not. But there's you and I, and your father, and of course Charlie eats like a horse. And then Sam, and Aunt Gertie, and I told Mabel she could stop by at some point today. And no one knows when Molly is coming up. Charlie said her little sister's birthday is the 22nd, and she wasn't sure if she should come up before or after the celebration. But she doesn't live that far away, so I don't see why she couldn't come up now, and then come back for our Christmas dinner.'

Mia follows her mum outside. The cottage ghost's comment from earlier comes to mind, and she can't help asking, 'So are we assuming Molly is a real, live person?'

Penny giggles. 'Of course we are! What, do you think your brother is making her up?'

'I just think it's awfully convenient.' Mia steps in the footprints her mother made on her way down. The wind is blowing away from them, which makes conversation a little easier. 'As far as I know, no one has met this girl, and she has very plausible reasons to not be able to be here with us. You and Aunt Gertie were pretty merciless with him last year about his lack of a significant other. I wouldn't put it past him to invent someone just to keep you off his back this year.'

Penny tsks in dismay. 'Mia. That's just silly. Of course Molly is real. Charlie said he was video calling her just the other night! Besides,' she continues, elbowing Mia in the ribs, 'your brother is not clever enough to pull off that kind of deception.' Her frown deepens. 'And when have I ever pushed you children romantically? I know better!'

Mia chuckles, but sobers when she realizes that neither last year nor this year has *she* been subjected to the same scrutiny as Charlie. In fact, her family seems to avoid the subject of her love life like the plague. Does that mean they've written her off as a lost cause? James may have ghosted her, but she's only twenty-eight, for Pete's sake.

They tumble inside, shutting out the cold and unwrapping all their layers. Penny ushers Mia into the kitchen and hands her an apron. 'There are all kinds of fresh ingredients in the fridge. I'm sure you can pull something fabulous together. Just don't add too much salt. Your father needs to watch his sodium.'

'Sure, Mum,' says Mia, leaning in to peck her mother on the cheek.

Cheered by her mother's faith in her cooking at least, if not her love life, Mia rummages through the fridge, formulating a plan. Penny edges in beside her and pulls out a bottle of Chardonnay. When Mia looks at her sideways, Penny just shrugs, thin shoulders lifting delicately. 'What? It's Christmas. There's no unacceptable time to start drinking.'

Maybe her mother has a point. Maybe Mia should drink a little too. The wine might help with how glum she's been feeling. 'Pour me a glass too then, please, Mum?'

Penny makes a delighted little sound and turns to locate the wine glasses. Mia puts her choices on the counter and finds a cutting board and knife.

'Here you go, dearie.' Penny sets the full glass beside Mia's workstation.

'Thanks.' Mia cuts the butternut squash in half and begins peeling it. She's feeling slightly off-kilter and she hasn't even started drinking yet. Maybe it's the slight fuzziness of the residual travel fatigue, but meeting John this morning is feeling more and more surreal. Did all of that really happen? Was there any possibility that she had some kind of bizarre, stress-induced hallucination? 'Mum, was there ever a gardener who worked here on the property?'

Penny sips her wine, eyes squinting as she thinks.

'Mmm, yes. But that was years ago, I think. He worked for Grandpa Morris and Grandma Joan.'

'But they lived in London,' Mia objects.

'Once you were born, they did. They had to move for my father's job. There was nothing out here for them.' Penny sighs. 'My mother loved coming out here for the holidays, though. In fact, that's how we know Mabel's family! Mum would ring them up and let them know we were all coming down for Christmas. Mabel's parents would get the house ready. They'd air everything out and stock the fridge and such. Then the rest of the time all the furniture was draped in sheets and the rooms shut up like someone had died.' She shivers. 'I always found that a bit creepy, as a child.'

'What about when we lived here?'

Penny shakes her head. 'No, there was no staff when we lived here. Just us and Aunt Gertie. Golly, those were lovely years. You and Charlie used to just run amok, and I never had to worry. The worst that could happen to you was a broken bone or two. Do you remember when you caught that enormous bullfrog? You were convinced it was an enchanted Prince Charming, and I was so afraid you were going to catch syphilis or something.'

'I don't think you can catch syphilis from frogs, Mum.'

Penny sips her wine as she waves a hand to dismiss Mia's objection.

Mia mulls things over as she adds the chopped squash to a baking sheet and drizzles it in oil. So, there *was* a gardener who worked here in the nineties. She pops the sheet in the oven and starts slicing up a few pieces of thick bacon while a pan warms on the stove. 'So how long did the gardener work here?'

Penny shrugs. 'I don't remember. I don't think I interacted with him much. I'd have to look and see if Mum left any records – there might be a photo or two of him. When they did their Christmas parties, they always invited all the staff.'

'Who else did Gran and Grandpa employ?' The pan is warm, so Mia tosses the bacon into it and lets it crisp up, relishing the sizzle of the fat in the heat and the enticing smells curling up towards her nose.

Penny takes another sip of her wine while she thinks. 'Hmm. There was a cook too. Catherine I think was her name. She always said to just call her Cook so it's hard to remember. She cooked like you, Mia. All she had to do was look at whatever ingredients were available, and she would know exactly what she wanted to make. What are you making, by the way?'

'A squash and pear soup. With a little spice, I'm thinking.'

'And not too much salt,' Penny repeats.

'Yes, Mum,' says Mia patiently. The bacon sizzles away and Mia adds in sliced pears, onion and a few minced cloves of garlic. Penny sighs appreciatively at the smells emanating from the stove, content to drink her wine and make light conversation as Mia begins to carefully season the soup base.

An hour later, the soup has nearly come together. Martin wanders into the kitchen, sniffing like a bloodhound. 'Well, with smells like that coming from the kitchen, our girl must be home.' He leans in for a kiss on Mia's cheek and then reaches over to tweak Penny on the nose. Penny squeaks in protest and Mia turns back to the stove to hide her smile. For as long as she can remember, her dad has done that move, and her mum has pretended to be outraged. 'Mum, do we have any bread to serve with this soup?'

Penny shakes her head regretfully. 'I meant to grab some at the shop when I was in town but I forgot.'

Martin leans his elbows against the counter. 'Well, we can just send the boys for a few loaves when they come in. They should be just about done with the wood by now.'

As if summoned by his words, Charlie and Sam tumble in through the back door, laughing and stomping the snow from their feet as they carry armfuls of wood into the living and dining rooms. On their way back outside, they spill into the kitchen, while Charlie continues to protest.

'It was not cheating!'

'It was too, Charlie Robinson, and you know it.'

'Not at all. Mr Kittredge gave me the answer sheet by mistake. I thought I'd just caught a lucky break, that's all.'

Sam shakes his head, chuckling under his breath. 'Whatever you need to tell yourself to sleep at night, Charlie.' His head swivels suddenly, like he just picked up a scent – literally. 'Whoa, what smells so good?'

'Mia is cooking us all lunch,' Penny informs him from her perch at the island. She's started her second glass of wine, and her spirits are high.

'Oh, are you making the little pigs in blankets that

I love?' Charlie pleads, striding through the kitchen to stand beside Mia. 'Nah. It's just soup. Bummer.'

'Well, you can just not have any then,' Mia retorts. She glances over at Sam, whose cheeks are flushed from the cold. His eyes are sparkling. He grins at her, then returns to his argument with Charlie. Their bickering fills the kitchen as Mia stirs the soup, darting little glances at Sam. His coat is sprinkled with wood shavings, and there are melting snowflakes in his hair. He's shaved since she saw him first thing this morning, and she has to force her eyes away from his incredible jawline. She should describe to John how annoying Sam's good looks are . . .

. . . *if John is real.* Maybe she fell asleep in the chair at the cottage and dreamed it all up. Then again, how did her luggage get there? She certainly didn't lug it through the snow again. She quickly scans around her. If that did really happen, is John wafting around the big house somewhere? Will she be able to pretend he's not there if he appears suddenly? Because she really doesn't want to do something embarrassing like scream . . . especially in front of Sam.

'So, Sam,' Penny begins. 'It's so nice having you here with us this week.'

'Yeah, we needed some free manual labour,' Charlie teases. 'Come on, Sam. Another trip or two will fill up all the wood boxes.' He tugs Sam towards the door, calling over his shoulder, 'You all should have seen Sam chopping wood out there. Took to it like a natural. He's a regular lumberjack.'

The image of Sam wielding a heavy axe, logs splitting

apart from the sheer force of his swing, rises up in Mia's mind. Had he set aside his heavy coat while he chopped? Rolled up his sleeves? Sam has great forearms. Must be all that tennis playing. Had he spread his legs, bracing them against the snowy ground so that he could lean into every swing . . . A little tingle of desire skitters down her spine, and her eyes widen in alarm. No. Time to slam the door on that mental picture. She will focus solely on cooking. Pulling out her phone, she types a quick text to Lucy to distract herself.

You'll never believe who's staying for Christmas . . .

Lucy's reply comes almost instantaneously. *Who??? Wait, did James surprise you up there?*

Mia snorts. *As if. No, my idiot brother invited Sam Williams.*

THE Sam Williams? The one who deserves to be hogtied and slowly roasted over an open flame?

The very same.

Oh Mia! I'm sorry. That's a tough break.

As the boys head back outside, Penny gently but firmly nudges Mia. 'Put your phone away, dear, before you burn the soup.'

Disgruntled, Mia complies, deciding it's not worth the argument. Penny sighs. 'I can't believe Sam's family made plans that didn't include him. Can you even imagine? When Charlie told me it just broke my heart. But Sam's parents have always been like that. Too absorbed in their own lives to pay much attention to their children.'

'His dad was always the sort to prefer a good book over a human interaction,' Martin adds. Mia smiles to herself.

Her dad loves a good snark session. She has a theory that she actually inherited most of her sarcastic wit from her father. He's just surprisingly good at keeping it under wraps.

Penny and Martin continue talking about the Williamses as Mia moves around the kitchen, cleaning up her mess and rinsing dishes before adding them to the dishwasher. When Charlie and Sam come back in, their wood-stocking mission completed, the kitchen is more under control and Mia is feeling less rattled by their presence.

'Tell us what you're up to these days, Sam,' Penny coaxes. Sam and Charlie have both collapsed into the breakfast nook, laughing at how out of breath they are.

'Not much to tell, Mrs Robinson. I've just taken on a new job at Pembley Sanders. That's why I wasn't able to join my family on the cruise – I'm still in my probation period.'

Of course Sam's a job-hopping derelict, Mia thinks as she wipes down the counters. Probably hasn't held down a job for more than a year since he graduated.

'Is it full time work?' Martin asks.

'Yes, and hopefully fewer hours than the last place. The benefits were fantastic – they even provided company housing – but all I did was work. My boss had no concept of work–life balance.'

Mia snickers under her breath. Ideally Sam's boss was a fire-breathing dragon who also incinerated him on a daily basis.

'The new job's not glamorous in the slightest, but it pays the bills and then some.'

'Are you saving up to buy your own place?' Penny motions for Martin to gather up a few more wine glasses.

'Yes, that's the goal. I'll need to save for another year or so. Then I'll be able to start the house hunt. I'm not looking for anything too extravagant. A couple of bedrooms and maybe an outdoor space if I'm lucky. Although I'm not thrilled about the idea of moving again. I'm just getting settled into the new place. Still have a few boxes left to unpack.' Sam crosses one ankle over his other knee, exposing his sock. Mia is at first thankful that he's no longer barefoot, then irritated by the whimsical llamas in rain boots sprinkled all over the bright purple hosiery. Doesn't the man have the decency to dress like a grown-up?

Martin chuckles. 'I think we still have a few boxes in the basement from when we moved to London years ago. You're doing all right, son.'

'Pity you don't have anyone to share the new place with . . .' Penny hints, her meaning rather obvious, but Mia has to give her some respect. Penny's fishing for information and she's not ashamed to go after it. 'Your good looks will be wasted if you don't find someone soon.'

Sam chuckles. Mia glances over at him. Martin has poured both him and Charlie a glass from a new bottle of wine. Sam nods in thanks, and Mia sees that the back of his neck is a little red. *Interesting.* She didn't know Sam Williams was capable of feeling embarrassment. Maybe now he would understand a little bit of what she'd felt all those years ago.

Martin chimes in as he returns to the seat beside Penny. 'I ran into your mother at the pharmacy last year. She said your sister is married with two children. Have you thought about whether or not you want kids too?'

'Ah, I'm not sure,' Sam hedges, now visibly uncomfortable with the spotlight being squarely placed on him. 'Charlie, when is Molly coming up here?'

Charlie grins like a cat with a mouse. 'Oh, no. You're the one in the hot seat right now. Don't try to tap me in.'

'Yeah, leave your fake girlfriend out of this,' Mia pipes up as she pinches sprigs of rosemary on to a plate for the garnish.

Charlie's mouth drops open. 'What? She's *not* fake. Why would you say that?'

Mia shrugs. 'I'm just saying, I've never actually met her. From what Mum says, none of us have.'

'*I've* met her,' Sam says supportively.

Mia jabs the air in his direction with her wooden spoon. 'You don't count. You're an untrustworthy witness.' Sam raises his hands in mute surrender.

Turning back to the oven, she bends to pull out the roasted squash. She'll blend this up, add it to the sautéed ingredients, and then she's planning to whisk up some sour cream and milk to dot in each bowl as it's served.

'Is there anyone you're interested in currently, Sam?'

Mia is appalled to realize that she wants to hear his answer to Penny's question. Very badly. Distracted by her rogue thoughts, she dumps the squash into the blender and jabs the on button. The machine roars to life, drowning out Sam's response.

'Ack!' Mia frantically hits the power button again, and the machine chokes off. The upper cabinets are now coated in little bits of bright orange puree. In her distraction, Mia forgot to place the lid on the blender, and now there is squash everywhere.

'Are you all right, darling?' Martin half rises from his chair, and Charlie and Sam both swivel to look at her.

'I'm fine.'

'That's quite the mess,' Penny observes. 'Is the soup ruined?'

'No.' Mia pushes away her annoyance and grabs a rag from under the sink. 'There's plenty left and this will clean up easily.'

'Let me do it,' Sam says, coming to stand beside her.

She's about to protest, but really, doesn't he deserve to do more? He could clean every inch of this house, chop all the wood on the property, and they still wouldn't be even. She tosses the rag at him. 'Be my guest.'

Sam works quietly beside her while the others carry on with their conversation. Mia is finding it nearly impossible to stay focused on her task. She's thankful that the growl of the blender hides her pounding heart, in disbelief that Sam is still able to rile her up so easily. Sam moves with unconscious athleticism, and she watches him from the corner of her eye. His fingers flex around the rag he's using to clean, and Mia only has to close her eyes to recall the sensation of those same hands sliding into her hair. Shivers run up and down her back. In an effort to push away the memories, she forces her focus back to blending the squash, pouring it into the other ingredients once it's smooth. She tastes it once more, and mutters, 'Needs some nutmeg.' She's about to rummage through the spice cabinet again when the little nut grater appears at her elbow.

'This what you're looking for?' Sam smiles at her, and there's an apology in his eyes. She can see it. She could have it too, she knows this. He would say all the right things, and she wouldn't be able to do anything except forgive him. He leans closer, and she breathes in a whiff of that enchanted forest again. The smells of the soup are replaced by a spicy, knee-weakening aroma. Mia's ovaries cry out in protest.

But she is not that weak. She won't be wooed by a pair of warm brown eyes and an apologetic smile. Instead, she snatches up the nutmeg and purses her lips as she peruses Sam. 'If you two want to have any of this soup, you'd best get yourselves to town to buy that bread. It'll be ready in half an hour and I'm not planning to serve it cold. This isn't a gazpacho.'

Charlie reluctantly shoves back from the table. Sam shoots her a tentative look. 'Any chance you want to join us, Mia?'

She plants her hands on her hips and scowls at him. 'Any chance you've invented a time machine and can now undo the past?'

Sam's smile fades and he ducks his head. Charlie claps him on the shoulder in an attempt at camaraderie and heads out. Sams follows him without another word. Mia checks her phone, and mercifully, there is another text from Lucy.

I hope you're plotting revenge on Charlie for doing this to you. I'm thinking Veet in his shampoo. Or should we shave his legs while he sleeps? Ooh, just one of them. That will teach him, the hairy weirdo.

Mia smiles, cheered by her friend's fierce loyalty. *I love it.*

Her phone vibrates a second later with another text from Lucy. *Is Sam still hot though?*

Unbelievably. It's infuriating.

The nerve. He could have at least got a little fat or developed a skin condition or something.

See, this is why she loves Lucy. Girlfriend's got her back, and they practically share a brain. Mia slides her phone into her waistband and tunes back into her parents' conversation.

'Well,' Penny is giggling as she refills her wine glass for the third time, 'I'm just saying. If I were thirty years younger, I would offer to have Sam's babies.'

'Mum! Don't be gross!'

'What? That boy is absolutely scrumptious,' Penny defends.

Disgusting. Her parents have always been a little inappropriate, though. Mia should be used to it. Shaking her head, she hunches over the stovetop, making the last few adjustments to the soup while her father's belly laugh fills the kitchen.

7

JOHN

20 December

It's always a welcome change to have the family up at the house. He always appreciates the disruption to otherwise predictable days, the continual hustle and bustle. It definitely beats his regular routine of selecting yet another book from the library and curling up in an armchair that he can't quite feel.

Striding down to the gardener's cottage, he avoids the stone walkway that leads to the back of the cottage and suppresses a shudder. No need to revisit *that* place. Without much effort, he can still recall the decidedly odd sensation of standing beside his mortal body lying there on the path, watching himself take his last breath. It was deeply troubling, and is not something he cares to relive with any regularity. Instead, he lets himself into the cottage, calling out what he hopes is a cheery hello.

'I'm upstairs,' Mia calls out.

'Mind if I join you?'

'Be my guest.'

John takes the stairs two at a time. He's always liked doing that. Perks of having long legs.

'So, you really are real,' Mia muses. 'Not a figment of my imagination. Or—' she pauses, scrunching up her forehead. 'Am I imagining things now?'

'Like it or not,' John assures her, 'I'm really and truly here. Unlike your brother's girlfriend, who I'm honestly not sure even exists. Have you actually met Molly?' Mia shakes her head. 'That's what I thought.' He looks at Mia. She is sprawled across the top of the bed, hair in disarray, pyjamas rumpled. There is a smattering of crumbs across the coverlet.

'So, the pity party is still in full swing, I take it.'

Mia sticks her tongue out at him and returns her attention to the ancient magazine she's flipping through.

'I'm curious. What's the plan, exactly? You're going to hide out here all week and then sneak back to London?'

'Basically,' Mia mutters, without even looking up.

'And who, exactly, are we avoiding?'

Mia purses her lips. 'Well, Mum and Dad have decorated every inch of that house. You can't turn a corner without bumping into a garland or a bauble or a candy cane. It's oppressively festive. Down here I can breathe.'

'Are you saying you don't like Christmas?'

She lets the magazine fall closed. 'I'm twenty-eight, you know.'

John clicks his tongue in what he hopes is a sympathetic

81

way. 'Far too old for Christmas magic. So that's why you've become a borderline hermit. What are you even eating down here? I imagine the cupboards are pretty barren.'

'Yes, well, I found some crackers. And tuna.'

John grimaces. 'Rumour has it you cooked an amazing soup yesterday. Could have put Gordon Ramsay to shame. And yet, here you are, eating crackers and canned fish in your jammies.'

'At least I'm not having to make casual conversation with Sam.' Mia swipes the crumbs on to the floor. 'Is there a broom around here?'

'Downstairs by the back door.' John settles himself on the dormer window seat. When Mia returns, he studies her body language as she sweeps. 'This Sam has you all tied up in knots.'

'He's not supposed to be here,' she mutters, contorting her body to reach the broom under the bed.

'He seems nice enough,' John ventures. He's wildly curious to find out the reason Mia hates Sam so much. And he has a hunch that if he pushes just the right amount, she'll spill the tea.

'That's how he does it,' Mia returns bitterly. 'He's a handsome, silver-tongued devil.'

John guffaws. 'How intriguing. Care to share more?'

'You wouldn't believe me if I told you.'

'She says to the ghost that only she can see.'

This garners a small smile from the angry one. She sobers quickly. 'He humiliated me.'

John folds his hands on his lap and leans back. Mia

twists her lips from side to side, and then, finally, gives a quick nod.

'Sam and I knew each other all throughout school. We'd all gone to the same secondary school – Charlie, Sam and I. Sam and Charlie both played tennis and hit it off right away. Charlie was never the kind of brother who was annoyed by his little sister hanging around, so I knew all his friends. He also wasn't that popular with the girls – that's the Robinson genes for you – but Sam was a different story. He's unbelievably hot, you know? Perfectly brown hair that falls over his head in that clichéd way. Warm eyes that draw you in, make you feel like you're his whole world. I've always preferred blue eyes, but Sam's are so inviting. Plus, he had this clear, smooth skin, as though he wasn't a teenager like the rest of us. Every girl at school was drooling over him.'

John can't wait for her to go on. 'Did you two date in school?'

Mia shakes her head. 'No, Sam was focused on getting good marks, and playing tennis, of course. He was nice to everyone, but never really dated. But then the boys finished and went to university. I moved on, to some degree. I wanted to take a gap year to travel around the world after school, explore some of my culinary interests. But my parents were adamant that I go to uni like Charlie. It took me by surprise that they felt so strongly about it, so I just gave in. I have my whole life to travel, you know?'

John only nods, not wanting to interrupt.

'Anyway, we all ended up at university together. That's where I met Lucy, gem that she is. She was in the room next to me. I loved living in halls. Sam and Charlie were in halls too, even though they were older, because Charlie had long labs to get through and Sam was so devoted to tennis. It was just easier to live right there.' Mia sighs. 'And even though I thought I'd put Sam behind me after he left school, I fell right back into the crush once he was living so close to me. I really, *really* fell for him that year. He could make my day by just saying hello. Or walking me to my lectures. I'd be on cloud nine the rest of the day. We just got along so well. I'd come and watch him practise, and we'd make small talk during warm-up and cooldown. It was just . . . magical. I never took Sam for a player, but in the end, that's who he was.'

John frowns. 'Surely not.'

Mia shrugs. 'I don't know how else you could interpret it. We spent loads of time together. He would say the nicest things to me, share the poems he'd written, things like that. And then things started to shift. Lucy was dating this rugby player, and Charlie had a really heavy courseload that term, so Sam and I were spending more time alone together, and things were changing between us.' Mia looks off in the distance. 'At first it was just the subtle stuff, you know? He'd brush against me. Hold my hand. Hug me in celebration when he won a match. But then there was that night in his halls . . .'

John squirms in his seat. He doesn't want to press Mia, but he's dying to hear the rest of the story. He bites the inside of his cheek as he waits for her to continue.

'I'd dreamed of that moment for months. At first we were just hanging out, but then he put an arm around me, and then—' Mia's voice hitches. 'I kissed him first. He didn't respond right away, and I worried that I'd misread the signals. But then he kissed me back. And it was everything I ever dreamed of. There was always *so much* chemistry between us. It just . . . worked. Felt like the most natural thing in the world.'

'So you slept together?' John asks.

'Almost. Some idiot pulled the fire alarm and we all had to evacuate. By the time we got outside, Sam must have had second thoughts. He just gave me a sheepish grin and offered to walk me back to my hall. Obviously, I was disappointed, but then he reached out the next day and invited me to go swimming with him. His coach had got him access to the uni pool after hours so that he could get in some extra cardio. Something about the water being easier on his knees than running, I don't know. I told Lucy about it, and she was like, "This is your chance! It will be just the two of you, and you can finish what you started the night before!" And I thought that was a great idea.

'Obviously, that late in the evening, we would have the pool all to ourselves. So, at that point I was trying to figure out which swimming costume to wear. It was between the red one piece that made my legs look amazing, and the blue halter top, with the little bow right between my boobs.

'Sam called me that afternoon to make sure I was coming. It wasn't a long conversation, but when we were hanging up, he said, "OK, see you tonight, love you, bye." '

'Wait,' John holds up a hand. 'He said he loved you?'

Mia nods. 'He'd never said that to me before. And I was just . . . over the moon, you know? Like this was better than anything I could have imagined.'

John smiles, thinking of his own crushes and unrequited loves. Like that rangy boy in his maths set with the tiger eyes. 'Indeed.'

'I remember thinking that this time with Sam was going to entirely erase the memory of my disappointing encounter with Christopher Jones and his slimy fish-faced kisses. Lucy told me to bring both of my swimming costumes, and decide which to wear once I got there. Sam had texted me the code for the building, and it was completely deserted. We had the place to ourselves. But once I was there, looking out over the water, I had another idea. I dropped my clothes piece by piece on to the poolside bench, kicked off my slides and slipped into the water in nothing but my birthday suit.'

John nods. 'I always had you pegged for the bold kind.'

Mia grimaces. 'Well, Samuel Williams was the kind of boy you take risks for. The kind of boy for whom you leave it all out on the table. So, I went a little deeper into the water, and I was trying to figure out exactly how far I should go. I was thinking I didn't want to leave anything up to interpretation, you know? I finally picked a spot that was just deep enough to show off my shoulders, decolletage and the tops of the girls. I was in a spot where all I had to do was press my toes into the floor, and I would rise up a few more inches, making my state of undress unmistakable.

'I heard some noise, so I dipped beneath the water one

last time to make sure there were no stray hairs clinging to my face. Then I saw Sam. In all his Sam glory.

'He came right to the edge, grinning and saying hello. I pushed my toes against the tiles and rose up, and Sam stumbled to a halt with the strangest expression on his face. At first, I was thrilled. My plan was working and Sam was speechless. I said, "Want to come join me?"'

Mia sighs, wrapping her arms around her waist. 'I'd never felt so bold. So powerful. So fully in control of my own destiny. Sam looked at me, his eyes bouncing from my chest, to my face and back down. Then he glanced over his shoulder. I told him the water was perfect, and I moved closer to the shallow end, until the water was only at my belly button. Sam didn't move, but I had come too far to back out now. I was all in at this point. So, I took a few more steps, and at that point the water was below my hips. Sam came closer, and that's when I heard the other voices.'

John covers his mouth. This story is not turning out the way he expected.

'Nearly a dozen other guys burst into the pool building. And – get this – it was most of Sam's tennis club, and – horror of horrors – my brother Charlie.'

John's gasp is involuntary and one hundred per cent genuine.

'One of them yelled out, "Oy, Sam! This is incredible!" And that's when I realized that I was an idiot. I looked at Sam, and I was just flooded with these feelings of betrayal. He said, "Mia, I'm so sorry. I don't know how you misunderstood—"'

'Wait a minute,' John objects. 'He thinks *you* mis-understood?'

Mia nods, and there's a spark of anger in her eyes as she reminisces. 'I was so stupid. So, there I was, freezing cold now, making a mad dash for the ladder and my clothes. But they're all on that bench, remember? So, I would have had to run buck naked to the bench and they were *all* going to see me. Even Charlie.'

John makes an appropriately sympathetic sound. This truly is worse than he could have imagined.

'At that point I understood it was all some sort of sick joke. Sam came towards me, and he said again that it was all a misunderstanding. He tossed me his shirt, and I frantically pulled it on and dashed out of the water. Then everything was a blur. I was at the bench, pulling on my clothes, and I remember throwing his wet shirt back at him. Sam was spouting more nonsense, and I just ignored him, and the idiots who were snickering as I stomped past them. I didn't even know where Charlie was – I just ran the whole way back to my room.'

John had lived through quite a few humiliating events in his lifetime, but nothing on this level.

Mia sweeps the crumbs into the dustpan and empties it in the nearby bin. Then she flings herself back down on the bed and groans. 'I was such an idiot. I let his sweet talking and good looks blind me to the fact that he was just playing around with me, and I meant nothing to him. But I learned an important lesson that night. Never leave anything up to interpretation. And never trust Sam Williams.'

'Did he ever explain himself?' John asks, perplexed. From what he's observed so far, Sam seems like a solidly decent chap. This story doesn't quite add up – but maybe that can just be chalked up to Sam's immaturity. 'Or at least try to make a proper apology?'

Mia snorts. 'I never gave him the chance to. We only had a few months left in the academic year. I never talked to him again. I deleted his number and blocked him on socials. Lucy helped me avoid him for the rest of the term, which wasn't that hard to do since I knew his class schedule and practice times. And after he graduated, I forbade Charlie from ever bringing up his name.'

'Ah.'

There's a glimmer of tears in Mia's eyes. 'He humiliated me. And I really haven't tried to be with anyone else since. Lucy calls me the "first date only" girl. James is the first guy I've seriously dated since that all happened. And look how that turned out. There's apparently something about me that says "please use me and discard me".' John starts to object, but Mia interrupts him. 'It just feels awful, you know? To have finally allowed myself to think another guy was interested only to be let down once more. You'd think I'd learn.'

John sighs. 'Well, your hatred of Sam makes perfect sense, now. That's quite the origin story.'

'So, you agree with me.'

'Totally. But I'm not sure what your plan is from this point. Are you just going to hide out in this cottage for the rest of the week to avoid him?'

Mia shrugs. 'That was my plan . . .'

Holly Whitmore

John considers their options. He wouldn't mind just sitting in this cottage, talking to Mia all week. But, then again, an opportunity like this rarely presents itself. 'You know what I think?' John drums his fingers together. 'I think Sam didn't suffer enough for what he did to you. And we have him as a sort of captive audience while he's here.'

'What are you suggesting?' Mia sits up, interest brightening her features.

'I have a few abilities that may come in handy. Were we to decide to harass Sam a bit.'

'Ooh. Harass him how?'

'Well. I am, as you know, a ghost. So, I could use some of the powers I've been granted to drive him crazy.'

'You're going to haunt him?' Mia bounces on the bed, eyes sparkling.

'Well, I'm not going to drape myself in a bed sheet and float through the corridors, if that's what you're thinking. But I imagine we can make Sam's life quite a bit more interesting, if you know what I mean, while he's here.'

Mia claps her hands and cheers. 'Yes! This is an amazing idea! You can turn on his light all night while he sleeps. Or! I know. You could tie knots into all his shoelaces. Hmm, that one's not very good. Let me think about this for a second.'

John leans back against the cool window glass and smiles. It feels good to have a purpose again, after so long stuck in the in-between. He has never been able to work out why he's stayed tethered to this realm, but as Mia continues to throw out ideas enthusiastically, John begins to wonder whether helping her really could be the key to freeing himself from limbo. Mia deserves to find some healing from the terrible treatment she's received at the hands of the men she thought she'd had a future with. And if it helps to finally liberate John too . . . Well, there is no harm in trying.

8

JOHN

21 December

John has to admit, it's really fun, this sneaking through the corridors. Maybe he's been missing out for the last thirty years. He found a lot of comfort in being an 'honourable' ghost, but perhaps the haunting sort have more fun. Maybe Mags had had it right after all.

He tiptoes down the corridor towards the guest room where Sam is staying. The door is ajar, and John carefully slides it open far enough to slip inside. His heart is pounding in anticipation.

It's not quite four in the morning. Sam is sound asleep on his back, one arm flung above his head. His mouth is slightly open and there's a faint whistling sound as he breathes. He really is an attractive man – John can see why Mia was gaga over him in school. Truth is, John would have been too. As it is, Sam's a little young for his tastes now. John steps through the room, taking note of

Sam's cardigan draped across the chair in front of the little writing desk, upon which Sam has arranged his speaker, his pen and, for some reason, a banana. John bends over and quietly replaces the pen with an identical one – that's all dried out.

This is one of the first pranks they've come up with. Mia had found a whole pile of the kind of pens that Sam uses in the back of a desk drawer, and she and John uncapped them all last night while they were plotting. Every chance John gets, he'll swap Sam's working pens with the dried-out ones. It's a silly little thing, but seeing Mia's delight at Sam's bewilderment will make it more than worth the slight headache he got from the pen fumes as they met their demise.

After swapping the pen, John swipes the Bluetooth speaker off the desk and tucks it carefully under the wardrobe before fading back against the wall and clearing his throat surreptitiously. How does the song begin? He and Mia spent over an hour last night selecting which carol John should begin with today. Ah yes. He straightens up, recalling his old music teacher's voice training from the early seventies. He lowers his diaphragm and mentally finds the note.

Everything is set. It's showtime. John's going for a nice, melodic voice, with just a touch of creepiness. Nat King Cole with a ghostly essence, if you will. He draws in a deep breath and begins. *Chestnuts roasting on an open fire. Jack Frost nipping at your nose. Yuletide carols, being sung by a choir and folks dressed up like Eskimos . . .*

Sam rolls over and moans, burrowing deeper into

the covers. Well, that will never do. John raises his voice slightly and launches into the next line . . . *Everybody knows a turkey and some mistletoe help to make the season bright . . .*

'Argh!' With a groan, Sam launches himself out of bed and over to the desk where he stands bleary-eyed, blinking down at the empty surface. 'Where's it gone?'

John continues to sing, snickering under his breath. Sam searches the room, his movements becoming more frantic as the song continues. When he gets down on his hands and knees to peer under the wardrobe, John hurries through the next line . . . *To see if reindeer really know how to fly . . .*

'Got you!' Sam mumbles, fumbling to pull out the palm-sized speaker. 'How did you get down there, anyway?' He jabs the power button and returns the speaker to the desk, sighing impressively.

John snickers once more, and continues to sing . . . *And so, I'm offering this simple phrase . . .*

'No!' Sam stabs futilely at the power button and John pretends to have the device respond each time, only to continue the song again when Sam sets the speaker down. Sam is growing increasingly agitated, pressing all the buttons on the control panel, whacking it on the desk surface and running over to check the settings on his phone. As John reaches the end of the song, he has to work hard to control his laughter.

Merry Christmas . . . to Sam.

Sam freezes, eyes wide and wild as he stands in the middle of the room. 'Wait, what?' John leaves him there to ruminate and slips back into the corridor, chuckling as he goes. He's now confirmed his theory. There is definitely fun he's been missing out on.

Later that morning, when Sam stumbles down the corridor and into the bathroom, John grabs the speaker and hurries after him. Bracing himself, John launches through the walls and the porcelain sink, pausing just long enough to plant the speaker on the top of the medicine cabinet. Then he plunges back into the corridor, pressing a hand to his belly and working to calm his breathing. Once the nausea has settled down again, he takes this opportunity to wander back into Sam's room and snoop around. His initial thought is to find other ways they might be able to mess with Sam. He could always resort to Mia's idea – tying shoelaces together – or mismatching socks. Then it occurs to him – better to simply hide one of each of Sam's outrageously patterned socks so that pairs cannot be made. After he removes one sock from each pair, John hides them on the top of the wardrobe and looks around the room. His gaze lands on the small brown notebook on the desk. What exactly does Sam jot down every two seconds anyway? Flipping through a couple of pages, he scans the scribbled lines.

> *Gently drifting from the sky,*
> *A quiet descent, soft breath.*
> *The world lies still.*
> *Each flake unique, fleeting,*
> *Carrying the weight of winter's silence.*

So, Sam fancies himself a poet. Interesting. And actually, the poems aren't bad. Poetry is very much a matter of personal taste, but John can appreciate the construction and play of the words.

Down the corridor, the water turns on, and John gently closes the notebook before swiftly heading out of Sam's room to the landing and takes up his station just outside the closed bathroom door. He readies himself once again and begins to sing. Only this time, he adds a bit of personal flair. *Chestnuts roasting on an open fire. Jack Frost nipping at Sam's nose.*

'Oh, come on!' Sam's shout is muffled by the sound of the shower, but it still makes John laugh. He continues singing, sending his voice through the speaker and personalizing the song at every opportunity. When the line becomes *Sam Williams knows a turkey and some mistletoe . . .* the water shuts off abruptly. Sam starts swearing profusely. Amused, John takes a seat beside the Christmas tree that someone carted up here last night. It's still barren, waiting to be decked out in all its festive finery, but it's a lush, healthy tree with symmetrical branches and a deep, rich colour. As John sits admiring the tree, Sam comes barrelling out of the bathroom in nothing more than a towel. His feet slap wetly on the wood floor as he stomps down to Charlie's room and throws open the door.

'All right, man, *enough*!'

'What on earth – what is your problem, Sam? Sorry, babe. I'll have to call you back.' Charlie tosses his phone on to the bed and extricates himself from the covers. 'Have you lost your mind, Sam?'

'Just about, and I'm sure that's the intention. Enough with the music.' Sam is wild-eyed. 'I don't know how you're doing it, but well done. Very funny.'

'Mate, I literally have no idea what you are talking about. Do you know how unhinged you sound right now? And also, you're dripping all over my floor. Do you mind?'

Sam glances around the room, and then back at Charlie. 'So, it's not you?'

Charlie raises his eyebrows and screws up his lips. 'Considering I have absolutely no idea what you are talking about, I'm going to take a wild guess and say it's one hundred per cent not me.'

Sam backs out of the room, shaking his head. John smiles at the look on his face – he's never seen someone so bewildered. Sam takes a couple of deep breaths and then stomps back down to the bathroom. There's a clatter and a sizzle, and then he continues on to his room, his clothes bundled against his chest. Curious, John peeks into the bathroom. The Bluetooth speaker is bobbing in a few inches of water, a slight smoky smell wafting up from the contraption. Snickering, John leaves Sam to his own devices and heads downstairs in search of Mia.

He finds her in the kitchen, assembling some sort of collection of meats and cheeses on a wooden board. 'Well, hello there, what are we up to this morning?'

Mia smiles at him, brown eyes sparkling. Beneath her apron, she's wearing jeans and a fuzzy grey sweater, and those ridiculous slippers are on her feet again. 'I'm putting together a charcuterie board for lunch.'

John gives her a blank stare, and she giggles softly to herself. 'Basically, you just place meats and cheeses and crackers in a pleasing design on a board. Everyone can snack to their hearts' content after oohing and aahing over how pretty it looks. I can make the salami into little flowers, see? And then I'm going to do some sugared cranberries. And maybe a baked brie.'

John leans back against the counter, crossing his legs at the ankles. 'You really like this stuff, don't you? Cooking and what not.'

Mia looks up from her flower assembly. 'I'm never happier than when I'm in a kitchen.'

'Which is why you work at a hospital gift shop,' John observes. 'The connection is obvious. I don't know why I didn't see it before.'

Mia shrugs. 'I considered culinary school. But I don't want to work food service hours. That's no kind of life. Working at the gift shop, my evenings are my own. It means I have the time to get creative.'

John sucks on a tooth. 'Makes sense. By the way, I've had some fun of my own this morning.'

'Now where did I put my glasses? I swear, I'd misplace my head if it wasn't attached.' Aunt Gertie shuffles through the room, patting Mia on the back and then continuing in her search. Mia waits until she's round the corner and then whirls back to John.

'How's it going?' she asks in a hurried whisper.

John smiles broadly. 'Better than expected. I'm having a blast, for starters. And Sam pitched his speaker into the sink. It was spectacularly dramatic. Five star experience.'

Mia's eyes grow huge, and her smile is even wider. She's about to respond when Aunt Gertie makes her way back into the room, glasses now located. 'Mia dear, I've just come home from visiting Mr Thrumble. The man's pantry and fridge are basically empty. I don't suppose you'd mix up a few pot pies that I could take over to the man? I feel bad, it being Christmas and all.'

'I'd love to.'

'Wonderful. I'll bake some biscuits to take over. And then we'll have some for the ghosts as well.'

John startles, and Mia cocks her head, looking down at her aunt. 'Sorry, what?'

Aunt Gertie gives her a patronizing smile. 'You heard me right. This time of year, the ghosts appreciate a little attention and love. What?' She sighs, rubbing at a spot beside her eye with a gnarled finger. 'I can assure you there are more than a few unexpected guests here at Willowby Manor.'

'Oh, I don't believe in ghosts.'

'No one does, dearie, till they do.' And with that vague comment, Aunt Gertie nips a piece of pepperoni and pads away, humming to herself. John and Mia swap amused glances, and Mia is about to comment when Sam tumbles into the kitchen, a wild look on his face.

'Oh, hey, Mia. Ah, good morning.'

Mia gives him a sullen grunt, focusing instead on her charcuterie. Sam watches her for a beat with a regretful look on his face. Then he turns away and pulls out sliced ham from the fridge and a loaf of bread from the pantry. He rummages through a drawer and locates a knife, and gets to work. John's gaze flicks between the two of them, amused by the concerted effort Mia is making to completely ignore Sam.

'So,' Sam begins tentatively. 'Any chance you've heard any music this morning?'

Mia lifts her head slowly, lips screwed up in a sarcastic grin. 'Nope. In fact, it was blissfully silent until you barged your way in here.'

'Oh.' Sam's face falls, and he returns his attention to his sandwich making. Mia sneaks a glance at John, who has straightened up and is clearing his throat. John waits until Sam has scooped out a large spoonful of mayonnaise, and then begins to sing once again.

. . . *Tiny tots, with their eyes all aglow, will find it hard to sleep tonight* . . .

Sam jumps a mile, launching the spoonful of mayonnaise with a screech. Mia drops her head, the curtain of her hair obscuring her face and hiding her laughter. 'Mia, you hear that, right?'

In an impressive display of self-control, Mia meets Sam's gaze with a perfectly calm expression. 'Sorry? Hear what?' She avoids looking at John, who's continuing like he hasn't a care in the world.

. . . *They know that Santa's on his way, he's loaded lots of toys and goodies on his sleigh* . . .

Sam's eyes are wild. 'You *really* don't hear that?'

Mia's tone is gloriously sarcastic. 'I hear you getting all hysterical. And I *see* you making a mess of my kitchen.'

Sam grimaces at the splattered mayonnaise. He grabs a towel and wipes it up, hands shaking. Over his bent head, Mia meets John's gaze, and he shoots her a wink.

. . . and Sam Williams is gonna spy, to see if reindeer really know how to fly . . .

'For the love of God,' Sam groans. 'Make it stop. Please.'

'Well, since you said please,' Mia quips, eyes sparkling now. 'Let me see if I can help.' She raps on the counter with a wooden spoon three times. 'Attention all ghosts of Willowby Manor, can you give Sam Williams a break?' Mia crosses her arms and spears Sam with a glance. 'Happy now?'

Sam waits for a beat, listening intently. When no music continues, he sighs and takes a bite of his sandwich. 'Yes. Much better. Thank you, Mia.' He sags against the counter and doesn't say another word until he finishes eating. John gives Mia a conspiratorial nod and she mouths 'thank you' to him as he walks out of the room.

9

MIA

'You know the fake trees can come pre-lit, right? So, remind me again why both of our trees have to be fresh?' Charlie asks this as he lugs another cardboard box on to the upstairs landing.

'A fresh tree brings more Christmassy cheer, obviously.' Mia opens up a stepladder and makes sure the safety locks engage.

'Mum!' Charlie turns to locate Penny, his tone outraged.

'Mia, don't be snide with your brother,' Penny admonishes. She pats Charlie on the shoulder. 'She's just grumpy. She's been like this since she got here. I'm sure she didn't mean it, sweetie.' Penny pulls open a cardboard box and sighs in delight. 'Ah, yes, here they are.' She removes a smaller box and carefully places it on the bench in the corridor. 'And, to answer your question, the reason we have fresh trees is called compromise.' She looks over at where Martin is untangling a strand of lights. 'It's what makes a marriage work.'

Mia carefully climbs the ladder to assist her father as he begins to hang the lights on the fresh tree. 'Actually, I'm feeling rather jolly today,' she says. 'Not sure what brought that on, but it's a welcome surprise.' She glances surreptitiously down the hall, where John is leaning against a doorframe, observing the family dynamics.

'Start the strand on that little sagging branch, Mia,' Martin directs. Then he announces, 'A successful marriage requires compromise, folks. Your mother has been after me for years to purchase artificial trees, but that would be a travesty. It's fresh or nothing.'

'Exactly!' Penny exclaims.

'I'm not following.' Charlie shakes his head. 'Mum wants artificial trees and Dad wants fresh ones. There are two fresh ones in the house. So how exactly did you guys compromise?'

'Well, when your father is old and senile, I will buy as many artificial trees as I want.' Penny smiles widely. 'See? Compromise.'

'Huh,' Charlie says.

Mia giggles. 'Makes perfect sense to me. Hey, Charlie, does your girlfriend's family do fresh trees or artificial?'

Charlie frowns. 'I'm not sure, actually. I've never met her family.'

Mia hides a grin. 'Hard to meet the potential in-laws when the person in question doesn't actually exist,' she teases, narrowly dodging Charlie's hand as he tries to smack her arm in retaliation.

'Martin, how long have you been doing the themed trees?' Sam asks as he lugs another box on to the landing.

Mia's gaze snags on the line of sweat that coats the back of his neck, making his skin glisten, reminding her of the days when she watched his tennis matches. There's just something about seeing him hot under the collar that she's always found mesmerising. It takes her a moment to tear her eyes away.

'Oh, well, let's see!' Martin visibly brightens. 'I started before the kids were born. Penny, I'm sure you have pictures around here somewhere. Penny is the official recorder for the family. But I think it was probably in 2000 that I really started getting into it.'

'You called it the tree of the new millennium! Ouch.' Mia pokes herself on a pine needle and pops the injured finger in her mouth.

'That's right!' Martin looks up at his daughter in approval.

'And I know we have a picture because we bought a new camera that year that I was so excited about. I'll have to look for it.' Penny turns to where Sam is unloading individually wrapped decorations from the box he carried in. 'Now, Sam, be careful with those. They're all glass, and most are antiques. That's why we don't put them up before our neighbourhood party.'

Mia groans. 'That's one of the reasons. Mum, do we really have to put those up?'

Martin sighs. 'You know we do. It's the first thing Aunt Gertie will notice when she returns from visiting Mr Thrumble.'

'Hideous things,' Penny agrees. 'But they've been in the family for three generations. It can't be helped. Carefully now, Sam.'

'Yes, of course,' Sam says as he works to open the next box.

'Charlie, have you found the other ornaments?'

'Mmm hmm.' Charlie straightens from where he was bent over another box, a crude clay ornament in his hands. 'This masterpiece is courtesy of Mia, 2005. It appears to be a Christmassy . . . ghoul.'

Martin laughs, and Mia pretends to glare at Charlie. 'It's a penguin, Charlie.'

His eyes widen comically. 'Oh, yes. Obviously. My mistake.'

Sam carefully lifts out one of the glass ornaments. 'Well, these are truly . . . beautiful? Just look at the colours of this one.' He holds it aloft, wincing slightly. The obnoxiously pink ornament is dotted with gaudy crystals.

John has slipped down the corridor and stops right beside Sam. With a quick movement, he knocks the ornament out of Sam's hand and on to the floor, where it shatters spectacularly. Mia gapes at the shards and then glances sidelong at John. He shrugs, a mischievous grin on his face.

'My goodness!' Penny covers her mouth with her hand.

'Oh, I'm terribly sorry, Mrs Robinson,' Sam says, looking horrified.

She presses her lips together and then smiles thinly. 'Of course it's fine. Just be more careful, dear.'

'Pass me some up here, Sam,' Mia chimes in.

Sam removes another ornament from the packaging. As he does, the glass ornament rubs against the thin plastic packaging, screeching horribly.

'Ugh. I had forgotten that sound. These really are the

worst, aren't they?' Charlie shudders as he hangs a felt stocking haphazardly on a lower branch.

Sam reaches up to hand Mia the ornament. John, who is several inches taller than Sam, simply bats it from his extended hand, and it goes flying.

'Sam!' Mia shouts, while Penny gasps. Sam pales, shaking his head.

'I'm so sorry, I don't know what—'

The pieces of the ornament are scattered across the floor, the garish colours winking in the soft lights on the Christmas tree.

'It really was a hideous bauble, wasn't it?' John asks Mia, amusement written across his face.

Mia, studiously avoiding making eye contact with John, looks at Sam. 'Bit of a butterfingers, aren't we?' she asks, her words laced with mirth.

'I don't know what's wrong with me today,' Sam mumbles, his ears turning red.

'Well, all you can do is try again,' Charlie encourages. 'It works better if you don't just toss them on the ground, though. They're fairly fragile, as you can see.'

'I'm not tossing them!' Sam protests, exasperated.

'If you ask me, it's no great loss,' Martin soothes in a stage whisper. He pats Penny on the back. 'No harm done, dear.'

'Of course, you're right,' she responds. Her unusually calm reaction leads Mia to believe that perhaps Penny was never a huge fan of these ornaments either.

Mortified, Sam withdraws another box of baubles from the container. Sliding off the protective sleeve, he lifts the entire package, the ornaments safely nestled in their plastic cushions. Moving with the deliberation of a mime, Sam takes two cautious steps towards the tree and holds the box up to Mia for her to take the ornaments.

John reaches between Mia and Sam, careful not to touch either of them and deftly removes several of the baubles. Without a moment's hesitation, he chucks them on the ground where they splinter, pieces flying into every corner.

'Honestly,' Mia begins.

'Good golly,' Martin observes.

Charlie just shakes his head.

'I'm *so* sorry,' Sam barks, his hand shaking. He tries to put the box with its remaining ornaments down, but John bats it from his hand, and the whole thing smashes to the floor.

Everyone freezes, looking to Penny who – after a stunned moment of disbelief – bursts into laughter. 'Sam! This is unbelievable!' Mia, relieved, begins laughing too as Martin starts to chuckle, and Charlie smiles widely. Sam looks between them all, bewildered.

'The boy has done us a Christmas kindness,' Martin says in between chuckles. 'Lord knows we've all hated those ugly things.' This makes Penny laugh even harder, until she's bent over, hands on her thighs as she tries to catch her breath.

'I'll get a broom,' Sam offers, cheeks flaming.

'Show – him – Mia,' Penny wheezes.

Mia swaps a wide-eyed, amused look with John, and then hops down off the ladder. 'You'll never find it on your own, I'll show you where we keep it. Come on, downstairs.' She gestures towards the staircase and Sam skirts the mess at his feet, looking entirely chastened.

They make their way down the stairs, the muffled sound of the others' laughter still faintly audible.

'I don't know what happened there,' Sam mumbles, shaking his head.

Mia glances at him sidelong as they reach the front hallway. 'You really weren't doing it on purpose?'

'No!' Sam nearly shouts.

'Are you sure?' She can't help teasing him a little more. She's enjoying this way too much, but it is so nice to finally feel a bit better. 'They were properly ugly. Maybe you were just trying to help us out, like Dad said. Heaven knows we've had to endure their hideousness long enough.'

Sam huffs out an approximation of a laugh. 'To be honest, I've never seen such ugly ornaments. I can see why your mum doesn't put them up until after her party.' He winces again. 'But I would *never* . . . I'm so embarrassed.'

'Mmm.' Mia leads the way into the kitchen and heads towards the cupboard on the side of the room. Seeing Sam so flustered has soothed her simmering anger considerably.

'No one likes feeling embarrassed.' Popping open the latch on the broom cupboard, she reaches inside and passes Sam the broom and dustpan. Sam makes a little rumbling sound of agreement and Mia's stomach flips unexpectedly. She's startled by the intensity of her reaction to him after all this time. Why hadn't that chemistry waned? Not even a little? Sam gives her a knowing look but makes no comment. He reaches up and runs a hand across her shoulder. 'You picked up a few cobwebs.'

But even after brushing away the offensive strands, his thumb continues to move, gently stroking along her collarbone. Mia's eyes fix on his thumb, hypnotized. Her lips part just as he seems to realize what he's doing.

'Sorry,' he mumbles, pulling his hand away quickly, before adding sheepishly, 'it's always been hard to keep my hands to myself when I'm around you.'

Mia can't help the smile that creeps over her face. She remembers having the same problem all those years ago, remembers how intoxicating it had been to touch Sam, like a drug she could never quite get enough of.

'It's good to see you smile, Mia.' Sam hesitates. 'I'm sorry that I ruined Christmas for you. I shouldn't have come.'

Mia's not sure how to respond. She didn't want Sam here, didn't want to ever see him, or be within the same fifty miles as him again. But she can't forget that look in his eyes when he told her that his family had all made plans without him. And she can't ignore the desire that had risen inside her at his touch.

'You have something so special here, Mia,' Sam continues. 'I don't mean about Willowby Manor, although this place is incredible. I'm talking about the community, the people I met on Saturday. And your family. There are relationships here that go back centuries. Now I know why you're always so grounded and calm.'

This makes Mia laugh. 'I think you might be the only person to ever describe me as calm.'

Sam chuckles softly. He's standing so close, and his expression is warm and open, the way it used to be when they spent time together. 'That's not what I meant. I just meant that you have a certain sense of belonging. You know where you come from and it gives you a stability that most people don't have. It's something very . . . special.' He steps back slightly and clears his throat. 'Thank you for letting me stay the week, even though it's obviously not what you would have chosen.'

Mia harrumphs. 'I didn't let you do anything.'

'No.' Sam smiles down at her. 'But you could have insisted that I leave. I'm grateful that you didn't.'

His words are doing something funny to her. If she's not careful, she'll forget the reasons why she hates this man. It would be too easy, when he looks at her with such admiration and care in his gaze. She feels the instinctive pull, the desire to move into him, to close the little space that remains between them. Mia forces herself to take a step back and looks around for a much-needed distraction. 'Looks like we're low on bin bags. Will you write them on the list on the fridge, please?'

Sam pulls the pen from his pocket and locates the pad magnetized to the fridge door. 'Argh,' he growls, as the pen proves to be dry. 'Why does this keep happening?'

Mia rummages in a drawer for a pencil. When she hands it to him, their fingers brush. His skin is warm, and a jolt runs up her arm at the contact. All she would need to do is close her eyes, and she'd be back in the cramped little bed, heart pounding after Sam had traced one of those long, artistic fingers down her cheek. She'd never felt so wholly desired. Agitated, Mia jerks back, breaking eye contact. 'Ah, I need to finish presenting. I mean, wrapping. The presents. Gifts. You know. For Christmas.'

'Sure.' Sam raises the cleaning tools. 'I have work to do as well. Happy wrapping,' he calls out as Mia beats a hasty retreat.

10

JOHN

Well, that is interesting. John watches Mia as she dashes up the stairs like her tail is on fire. He had followed Mia and Sam to the kitchen, set on wreaking more havoc given how much Mia had enjoyed his antics with the ornaments. He was thinking that perhaps he could dump some rubbish on Sam, or make the microwave keep buzzing over and over. Something that would drive Sam crazy, and make Mia laugh again, while also saving her from getting into a blazing argument with Sam. He could only imagine the bitter words being thrown around while the two of them were alone.

Instead, he'd seemed to have observed some sort of truce. Or at least a temporary cessation of hostilities. Sam and Mia had shared what seemed to be a heartfelt conversation, and, if he wasn't mistaken, Mia had even *laughed*.

John had been quite the busybody in his day. There was nothing he'd enjoyed more than matching up a couple based on their compatibility and he had always had a sense for these things while he was alive, and now he can't help but think that it really is a shame Mia is such a sworn enemy of Sam. They'd make a striking couple, and John can even imagine they might have a few things in common. Ridiculous footwear, for starters. He sighs and heads up the stairs after Mia. No use imagining the impossible. He has a feeling that Mia Robinson isn't one to change her mind. That girl has a stubborn streak the width of Africa.

Taking the stairs two at a time, he catches up to Mia in the corridor and follows her into her childhood bedroom. Once they're inside and the door is closed, Mia lets herself fall back on the bed, laughter bubbling up.

'John! This is working out so perfectly. His face when you tossed that first ornament on the floor! I thought he was going to throw up.'

'I was worried I was taking it too far. But let me tell you, Mia, I have no regrets. I've been staring at those ghastly ornaments for longer than you've been alive. It was time for them to go.'

'You've done the world a great service today.' Mia's voice is grave. Then she dissolves once more into laughter.

'You know where they came from, right?'

Mia shakes her head as she pulls out wrapping paper and tape from under her bed, then slides open a dresser drawer and starts taking out the gifts she'd stashed there when she arrived. John takes a seat up by the head of the bed.

'Mags told me they were gifts from a suitor. Apparently, some young man in town was interested in your gran. Joan was quite the catch when she was an eligible young lady, you know. Anyway, the man – I believe his name was Reginald – worked at the factory in town, and he would gather up all the ornaments that ended up as seconds and bring them to Joan whenever he visited. She thought they were atrocious, but she was too nice to say anything. Eventually, Gertie told him to stop coming. She was the one to break the news to Reginald that your gran was engaged to Morris.'

'I love that you know all of this.' Mia, having abandoned all pretence of wrapping gifts, is lying on her stomach, chin propped on her hands as she listens. 'What other juicy gossip can you tell me about Willowby Manor? Maybe listening to ancient drama will inspire a new way to mess with Sam.'

John leans back against the headboard and crosses his legs at the ankles. 'Well, the gardener died a tragic death here.'

'Pssht. I already know that one.' Mia brightens. 'Ohh, but I don't know how! Is it insensitive to try to guess how you died?'

'Of course it is,' John responds. But he waves his permission anyway.

'OK, let's see. You seem like a man who enjoys a nice bath. Did you fall asleep and drown?' John shakes his head. 'Wait, no. I think you fell asleep in your room with a candle on . . . No, that can't be it because the cottage would have burnt down. Also, do ghosts look the way they did when they died? Like, if you had your head cut off, would you have to run around headless?'

'Probably,' John quips with a serious face.

Mia's eyes widen. 'Truly?'

114

'I have no idea. But I don't think so, or else my head would be full of holes.'

'Ooh, a clue! OK, wait. Don't tell me any more. So, your head is a sieve – maybe you walked into some bird-shot? No? Hmm. I feel like I can get this if I just think hard enough.'

John starts to respond, but there's a tentative knock at the door.

'Mia?'

'Come in, Mum,' Mia calls, absentmindedly.

She's clearly still trying to figure out how John died when Penny steps into the room, her arms laden with photograph albums. She's changed into a pale green trouser suit with a striped turtleneck underneath the jacket. 'I thought you might like to look at these. Oh, were you talking to someone?'

Mia's eyes jump to John, and then away. Quickly, she flicks the bedspread over the small pile of presents in the middle of the bed. 'Nope! Ah, must have been the radio.'

Penny looks around Mia's room. 'But you don't have a radio in here, dear.'

Mia gulps. 'Ah, I meant the radio was on next door. In Charlie's room.'

Penny lowers the albums to the bed. 'Well, OK. These are all the albums I could find. They're not in any order, but I thought you might like looking at all of Dad's trees over the years.'

'Thanks, Mum.'

Penny gives Mia a little squeeze and heads out, closing the door behind her.

Mia tugs the thickest album into her lap and begins to flip through the pages. 'Oh, look. These are of Mum and Dad when they were young. Dating, maybe?' She flips a few more pages, then squints at another picture. 'Wow, Grandma Joan *was* a total hottie, you weren't lying. Look at her in her swimming costume.'

John gives the photo a cursory glance with a polite nod. 'Very nice. She actually looks a bit like my mum.'

'Really?' Mia peers at the picture again. 'How interesting. Oh, look! There are pictures of every single holiday party here at Willowby. Gosh. I think that's Mr Thrumble with hair.'

John chuckles, and Mia falls silent for a few minutes, absorbed in the photos.

'Ugh. This was my dad's moustache phase. Terrible idea. He looks like a serial killer. Oh, here's the millennium tree he was talking about.'

John shifts to peer over her shoulder. The tree in question is enormous, studded with lights and swathed in airy silver tulle. 'I remember that one now. Looked like a giant spaceship.'

'Mmm hmm. This is actually quite fun. No one prints out photos any more.'

This confuses John. 'Are you telling me no one takes pictures any more? Haven't I seen you snapping away on that little pocket phone you have?'

Mia smirks. 'You can just say phone. And yes, I have hundreds of photos on my phone. But we don't print them out. We just keep them in the cloud.'

John's confusion is evident.

'The internet was a thing when you were alive, right?'

'Of course,' John says. 'I went to the internet cafe once or twice.'

Mia's eyes widen. 'O . . . K. I've read about those. Things really have changed in the last few decades, haven't they?'

'Mmm. It remains to be seen whether that's good or bad.'

'Oh, I think it's good. People are much more open minded about a lot of things these days. For instance, it's not cool to bully people any more. Or poke fun at their weight or their freckles and things. It's all about tolerance, John.'

'Well, I'm sure there are some things people still aren't tolerant of.' Like being humiliated by a certain brown-eyed tennis player, John thinks.

'Sure, but I think it's mostly centred around religion and politics these days. Not about people's individual choices. Haven't you heard the expression "you do you"?'

John shakes his head.

'Well, it's just kind of this acknowledgement that we all have our own path to walk and should feel confident being ourselves.' Mia stares thoughtfully off into the distance. John watches her, wondering if the world really has changed that much since he died. Tolerance wasn't exactly the de facto response that he remembered.

As a child, he'd always been passionate about music, and particularly singing, but he'd been subjected to a fair amount of ridicule for it. His mum had always been very encouraging about it, but the other children at school had been ruthless. He had been teased relentlessly for an entire year, and John had been tempted to quit so many times. But that year he'd had the solo at the end of year concert, and he couldn't bring himself to miss out on that experience. Thankfully, Mrs Wicket had become head of music the following year, and taken John under her wing, until singing had quickly become the brightest spot in his life.

Shaking herself, Mia returns her attention to the albums on the bed. 'Wow, these albums really do go way back. Hey, you should be in here somewhere, shouldn't you? Mum said the staff were always invited to the Christmas parties.'

'It's very likely,' John offers.

'Oh, it's a shame Mags won't be in any of the pictures, though! I'd have loved to see her.'

John barks out a laugh. 'Mags was positively terrified of any and all technology when she came across it while she was stuck in limbo, so perhaps it's for the best she never came face to face with the business end of a camera. You know, her crockery-throwing antics were actually the inspiration behind the ornament tossing earlier.'

'Genius – thank you, Mags! God, Sam was *so* confused, it was brilliant.' Mia dissolves into giggles at the thought. At the mention of Sam, John is tempted to bring up the events that transpired in the kitchen, to see whether Mia might confess that perhaps Sam isn't all bad after all. But before he can work up the courage, Mia stops giggling and turns to him with a curious look. 'How was Mags able to pass over?'

John frowns. 'I have no idea. One day she was here, and the next she just . . . wasn't.'

'But *you've* never been able to pass over.'

'No. I have wondered if it had to do with how I died. Maggie fell down the cellar stairs and broke her neck. They were renovating that part of the manor when she disappeared, so maybe the link between her place of death and herself were severed? Of course, that won't happen to me, because I died outside.'

Mia looks up from the photo albums. 'Do tell.'

John shudders. 'Not much to tell. I was careless and left a garden rake lying out. Right on that stone path that winds around the back of the cottage. Wasn't watching where I was going, stepped on it, of course. I took the tines right to the back of the head.'

'Gross.' Mia grimaces. 'So, you bled out, then?'

John nods. 'It was off season, and there weren't many people here at the manor. Took too long for someone to find me.'

'That's horrifying.'

'Yes, well, it happened. And I've been stuck here since then, spending the last thirty years trying to cross over.'

It occurs to John that's not entirely true. It's not like he's exhausted every option. At first, there was a bit of novelty to being a ghost. Despite the indigestion, it was rather thrilling to be able to walk through walls. He'd played around with that for a year or two. Then he'd decided to read every book in the manor library, and that had taken quite a bit of time. But since then? He'd mostly been twiddling his thumbs, content to watch the months tick by without doing much about it.

'Can you leave the grounds?' Mia asks, peering at another set of Christmas pictures. 'Go into town, even?'

'I wish. The first year after the accident, I walked all over the grounds to find my boundaries. I'm fairly limited. I can go to the cottage, and the house obviously. And then about as far as the orchard. No further.'

'I would have lost my mind.'

John chuckles. 'Maybe I have. How would you know?'

'Fair,' Mia chuckles and then continues perusing the albums. 'Hey, wait a minute, I think this might be you!'

She spins the album around so John can see it. There's a group of people clustered by a Christmas tree, which is located in front of the bay window. But this is not a Martin Robinson tree. It's simply done up, with an angel tree topper and plenty of tinsel.

'Ah. This is all the staff at Willowby Manor the Christmas before I died.'

Mia studies the picture. 'You were a sharp-looking man, John. Quite the catch. Actually, everyone in this group is good-looking. Especially that redhead in the corner with the big shoulders. I've always loved a man with great shoulders. Although Sam has gorgeous thighs and I never minded those either . . .' Her voice trails off, seemingly lost in thought.

John nods. 'Lot of power in strong thighs. But I personally preferred the broad-shouldered type.'

'So the redhead worked here too?'

John swallows hard and shakes his head. 'No. That's Alastair McGregor.'

'Such a dashing name,' Mia observes. 'Who was he?'

'A friend,' John says slowly. 'We grew very close that year.' He sighs. 'I'm not sure how to talk about this. Alastair was a great guy. Funny. Charming. He had such a unique perspective on the world. I used to listen to him talk for hours.'

Mia sobers, dropping all pretence of teasing. 'This Alastair was important to you.'

John sighs. Mia is latching on like a dog with a bone, and he's not certain he's ready to get into all the messy details of his last few months alive. 'He was, at a certain point in my life. But by the time I died, we hadn't spoken in months.'

'Hmm.' Mia taps the photograph with a finger. 'Do you think this Alastair has something to do with why you ended up stuck in the in-between?'

It's not like this hasn't occurred to John over the years. After all, he's had a lot of time to think. But even now, after so much time, he's not ready to delve into that. 'Well, Mia, you're the first living person to be able to see me in thirty years, so, I would imagine that being stuck here has something to do with you.'

'I'd hate to think that you've been stuck here all this time just waiting for me.' Mia shakes her head. 'No . . . there's something more here.'

Sadness washes over him and he huffs out another sigh. 'I think I'm done reminiscing, Mia. I'm going to the cottage for a bit. I need some peace and quiet. I'm not used to all this excitement and energy.'

Mia's lips work from side to side as she looks at him. Then she raises her eyebrows and shrugs. 'OK. See you later then.' Setting aside the photo albums, she uncovers the presents and starts measuring out wrapping paper.

John lets himself out of the room, still feeling troubled as he walks along the corridor. When he was alive, he hadn't really felt the need to chase after his dreams, or anything like that, content with a simple, safe life. Alastair had been the exact opposite. It had both challenged and scared John and, ultimately, it's what had driven them apart. He stops briefly by Sam's room, peering through the cracked door. Inside, Sam is painstakingly wrapping up a small box. Compared to the hastily wrapped others on the bed, this present is a cut above. John lets himself in and moves closer so he can see who Sam addresses the gift to.

Sam pulls out his pen and – to John's surprise – marks the box for Mia. When he turns to place the wrapped gift on the desk, John deftly replaces Sam's pen for one of his own dried-up ones, and saunters back out of the room.

It's curious that Sam has a gift for Mia, John thinks. Could he unwrap it later and see what Sam's gift is? He debates the feasibility of this as he heads downstairs.

On his way to the back door, John passes through the kitchen and scoops up a few of the biscuits Aunt Gertie has put out. He takes a hearty bite and chokes slightly as the biscuit crumbles in his mouth.

Ugh. Dry as always.

11

MIA

22 December

The gardener's cottage is chilly in the mornings, even with a fire merrily crackling in the front room. Mia has never been more thankful for her enormous fluffy slippers from the flea market.

What started as a desperate attempt to replace her grandmother's earring has become one of her most cherished routines. She usually wakes up early, too excited to sleep in and miss potential deals. She would spend the entire bus ride, or trip on the Underground, plotting her attack. She always went to the jewellery stalls first, followed by the stalls with vintage clothes – some of her favourites. In fact, on her last treasure hunt, Mia had scored a pair of vintage Robert La Roche men's sunglasses that she absolutely adored. She sets them on the wonky dresser this morning, in the hope that the sun will peek out later on.

She is surprised by how much she's enjoying this visit, especially given how she'd felt that first morning waking up here at Willowby. She hasn't thought about James in ages, and with the benefit of a little bit of distance, she's gaining some perspective. Perhaps James wasn't the right one for her. He had seemed perfectly happy to let Mia do all the heavy lifting in their short relationship. Come to think of it, had he ever initiated in any way other than the physical? Mia had cooked for him, written him little notes and taken an interest in his career. What had James done for her? Mia comes up empty.

This week has been full of revelations. Mia had never pegged herself as someone who would enjoy being friends with a ghost, but life will always have its surprises. And after yesterday's antics, she doesn't even mind the fact that Sam is still here. It's been quite funny watching him react to the harmless pranks John is playing on him and it does feel like justice is being served, which Mia is finding immensely satisfying. And there's something else, too, about having him around again, a long-buried feeling slowly rising inside her. A feeling she isn't quite sure what to do with.

Mia spends the morning tidying the cottage, and then heads up to the big house, snow gear in tow.

'Good morning, Daddy,' she chirps. Martin is tucked into the sunny breakfast nook, his long legs tangled beneath the scarred table. The newspaper and a steaming mug of coffee litter the tabletop. She gives him a kiss on the cheek and then moves to the kitchen sink to wash her hands.

'You're up early,' Martin observes. He sets the paper aside to focus on her. 'Cooking again?'

'Of course,' Mia responds. 'We'll need lunch, won't we? And I have a hankering for gingerbread.' Rummaging through the fridge, she pulls out a whole chicken and begins prepping it.

'Your mother and I are headed out in a bit to visit the Fletchers. From what your mother says, Dot and Earl are thinking of moving to Malaga.'

'I don't blame them,' Mia responds absently. She's searching for her mother's kitchen shears. 'If I could get away from winter, I would. Although I always prefer a white Christmas.' As she says it, she suddenly remembers a mostly jokey argument with Sam years before where he'd been adamant that snow on Christmas was too clichéd and predictable to be enjoyable. It brings a reluctant smile to Mia's face as she recalls how shocked she'd been by the revelation.

Martin chuckles. 'The snow has never bothered me. But your mother has started making noises about spending the winters somewhere warmer.'

Mia makes short work of chopping the chicken carcass into several pieces. 'Would you mind finding the peeler for me? Mum must have reorganized since the last time I was here. I can't find anything.'

"Course, darling.' Martin slides to his feet and works his way methodically through the drawers, eventually handing her the tool. 'How're things at the hospital?'

'It's been good. Sometimes they have me sub in at the front desk if someone calls in sick. I spend a lot of time checking IDs and printing visitor badges. On the plus side, I get to chat with a lot of random people, and help them figure out where their loved one is staying. But it's pretty dull when it's slow. Thank goodness for the book club.'

'You gals read anything good lately?'

'Mmm, a couple of memoirs. Oh, and a thriller about this female serial killer who returns to the same wellness resort year after year to exact revenge on the staff there. That one was a page turner.'

'Send me the link,' Martin says. 'Your mother bought me a Kindle and I'm learning how to use it.'

'Look at you all hip and with the times.' Mia peels several parsnips and chops them into large pieces. 'How's retirement?'

Martin sighs. 'You know, I'm thinking about picking up some part-time work. Your mother says I'm in her hair too much now that I'm home all the time. You want me to chop that onion for you?'

'Absolutely. You know I hate cutting those. I always cry.'

Martin chuckles and sets himself up with another cutting board and knife. As he slices the onion into thin pieces, he hums to himself.

Thinking about what John's told her of his musical career, Mia asks, 'Did you ever act or sing while you were in school, Daddy?'

Martin laughs. 'Oh, yes. I was in a production of *Treasure Island* that brought down the house. It wasn't a musical, but the acting was unparalleled.' He gives her a wink. 'For a school production, at least. It was quite fun. That's actually where your mother and I met, you know.'

'I thought you met when you were both working at the fish and chip shop in uni?'

Martin shakes his head. 'That's when we went on our first date. But we actually met during that production. I don't think your mother even knew of my existence then, but I was captivated by her. She just had this energy about her – like she could take on the whole world and make it better. I took one look and fell in love. Even considered proposing that very minute. She was dating some athletic chap at the time, what was his name? Ah, that's it – Thomas Higgins. Can you imagine your mum as a Mrs Higgins?' Martin shakes his head. 'Doesn't suit her. Anyway, they were fairly serious, so I kept my distance. But I just felt like we were meant to be, you know?'

'Aw, Dad, that's so lovely.' Mia scoops the sliced onions into the pot and quickly peels several purple carrots. Martin peers at her, a perplexed expression on his face.

'Such a strange colour for carrots.'

'They'll taste almost exactly the same,' Mia assures him. 'But they look even prettier.' She chops the carrots into thick pieces and tosses them in with the onions and parsnips. After washing her hands, she asks, 'So did Mum remember you when you met up again at university?'

Martin lets out a laugh. 'Not at all! She actually walked up to me and introduced herself. I can still hear the way she said it – a little shy but with a touch of excitement. "Hi, I'm Penny Clarke. Do you want to grab a drink after our shift ends?"'

'And of course you said yes.' Mia arranges the chicken over the chopped vegetables and adds a few pieces of butter on top. This conversation is reminding her of the first time she met Sam, and despite her best efforts to ignore it, she's feeling nostalgic. She'd been thirteen and painfully awkward for the whole interaction, for which Charlie had mercilessly teased her afterwards, but honestly who could blame her? Sam was literally the hottest guy in school and he'd seemed genuinely interested in talking to her – it was enough to make any teenager weak at the knees. She'd been so enthralled by him that she'd spent most of the school year daydreaming about Sam asking her out on a date.

Martin nods. 'Of course. I was so happy to see her, and obviously I remembered her. But what blew me away was I still felt exactly the same about her. As if no time had passed. The same thrill of excitement, the same anticipation and desire to spend the rest of my life with her. When you find the right person, there's just something about them. You just know – or at least your subconscious does. Even if it takes a while to end up together.' He grabs a dishcloth and wipes down the counter where Mia was working. 'Love doesn't just fizzle out after a certain amount of time. Not if it's the person you're meant to be with.' Martin looks off into the distance, smiling as he allows himself to be lost in his memories. His words have struck an unexpected chord inside Mia, and she finds her chest growing tight as the memory of Sam saying he loved her all those years ago resurfaces. She grips the edge of the sink firmly, willing the wave of emotion away.

After a few moments and some steadying breaths, Mia turns round to her dad, just as he goes on, 'Now, your mother, she was talented. Could light up a room. She always came so alive on stage. When she was in a production I would go to every one of her shows. And I'd just sit there in the front row, in awe of how comfortable she was in front of a crowd. Just incredible.'

Her dad lapses into a comfortable silence, and Mia moves some of the dirty dishes to the sink. Hearing her father's version of how he and her mum fell in love has stirred up a confusing sense of longing in her. She'd always wanted a happy marriage like her parents', but the chances of it happening feel further away than ever.

'Dad,' she ventures after a few minutes, 'what if I never find someone like that? What if I'm meant to end up single for ever and alone?'

'Pssht,' Martin shakes his head. 'You've got plenty of time to find someone.'

'I'm twenty-eight.'

'Practically retirement age,' Martin teases her.

'I'm serious.'

'So am I,' he replies gently. 'You've got plenty of time, Mia bella. Just keep yourself busy, like you've been telling me you are, and when the time is right, it will happen. And in the meantime, you have a job you enjoy, you've got good friends, a comfortable place to live. Speaking of, do you think you'll stay down in London for a while longer?' Martin pours himself another cup of coffee and sits back down at the island.

'I do, Dad. I like living in London, for the most part.'

'Well, if you're happy, then so am I,' Martin responds. 'Of course, we miss seeing you here. Never thought that both my children would end up living so far away from Worcester. Sometimes it feels like I'm missing out.'

'You should get Instagram, Dad,' Mia teases as she pours stock into the pan. 'Charlie and I are both on there.'

'Don't know what that is. Can I put it on the Kindle? Here, let me do that.' Martin places the pot in the oven where it will cook until lunchtime. He rubs a hand over his jawline, his palm scratching on the stubble. 'Well, I'd better go and clean myself up. Your mother will have my head if I make us late. Hopefully everything is still working in the bathroom. I hear there was a bit of a mishap yesterday with a speaker or something.'

Mia snickers under her breath but puts on her most innocent expression. 'I hadn't heard about that.'

Martin shakes his head at her, but doesn't argue. 'Well, darling, Sam is a nice boy, but I don't blame you for feeling the need to punish him a little more for what he did to you.' His words take Mia by surprise, and she pauses to look at her dad.

Martin shrugs. 'You were always the prankster, Mia. Used to drive Charlie crazy. It's not a stretch to think you're exacting a bit of revenge on that Williams chap. But don't take it too far, Mia bella. You don't want to cross a line you'll regret someday.' And with that gentle admonishment, he heads out of the kitchen.

Mia starts cleaning up the colossal mess she's created, thinking over her father's words. They've soothed some of that anxiety that always lives inside her because maybe he's right, and she does still have time to figure out her love life. But even though she's gained clarity where James is concerned, she can't ignore that her feelings about Sam are more confused than ever. She's hated him for such a long time and there's still a stubborn part of her that won't let go of the pain that's tied up with her thoughts of Sam. But it's also become harder to deny the very real feelings she had for him before everything went wrong between them. And today, there's been a flutter of those familiar old feelings inside her, closer to the surface than they have been in years. She's not entirely sure she's ready to face up to what that might mean.

With the kitchen cleaned up and a batch of ginger-bread resting in the fridge, Mia checks her phone. There are a few texts from Lucy.

I should bring a gift for Tim's family, right? What says 'I'm cool and interesting and worthy of your son?' A fruit basket? Mia chuckles and starts typing out a response. Lucy has been dating Tim for almost two years, and although Tim had introduced her to his family a while back, this is the first Christmas they'll be spending together. He works in finance – an area that Mia finds quite dull, to be honest, but he treats Lucy well, and that's really all that matters.

Not a fruit basket! You're not seventy. Bring them a nice houseplant and a good bottle of wine and you'll be set. Don't stress! They already love you!

Once the text shows as sent, Mia layers on all her snow gear and heads outside. It's brilliantly sunny, thankfully. She can practically feel her vitamin D deficiency increasing every day further into winter. She fishes out her new sunglasses and slides them on. Charlie and Sam are hard at work, as they've been every day it's snowed, shovelling all of the various paths that crisscross between the driveway, the big house and the gardener's cottage. From a distance, Mia allows herself to admire the smooth way Sam works. He's discarded his heavy coat and scarf, and is working in just a short-sleeved shirt that displays his muscled arms. Biceps flexing, he hefts the snow over and over, intently focused on his task. Sam wears the same expression he does when he's playing tennis, and warmth pools in Mia's stomach. She shifts from one foot to the other, letting her mind drift for a few moments while she waits for John's arrival.

One of the things Mia had loved about Sam was the fact that he was able to wholly devote himself to whatever he was doing. When he played tennis, he did so with abandon, everything else fading away. At the end of his matches, she could always spot the exact moment the rest of the world would come back into focus for him. The first thing he always did was to search the stands, seeking her out, and as soon as he spotted her he'd gift her with one of his brilliant, joyful smiles. The memory of that feeling, knowing he would always look for her first, still tugged at her heart. She missed being the recipient of those smiles.

Mia bounces on her toes and listens to the snow crunching under her feet. It's perfect snowball snow. She's wearing her warmest mittens and the fleece-lined leggings that Mum gave her last year for Christmas. She is preparation personified.

Charlie and Sam are racing to see who can shovel the last few feet of the walkway. Charlie's approach is haphazard, flinging snow in every direction as he works to clear the path. Sam is more calculating, clearing the snow in neat rows so there's no rework. As she watches, Sam scoops up a shovelful and deposits it beneath a bush. While his back is turned, Charlie dumps an entire load of snow into Sam's portion, and then hurries back to his territory.

'Cheater!' Mia calls out, bending down to scoop enough snow for a snowball. John's not here yet, but she can't let Charlie get away with his trickery. Packing it carefully, she lets the snowball fly towards her brother. It glides through the air, smashing harmlessly into the freshly shovelled drifts feet away from Charlie. She's never had great aim.

Charlie glances at her, shakes his head and surreptitiously dumps another shovelful of snow into Sam's area.

'OK, that's it!' Tucking the vintage sunglasses into a pocket for safekeeping, Mia rushes down towards where the guys are working, until she's close enough that she's confident she won't miss. She fires off another snowball, this time hitting Charlie on the chest.

'Hey!' His protest is a mixture of laughter and shock. 'You actually hit me!'

'Lucy has been taking me axe throwing,' Mia retorts, as she lets another one fly. This one goes wide as well. 'Sam! Watch out!'

Sam startles, looking up from where he is methodically scooping snow. He dodges the flying snowball and looks around, bewildered. 'What's going on?'

'You started without me?' John's voice comes from behind, lightly outraged. 'Well, then. Let's get on with it.'

Mia crouches beside him. 'Charlie and Sam were racing, and Charlie was cheating. I had to do something.'

'Hmm.' John doesn't say anything else, since he's focused on forming as many snowballs as he can. He scoops snow with his bare hands and packs it quickly.

'Aren't you cold?' Mia asks, crouching beside him. John's only wearing his argyle sweater and those thin pleated trousers.

'Nah, it's great out here!' Charlie yells back, launching a hastily packed snowball in Mia's direction.

She dodges it, giggling. Then whispers, 'He thinks I was talking to him.'

'Better be careful,' John admonishes. 'You can't have people suspecting you talk to ghosts. And, to answer your question, I truly wish I could feel the cold. Or taste the biscuits your Aunt Gertie leaves out. Or feel any kind of sensation other than this clammy, damp feeling that's always inside of me.'

Mia stares at him. 'John. That's awful. I didn't know.'

'Don't worry about it. We have a snowball fight to win.'

While they've been exchanging furious whispers, Sam has barricaded himself beside the cottage with his snow shovel and a nearby wheelbarrow and is assembling his own arsenal. As Mia watches, he lets two fly in Charlie's direction. The first sails harmlessly overhead, but the second smashes against Charlie's leg.

'Augh! OK, that's it. You're both goners.'

The fight rages fast and furious, and with John's

assistance, Mia is credited with several direct hits to Sam's midsection and back.

'Why do I feel like you're only targeting me now, Mia?' Sam calls out.

'I don't know what you're talking about,' Mia sing-songs.

Charlie bends over, scooping up a handful of snow and packing it into a ball. He lobs it, smacking Mia right in the shoulder. She screeches as snow slips beneath the collar of her jacket, and Charlie roars with laughter. Sam covers his own laugh with a cough and darts behind the barricade he's constructed, wisely taking cover.

'I'd like to see you match that one, Mia Tia,' Charlie taunts. 'Your aim has always been abysmal!'

Anger sparking at her brother's challenge, and that stupid nickname, Mia scrambles to put together her own snowball, leaving John behind. She chucks it, hitting the back of Charlie's head with startling accuracy as he rushes away from her.

Then, running towards Charlie, Mia fires off the remaining snowballs she's prepared. Only one hits its mark, but her satisfaction is immense as Charlie lets out an outraged yowl.

'Oh, you're going down, Mia.' Charlie launches a rapid fire of snowballs, and Mia is forced to retreat from the relentless onslaught. She backs up a few feet at a time, crouching as she forms her own ammunition. She's so engrossed in the fight with Charlie that she's lost track of both Sam's and John's whereabouts. She scrambles back again as Charlie launches a particularly large snowball straight at her face. With her hands full of the ball she's packing, she can't block the incoming snowball, and it hits her full on.

'Agh! Charlie, I'm going to kill you!' This is what Mia intends to say, but the words come out all garbled as she spits out a mouthful of fresh snow. Her face is stinging and she can hardly see. She stumbles backwards, and suddenly she's thrown off balance, having collided with some unknown object.

'Mia!' Sam's shout penetrates her confusion. She's falling, but Sam angles himself behind her, his body pressed against hers as his strong arms wrap around her, breaking the impact of her fall. They crash to the ground in a tangle of limbs, snow spraying up in every direction.

'Ceasefire!' Sam yells again, but the command comes too late. Mia blinks away the snow obscuring her vision just in time to see a firmly packed snowball smash into the side of Sam's head. 'Ow! You lousy bastard! Quit it!'

'Oh no,' Mia murmurs. Sam shakes his head, wincing as the snow slides down beneath his collar. There's a bright red spot on his temple where the snowball found its mark. 'Are you OK?'

Sam is half propped above her, and he ignores her question as he looks Mia over somewhat frantically. 'Did you get hurt when you fell?' He yanks off his gloves in an impatient motion, and then gently, ever so gently, brushes the snow off her face. 'That snow can be sharp when it's packed that tight. Did it cut you?'

Mia stills beneath his touch. His fingers glide over her forehead, nose and cheeks, checking for injuries, and the concern written across his face tugs at something in her chest.

'I'm fine, Sam.' She feels an unexpected need to reassure him. When he reaches her lips, he pauses for an eternity, his gaze dropping to where his hand is brushing against her flushed skin.

Sam huffs out a little sound of appreciation as he stares down at her, still half cradled in his arms. 'For God's sake, Mia. How are you still this pretty?'

Warmth curls inside her at his words, the sensation only heightened by the feeling of Sam pressed up against her. She realises with a rush how much she's missed this, the way they fit so perfectly together, his weight alongside her, the heat of his body wrapping around her.

Shaking his head as if he still can't quite orient himself, Sam brushes more snow from Mia's hair. He takes his time, and she has the distinct impression that he's prolonging the contact on purpose, and she can't seem to find the will to object. He's studying her, as if reacquainting himself with her features, and she realizes that she's doing the same to him. A tender smile blooms on his face, and his eyes crinkle. 'Your cheeks are all pink,' Sam says, his voice low enough that the words are clearly only meant for Mia. 'And there's snow crusted in your eyelashes.' Gentle laughter rumbles in his chest. 'You look ethereal . . . like an ice princess.'

Lying there in the snow with Sam, Mia doesn't think about how much she's hated him for the last six years. She doesn't think about the humiliation of that night in the pool. She thinks about those precious, intimate moments they shared years ago, and the way that Sam used to make her feel. Cherished. Important. Tentatively, Mia lifts a hand and presses it to Sam's chest. His eyes slide closed and he swallows. He shudders at the contact and Mia exhales. Finally, she twists to prop herself up on an elbow.

Sam's eyes reopen and they lie there for a long moment looking at each other, neither one breaking eye contact. Then Sam sucks in a breath and offers up a single word. 'Truce?'

It's a weighted question, pregnant with significance. Mia knows he's not referring to the snowball fight. 'Yes,' she whispers.

Hope ignites in Sam's eyes, but he doesn't say any more. Instead he pushes himself back to standing and reaches a hand down to help Mia up. After a second's pause, she lets him pull her back to her feet. Sam gives her one of his easy smiles and turns to shout out, 'It's over, Charlie!'

'Copy,' Charlie replies. 'Good thing. My toes are frozen solid.'

'Mine too,' Sam mourns. Mia glances past where Sam stands to meet John's mischievous gaze. He waggles his eyebrows at her, clearly satisfied with the success of this latest endeavour.

'Lunch should be ready by now if we want to head inside,' Mia offers.

Charlie's stomach growls so loudly they can all hear it. 'I guess that's a yes.'

12

JOHN

It's been nice, having the house full all week. As John trails inside behind Mia, Sam and Charlie, he soaks up the sounds of laughter and conversation. Mia hops around on one foot, trying to unzip her snow-soaked boot, and Charlie keeps nudging her just enough to keep her off balance while howling with laughter. Sam, after removing his boots and carefully hanging up all of his outerwear, takes pity on Mia and steadies her with one hand under her elbow. Which, surprisingly, Mia allows him to do. She also doesn't tease Sam when she notices his mismatched socks, which John had been counting on. 'Are those rock-star avocadoes?' she asks innocently.

'Ah, yeah.' It's hard to tell if Sam is blushing or if his cheeks are still red from their time outdoors. 'Half my socks have gone missing, unfortunately. And these glowing bookworm ones are my favourite.'

Mia flashes him a look that, for once, isn't full of venom. Interesting. It seems that this cold war might be coming to an end, and John has a theory in the back of his mind that he's quickly becoming sure of.

'Please tell me that food is ready,' Charlie moans as he dashes towards the kitchen. John steps back quickly to avoid Charlie barrelling straight through him. Walking through walls is unpleasant enough. Having a whole person step through his incorporeal body is the worst kind of sensation. John likens it to going on one too many carnival rides in a row. The world starts spinning in a very unpleasant way. Plus, he's surmised that it must be unpleasant for the other person as well. They always stop and shudder, and make a comment about 'someone walking over my grave'.

Mia and Sam follow Charlie, walking at a more normal pace.

'Oh, hey, Mum,' Mia calls as she walks to the fridge. Penny and Martin enter the kitchen, both dressed up. Mia removes a rich brown glop of dough wrapped in clingfilm. 'Are you guys heading out soon?'

'We're on our way right now, dear. The Fletchers have asked us to lunch at The Hairy Dog.'

'Shame.' Martin shakes his head. 'Because what you whipped up this morning smells incredible. Much more appetizing than hairy dog.' He winks at Mia, and she giggles in response.

Charlie is pulling the heavy cast-iron pot out on to the stovetop. Using an oven mitt, he lifts off the lid, then audibly groans. 'Oh my God, Mia. I don't know if you've outdone yourself, or if I'm just that hungry. I need a fork. Stat.'

'Don't you dare stick a utensil in there like a Neanderthal,' Mia chides. 'Grab some plates, and we can all sit down. I'll serve us up.'

Charlie makes a sound of protest, but Sam crosses to the cabinets and pulls out a stack of plates. John sniffs the air – the chicken is fragrant and the root vegetables have cooked down into a delightful concoction that he wishes he could taste.

'I don't suppose we have time to share a few bites,' Martin asks, looking at the chicken longingly.

Penny checks her watch. It's the silver one that Martin gave her a few Christmases ago. 'We really can't, Martin. You know how Earl gets about tardiness.'

Martin sighs the anthem of the long-suffering, then looks straight at Charlie and Sam, his glare perfectly menacing. 'I'm having some of the leftovers this afternoon. If you two chuckleheads polish it all off, you're sleeping in the snow tonight.'

Mia giggles again and pats her father on the arm. 'Don't worry, Dad. I'll make sure they save you a plate.'

'Fine, we'll leave him some. Can we eat now?' Charlie calls out plaintively. 'I'm going to pass out from hunger.'

Mia rolls her eyes, and Sam quips, 'Good news, folks. There'll be more for us.'

'Come on, Martin. We simply cannot be late!' Penny kisses Mia and Charlie on the cheek and tugs Martin towards the door.

John leans back against the wall beside the breakfast nook and settles in, crossing his arms over his chest and his legs at the ankles. As he watches the Robinsons together, a pang of nostalgia hits him. This is what happens when you die in your thirties. He'd never spent much time thinking about the future when he was alive, too concerned with the now. Even once Alastair had come on the scene. But now, seeing Mia and Charlie banter, and Penny cajole Martin out of the door, he can admit to himself that he would have liked to grow old. Have a family. Enjoy a home filling up with his children and their significant others, welcoming them home at Christmastime, and catching up on all the happenings in everyone's lives. Maybe even bouncing a grandchild or two on his knees.

He knows he'll never be able to find that happy ending for himself, but that doesn't mean he can't help Mia find hers. Perhaps that's why he has had to stick around all these years. Perhaps, left to her own devices, Mia would end up sad and alone like John. But he can help ensure that doesn't happen to her, and he knows exactly where to start.

John had already had his suspicions, but after Sam's heroics at the end of the snowball fight and Mia's subsequent lack of animosity towards him, the attraction between the two of them is now obvious. John is certain that it won't take too much effort to push Sam and Mia together. All they need is a subtle nudge in the right direction.

The three young adults are absorbed in their meal, too hungry to make much conversation. Sam scarfs down his first helping, and true to his word, scoops up a hearty portion on to a plate that he carefully places on the counter.

Then he refills his own dish and makes short work of finishing that helping as well.

'That snowball fight was really something, wasn't it?' Charlie exhales, finally satiated. 'Reminded me of the battles we used to have here as kids. Do you remember, Mia?'

Mia has moved to the counter, where she's rolling out the dough she made earlier. 'I do. We had those toy machine guns – who gave those to us?'

'It had to be Grandpa Morris. Any excuse for him to tell us his war stories. And then we'd play out our own war with Ben and Stanley,' Charlie reminisces. 'Each team had their own bases, and we'd run all over the gardens, hiding behind trees and pillars . . . man, that was so much fun.' Charlie says this to Sam, who's gathering up the dishes and walking them over to the sink.

'Sounds like it.'

'They weren't very good at it, if I remember correctly.' Mia arranges the biscuit cutters across the dough and presses them all down. 'And little Stanley was a bit of a cry-baby.'

'A bit!' Charlie laughs. 'That's something of an understatement. Remember when he took one of your dolls from your room and tried to hang her from the rafters in the chicken coop? You were so mad.'

'Beth was my favourite dolly!' Mia objects.

'I don't remember all the details. I just remember you were spitting mad, and after rescuing Beth, you grabbed Stanley by the ear and dragged him all the way down to the road. You kept threatening to tie him up and leave him there with a sign that said – wait, let me get this right – "Free boy to a good home. Or a bad one." '

Sam's jaw drops and he lets out a startled laugh. 'Wow, he must have been terrified.'

Charlie snickers before continuing the story. 'Stanley was so upset and when you finally let him go he ran to Uncle Fred and cried for over an hour.'

Mia shakes her head as she carefully transfers the biscuits to the baking trays. 'Mum grounded me for a week, and Dad made me miss dinner that night. But I still think Stanley got off easy. He deserved worse for what he did.'

'Something you should know about Mia,' Charlie announces to whoever might be listening. 'She can really hold a grudge.'

Sam says nothing and simply continues carrying dishes to the sink, but John has the distinct impression that he winced.

'Yeah, well, I might hold a grudge, but at least I didn't pee so often in the garden that I killed Mum's roses.'

Charlie lets out an offended gasp. 'You knew?'

'Of course I knew,' Mia scoffs. 'We only had the one bathroom up here, remember? I would have peed outside too if I could have got away with it.'

'You can't tell any of these stories once Molly gets here,' Charlie begs. 'I've just about convinced her I'm not a yob like her past boyfriends.'

'So, I shouldn't mention how you refused to take a shower for two weeks when you were thirteen because you insisted you didn't stink? The headmaster had to call Mum because the teachers were complaining.'

'Ugh. That's disgusting, Charlie,' Sam chimes in. 'Mia, feel free to tap me in if you need any more embarrassing stories about him – I've got a few winners.'

Mia and Sam swap looks, and Mia laughs under her breath.

'Those are exactly the kinds of stories you shouldn't share, Mia.' Charlie looks at her beseechingly. Then his gaze turns mischievous. 'Of course, I could talk about that time when *you* were in secondary school and you forgot your homework, so you poured ketchup all over your trousers and pretended you'd got your period so Dad would come pick you up.'

'You wouldn't dare,' Mia threatens.

'Try me,' Charlie grins.

The siblings continue to reminisce while Mia bakes up the biscuits. Sam keeps himself busy by washing the dishes and sweeping the floor. Eventually, he takes up a spot on the stool opposite Mia and pulls out the notebook from the pocket of his cardigan. He jots down a few words, and when he sets the pen on the counter, John creeps forward. When he's confident no one is paying attention, he swaps the fine line Sharpie for one in his own pocket.

Sam listens a little longer, and then uncaps the pen and tries to scribble down a few more words. But the pen proves to be dry once again. 'What the—? Why does this keep happening?'

'What's the matter, Sam?' Mia asks, too sweetly. Her eyes are sparkling with mischief.

'My pens are still drying up overnight.' Sam pitches the pen into the bin, shaking his head.

'These gingerbread men just need a couple more minutes to cool, and then I'm going to ice them. Anyone want to help?'

'Do we get to eat some if we do?' Charlie asks, fingers creeping towards the nearest cooling rack. Mia swats him away.

'Yes. Lucky for you, I pay in biscuits.'

'Perfect.' Charlie dons an apron as well, and then glances up at the clock over the sink. 'Oh, bother! I've completely lost track of time. Molly's train is getting in right now!'

'Wait, for real?' Mia blinks in surprise. 'She's actually coming?'

'Of course she's coming! I told you she was. Man, I can't be late. I gotta go.' Charlie yanks the apron back off and balls it up, chucking it at Sam. 'Sam, I nominate you as Mia's assistant. Mia, make sure you keep a few biscuits for me. They'll be my referral fee for finding you such a competent assistant.' And with that, he rushes out the door, muttering about how long it will take him to make it down to the train station in Worcester.

'Guess it's just the two of us, then,' Sam says apologetically. 'I am happy to help, though. If you'll have me.'

'Beggars can't be choosers,' Mia quips. But then she gives Sam a sincere smile. 'I'd love the help. I always start out so gung ho when baking these. And then peter out after the first dozen or two.'

Sam and Mia are going to ice gingerbread men together? Oh, this he can work with. John waits patiently as Mia starts gathering up her ingredients, looking for an opportunity. When her back is turned, he scoops up the icing sugar from the counter and places it high on the top shelf over the stove, where he's sure Mia can't reach it.

'OK, so we've got the cream of tartar. Oh, and I wanted to add a little almond flavouring. Could you beat the egg whites for me, please?'

'Sure thing,' Sam responds. 'You know, I was thinking, we should probably have one of the biscuits before they're iced. Then after we're finished, we can have another. For comparison's sake.'

Mia snickers, and then forces a serious look on her face. 'I think you're right. How else will we know which delivery method is preferred?'

'Exactly.' Sam holds out two biscuits, carefully arranged on his outstretched palm. 'You choose first.'

Mia peruses them carefully. 'Hmm. I think I'll take the angel.'

'Fitting. I'll take the snowman.'

For a moment, the only sound is the biscuits crunching as they chew. Sam sighs in satisfaction. 'I don't know, Mia. That's going to be hard to top. Those are already delicious.'

'Thanks.' Mia gives him a sincere smile. She glances around. 'Oh, now where is the icing sugar?' She opens and closes a few cabinets, moving items around as she searches. Finally, she spies it in the upper cabinet and sighs. 'Really, Mum? That can't be the most logical place for it.' After locating a disappointingly small step stool, she stretches up on tiptoe, just grazing the edge of the bag with her fingertips.

'Oh, come on,' Mia grumbles. 'What I wouldn't give for another inch or two.' She continues to grope around, trying to catch the edge of the bag in her fingers. Her shirt rides up as she stretches, exposing a few inches of creamy skin. After a few failed tries, she gives a frustrated little hop, pushing off the edge of the still warm oven. 'Ah! Hot!' Mia wobbles precariously, and Sam launches himself towards her, gripping her by the waist.

'Easy there,' he soothes as he steadies her back on the stool. Mia goes very still at his touch and doesn't immediately pull away. Sam's fingers skim the strip of skin that was exposed as she stretched. Once she's no longer wobbling, Mia turns around. Sam's hands are still at her waist, his thumbs brushing unconsciously along her skin.

'Thanks.' Her voice is subdued. They stay like this for a long moment, bodies nearly pressed together, the heat of the oven at Mia's back and the scent of cinnamon lacing through the air. 'I, ah, like your cologne.'

Sam's smile goes all the way to his eyes. 'Thanks.'

Neither one of them seems in a hurry to move away. Mia licks her lips nervously, drawing Sam's attention directly there. His smile turns slightly crooked, and moving slowly, he reaches up to brush a few stray crumbs from the corner of Mia's lips. His fingers linger just a few seconds longer than needed for the task.

Mia's eyes widen, and Sam drops his hand, stepping back awkwardly. 'Sorry. You had – there were some crumbs still there.'

'Don't worry about it.'

'Here, let me get that down for you.'

Mia doesn't move, so after a moment, Sam reaches around her head, snagging the bag of icing sugar and lowering it to the counter beside them. Mia watches him the whole time, and it's not until the bag is down and Sam steps back that she seems to shake herself.

'Well. OK then. Thanks for grabbing that.'

'No problem,' Sam says.

Mia's cheeks are flushed, and John could have sworn her pulse is hammering away in her throat. He silently congratulates himself for his foresight in removing the taller stool from the room earlier.

Maybe this will be easier than he expected.

13

MIA

If you'd asked Mia Robinson what she'd be doing three days before Christmas, she never would have thought to say *baking with Sam Williams*. But here she is, watching Sam whisk up an enormous batch of royal icing, and trying her best not to openly admire his forearms. She busies herself with laying out the biscuits, sprinkles and other decorations.

'So, you've obviously become a wonderful cook over the last few years, and a baker as well. What other superpowers have you acquired since I last saw you?' Sam's tone is carefully nonchalant, as if he's acutely aware of the tenuous truce they seem to have stumbled into.

Mia could make it all come crashing down, if she had a mind to. A sharply worded retort or a scathing reminder of why Sam's presence isn't warranted would do the trick. But she can't quite bring herself to do it. She's had a lovely day and although it pains her to admit it, Sam's been a part of that enjoyment. She decides to embrace the comfort they've so newly discovered.

'Well, I recently became the proud owner of my first houseplant.'

'Do tell,' Sam says. Mia spoons out a portion of the icing for him and they both set to decorating.

'Yes, well, it wasn't so much a decision to become a plant owner, as a plant chose me. There was a stall at this market I was visiting full of plants and I was briefly body snatched by someone who loves plants. Next thing I knew, I had bought three.'

'Wait,' Sam says, spoon held aloft as he thinks. 'I thought you said you just acquired your first plant. Not first *three* plants.'

'A very astute observation. One met a terrible demise on the tube home. I know we don't speak ill of the dead, but I kind of feel like this plant threw itself into harm's way. As if the very notion of coming home with me made it want to kill itself.'

Sam barks out a laugh. 'You can't be that bad a plant mum.'

Mia raises an eyebrow. 'You have no idea. And then, the second one . . . well, let's just say that I was overly aggressive in my watering strategy. It succumbed to the Great Flood of '24.'

'But you still have one.'

'Yes! I do. Thankfully for me, it's some kind of fern that loves water. And it's thriving, if I do say so myself.'

'Congratulations,' Sam offers sincerely. Mia pauses

to watch him decorate his biscuit. He's scowling at the cutout as he attempts to glue sweets on to the gingerbread man's icing waistcoat. The scowl is surprisingly endearing, and an errant lock of hair has fallen over his forehead. Mia has the strangest urge to reach out and brush it back into place. 'I myself am the proud owner of a goldfish,' Sam offers. 'But my roommate really takes the cake. He owns four giant lizards.'

'You're kidding.'

'I'm not, actually. I forget the species, but they're the size of a small dog. A medium-sized dog, in fact.'

'How did you meet this guy?'

'Well, he posted an ad for a roommate. There wasn't a lot of interest, so he offered to knock a hundred pounds off the monthly rent and I took him up on it.'

'The lizards don't bother you?'

'Not as long as they're caged.'

This makes Mia snicker, and she sets down her icing knife for a moment while she tries to picture the scenario Sam has described. 'Do you think that comes up when he goes on dates?'

Sam laughs. 'How exactly would that go? Hey, lady with whom I am having a first date. What are your thoughts on giant lizards that require cages half the size of my bedroom?'

Mia laughs so hard that her hand shakes, dripping icing on to the counter and all over another uniced biscuit. 'Oh no, look what you made me do. This one's ruined!'

'Only one way to salvage it,' Sam declares, scooping up

the biscuit and launching it into his mouth, his cheeks bulging as he tries to chew.

'The only way, hmm?' Mia tries to sound sceptical, but she's still laughing too hard.

Sam has to swallow multiple times before he can respond. 'Yep. I don't know, though. The dating scene is hard enough without bringing lizards into it.'

'Tell me about it,' Mia says, thinking of James. 'Seems like every other day you're bombing a date or getting ghosted.'

'All well and good as long as you're not the one doing the ghosting,' Sam says quietly.

There's an awkward pause, and Mia looks up at Sam who seems to be avoiding her gaze. Something close to regret coils in her chest as she thinks over his words, and before she can stop herself, she says, 'It happened to me recently.' She's surprised to find herself admitting it, but keeps going. 'I dated a guy for two months and then he up and vanished. Haven't heard a word from him in over a week.'

Sam looks at her with serious eyes. 'He can do one.'

'Sorry?' Mia's too startled to say anything else at Sam's uncharacteristic vehemence.

'If he's too dumb to know what he's got, then it's his loss. Don't give him another second's thought. He's not worth it.'

Touched, Mia drops her gaze back to her biscuit creations. For a long moment, there's no other sound in the kitchen besides the quiet scrape of the knives against the bowls full of icing and the pleasing clink of sprinkles in their containers. Mia's mind wanders in the silence, and she suddenly realizes John has disappeared. Maybe he slipped out a while ago without her noticing. She's been having such a nice afternoon, and all the sugar and laughter is making her feel mellow.

'Do you still do photography?' Mia asks, eventually breaking the silence. 'Didn't you win an award for your photos in school?'

'Mm, not any more,' Sam responds. 'It was fun, but a trip to Italy ruined me for photos here. The light there was just so magical. I wasn't happy with any of my photos once I came back.' He shrugs, as if this was no great loss. 'But I still write poetry. I'm always chewing on some sort of wordplay in my head.' He grins at her. 'If you see me staring off into the distance, I'm probably wondering if the words I've strung together make any sense at all.'

'Maybe you can show me sometime.'

Sam starts to respond, but there's a clatter in the hall. 'Tally-ho! We're home!' Martin's voice booms down the hallway. 'Where is my chicken?'

Mia giggles and pulls the carefully preserved plate from the fridge. 'Heating it up right now, Dad!'

'That's my girl.' Martin strides into the kitchen, tossing his coat on to the back of a chair. 'How's things here, have you had a fun afternoon?'

'Very much so,' Mia says as she heats the chicken on the stovetop. Then, under her breath, she admits, 'Surprisingly so.' It had felt like time spent with a very good friend.

'Earl says the thing he'll miss most about living in

England is the cricket matches.' Martin turns to Sam and asks, 'Do you follow cricket, Sam?'

'Can't say that I do,' Sam replies. 'I've always been more into tennis than anything else.'

'Do you still play?' Mia asks curiously, before she can think better of it. Visions of a shirtless Sam dousing himself with water after a heated match fill her head and she grimaces, trying her best to drive them out.

'Occasionally,' Sam responds. 'And I did try cricket a few years ago. I was fairly good at it, if I do say so myself.'

'You must be naturally athletic,' Martin observes.

Mia's mind wanders even further, thinking of . . . *other* athletic activities Sam might be good at that don't require much clothing. An image of Sam leaning over her, shirtless, as she lay on his bed surfaces, his shoulders flexing as he held himself up. She hasn't let herself remember that evening in this much detail in a long time, but now she can't seem to stop herself as she remembers his natural grace and athleticism, the ease with which he'd moved her. There was that one move in particular, when he'd picked her up and held her against the wall with just his core and lower body strength so his hands had been free to roam across her body. Mia feels her breath quicken slightly as she remembers how turned on she'd been, to the point where Sam had needed to pause for a minute so she could catch her breath. Could he still do that move?

The clatter of Martin's cutlery pulls Mia back to the present, and suddenly horrified by her lack of willpower, she mentally backtracks. Instead of thinking of a sweaty, shirtless Sam, Mia does her best to imagine him playing cricket. 'There's nothing sexy about that sport,' she mutters under her breath.

'What's that, Mia bella?' Martin asks, scraping the last of the chicken off his plate and into his mouth.

Mia glances at Sam, who's watching her curiously. 'Nothing. I was just thinking about cricket. When does the season start next year? We should go to a game. It's mostly older, out-of-shape men that play, isn't it?'

Both men look at her with blank expressions. As she replays in her mind what she's just said, Mia shakes her head. What is happening to her?

'I think there are probably all levels of fitness represented,' Sam cautiously volunteers.

'True. I'm sure some are studs. But the season hasn't even started yet,' Mia chirps. 'I'll make a note to call in the spring.' Martin just gapes at her as if she's lost her mind, and Sam looks equally intrigued and amused. Mia squares her shoulders and tries to steer the conversation towards something that won't remind her of her times with Sam.

'Dad, when did we last clean out the bathtub drain?'

14

JOHN

23 December

It would seem the ceasefire between Mia and Sam has lasted longer than anyone thought possible. John is tucked into a corner of the kitchen – not in the breakfast nook since he didn't want anyone to unknowingly sit on him – where he has been observing the Robinsons. Martin was the first one down, and after brewing up a pot of coffee, he'd spent an hour absorbed in the morning newspaper. It occurs to John that Martin seems to be the only one who reads the paper. Everyone else seems to read everything on their phones. Yet another thing that's changed since his time.

Mia came up from the cottage early this morning, and Martin had been effusive in his appreciation of her presence. It is not lost on John that Martin treasures his daughter, and seems delighted to soak up every second he can with her while she's 'home'. They shared a nice long conversation before the rest of the house woke up, swapping ideas for Martin's tree theme next year.

It is a bit of a foreign concept to John, this kind of relationship between Martin and Mia. Martin seems to feel the same way about Charlie too – thrilled to have his son around him for the Christmas holiday, and effusive with his praise and encouragement for how his children's adult lives are turning out. John's been thinking about his childhood with his mother – a quiet, overworked woman who'd raised him on her own. His mum had rarely talked about his dad, and had no other family to speak of. Holidays had been a day for his poor mum to finally relax and therefore had not been lavish at all. An only child, John remembered many a Christmas holiday had passed with him sitting and watching TV, willing away the hours until it was time to return to school and see his friends. In fact, it wasn't until he'd taken the job here at Willowby Manor that he'd really had any kind of disposable income whatsoever.

It's not that John's mum hadn't been supportive. He had never doubted her love for him. After all, she'd provided for him. Attended every one of his concerts. She'd just been a quiet, reserved woman, worn out by the challenges of life. Once again, John wondered what had happened to her after he'd died. It broke his heart to think of his mum living out her days alone. Did she ever have any visitors? John was intimately acquainted with the horrors experienced by years of solitude.

Which is probably why he looked forward to Christmases here so much. He'd grown especially fond of the

Robinsons over the years as he'd soaked up every minute of family togetherness. And even if helping Mia sort out her love life didn't help him pass through this ether into the afterlife, it wouldn't be a hardship to keep watching the Robinsons year after year.

After a bustling morning, the manor kitchen is still full of commotion. Mia and Martin are engaged in a heated game of draughts. Charlie and Sam have taken turns with the hot air popper and have filled an enormous bowl with popcorn, which they are now doing their best to eat in its entirety.

'Afternoon, dearies.' Penny breezes into the kitchen. 'Aunt Gertie said to let you all know she's lying down for a long nap, but she'll be raring to go again this evening. She was mumbling something about ghostly biscuits again before she went to her room. I worry about her. I think she might be losing it a little.'

Mia glances over at John, who raises his eyebrows. 'Oh, she's been leaving biscuits out for the manor ghosts every day. Says they deserve a little extra something because it's Christmas. I can make up another batch, I guess.'

Penny shakes her head. 'Why would you need to keep making new batches?'

Mia shrugs. 'Because the biscuits keep going missing?' This was said with another surreptitious glance John's way.

John winces. He actually despises eating the biscuits, since they all taste like cardboard to him. But he figures it's the polite thing to do, since it matters so much to Aunt Gertie.

'Boys, are you eating Aunt Gertie's biscuits?'

Sam shakes his head emphatically. 'I wouldn't dream of it.'

'Yeah, me neither,' Charlie agrees.

Penny pats Charlie on the arm and then begins fixing herself a sandwich. 'Oh, darling, whatever happened with Molly? I thought she was coming in on the train yesterday?'

Charlie pouts. 'She was, but her dad was giving her a ride to the station and the car blew a tyre. She missed the train.'

'And there hasn't been another one since?' Mia asks, her expression perfectly innocent.

Charlie glares at her. 'Of course there was, but her dad asked her to stay until the car gets fixed. Apparently, it had to be towed, and then they discovered the transmission was leaking or something. Anyway, her family asked her to stay. The mechanic assured them he'll have it done by the end of the day. Speaking of, I should go check in with her.' Abandoning the popcorn, Charlie lopes upstairs. Mia snickers under her breath.

'Something funny, Mia?' Martin asks, as he peruses the board.

'If that girl turns out to actually be real, I will eat my slippers.'

'Mia, don't be absurd.' Penny shakes her head while she waits for her bread to toast.

'I'm not being absurd!' Mia objects. 'I have legitimate doubts about her existence.'

'Well, of course you do. We all do.' Penny tsks. 'But I

think a better bet is to say if Molly turns out to be real, you will make us all beef Wellington for New Year's Day.'

'Ugh, no,' Mia groans. 'It's such a tedious and finicky dish to make.'

'But you most likely won't have to,' Penny reminds her. Martin chuckles and moves his piece.

'OK, fine,' Mia says. 'But if she's not real, you have to make those brioche buns that we all love, Mum. You used to make them every Christmas and you haven't in for ever.'

'Well,' Penny huffs, expertly hiding her smile, 'I got tired of spending my entire Christmas Eve in the kitchen. But, all right. If Molly doesn't show her actual, physical face by Christmas evening, I will make the brioche for New Year's Day.'

'Yeah!' Mia does a silly little fist pump. John chuckles under his breath. He's beginning to think Mia has a good chance of getting those brioche buns. Charlie doesn't seem like the deceptive sort, but it is odd that this 'girlfriend' keeps encountering so many delays.

'I suppose I'd better go pick up the ingredients for the brioche,' Penny says thoughtfully, glancing out the window at the swirling snow. 'Martin, will you drive me into town? We can get them while we pick up the turkey.'

'Of course, dear,' Martin says, unbending his lanky frame from the chair. He puts his palms on his lower back and stretches. 'Let me just get my coat. Oh, look, it's snowing again.'

'Aw, Dad, you can't leave. We haven't finished our game yet,' Mia protests.

'But we have.' Martin leans down and jumps her remaining pieces. Mia's mouth falls open, and Sam coughs. The cough sounds suspiciously like a laugh. Mia looks over at him, and Sam pounds himself on the chest.

'Sorry. Kernel got stuck in my windpipe.'

'Hmmph.' Mia tucks the game pieces in their box and stows it back on the shelf. After glancing outside, she shivers. 'Ugh. I'm freezing. I think this weather calls for hot chocolate and a film.'

'Oh, yes, please,' Sam agrees. He wipes the counters clear of stray popcorn kernels and sweeps it all into the bin. Martin and Penny call out their goodbyes and head for the front hall. Anxious for some fresh air, John follows them. If he ducks outside as they leave, he can avoid the dreaded indigestion. Martin and Penny make short work of donning coats and boots, and then they step outside. John is careful to step in their footprints as they tromp through the snow to the garage, so as to not draw attention to himself. After Martin and Penny enter the garage, John diverts back towards the house. He breathes in the crisp winter air and then walks around the back, waiting beside the kitchen window until he can catch Mia's attention to let him inside. Of course, he could open the doors by himself, but again, people tend to notice things like that.

The glow of the kitchen lights spills out on to the falling snow, and John sighs in appreciation at the sight. Mia moves back and forth within the kitchen, chatting easily with Sam as she works. Sam leans against the counter, listening. He grabs a mug and places it on the counter, and then brings down another at her instruction. John smiles in satisfaction. This whole matchmaking thing is turning out to be even easier than he remembered. Tired of waiting out in the snow, he walks closer to the window and raps on the glass.

Sam turns, startled, and Mia meets John's eyes over Sam's shoulder. John points in the direction of the door and Mia nods in understanding. She exchanges a few words with Sam, and whatever she says seems to soothe his nerves. A few moments later, the back door opens and Mia bends down, scooping up a bowlful of snow.

'Well, hurry up,' she admonishes quietly. 'I needed a reason to go outside, so I told Sam some nonsense story about how we always melt fresh snow into our hot chocolate. This better be worth it.'

John snickers as he steps inside. 'It will be a new Robinson tradition.' He follows Mia back into the kitchen.

'Got your snow?' Sam asks pleasantly.

'Ah, yep. This is the best kind too. Not too crunchy and not too fluffy,' Mia vamps, rolling her eyes when Sam drops his gaze to the bowl in her hands. 'You'll see, it adds the perfect touch.

'Does your family usually watch Christmas films?' Mia asks, as she pours the chocolate into the mugs.

'Ah, no, actually. It was never really a tradition growing up,' Sam replies. He clears his throat. 'We're not exactly close like your family is, Mia. Everyone had a TV in their own rooms, so what was the point of sitting together in the living room?'

Mia shakes her head. 'Well, that's a shame. But surely you've seen *The Santa Clause*?'

Sam shakes his head.

'*Miracle on 34th Street*? *It's a Wonderful Life*? *White Christmas*?' Mia clutches her heart. 'Oh my goodness, Sam. This is awful. How is it possible you were so deprived?'

'I didn't realize it was such an offence,' Sam replies.

'Well, lucky for you, we have several days of this holiday left. Enough time to get you mostly up to speed. Where should we start? Something light-hearted, not too serious. Oh, I know!' Mia claps her hands together. 'We'll watch *The Grinch*.'

'Is that the green guy?' Sam asks innocently.

Mia slaps her forehead this time. 'Sam. You're killing me. Here, grab your hot chocolate. Your Christmas cinema indoctrination begins now.' Mia heads for the family room, but she doesn't get far.

'What about the snow?' Sam asks, angling his head at the bowl on the counter.

Mia offers him a pained smile. 'Oh, yes, of course. Can't forget the snow.' She scoops a minuscule portion into her mug, and a slightly larger clump into Sam's. With a grimace only John can see, Mia takes a sip. 'Perfect. All right, let's get started.'

Sam obediently follows Mia and takes the seat beside her on the deep sofa. He sinks down into the fluffy cushions, carefully holding his cocoa aloft so that it doesn't spill. Mia is engrossed in finding the film and doesn't notice as Sam leans a little further back so that he can watch her. A small smile plays around his lips as Mia scowls at the TV, scrolling through countless other films. He seems captivated by the light playing over her features, and his expression softens even more as she takes another sip of the cocoa and sighs in appreciation. Sam's expression turns almost wistful at the sound.

John relaxes in one of the armchairs, considering what he's just seen. Sam has made no mention of girlfriends, past or present. Is it possible that he is still pining after Mia? The story Mia told about her humiliation at the pool was all from her perspective, but what if Sam had truly just made a mistake and forgotten to tell her others were invited? He could still have had a genuine interest in Mia, and might even feel terrible about what happened.

Having watched Sam over the last few days, John has the mounting suspicion that it all comes down to something that simple. Sam doesn't seem like the kind of guy to plan out something so brutally sinister and deceptive as the humiliation that Mia described.

Mia sends John a conspiratorial look, and he surmises that she's hoping he will continue to prey on Sam's sensibilities. Perhaps she wants John to fiddle with the lights and make them flicker. Or howl down the chimney or some other such nonsense.

Sam shivers from his place on the sofa. 'Mmm. It's quite chilly in here. Mind if I light a fire?'

'Knock yourself out.' Mia is clicking through film titles.

Sam lays the wood in the hearth, then strikes a match. The draught snaking through the room blows it out, and he lights another, with enough gusto to make John smile. This one also blows out.

'What in the world?'

Mia snickers under her breath and darts another

look at John. She clearly thinks he's responsible for the draught. Somewhat frustrated, Sam pulls a third match from the box and strikes it. Taking pity on the man, John crosses the room and positions himself so that his body is blocking the draught. The match stays lit, and Sam is finally able to light the logs.

'Now we're in business,' Sam crows triumphantly.

Fires are inherently romantic, or at least John's always thought so, and he begins looking round to see if there's anything else he can do to set the mood. It would be a shame to waste this rare moment where Mia and Sam are alone and on good terms. He quickly strides over to the light switch by the door and dims the lights so that the room is bathed in a golden glow. The fire crackles heartily and Sam burrows back into the cocoon that Mia has created on the sofa. He picks up his hot chocolate and takes a long sip. Mia's attention seems to be trained on Sam as he tilts his head back, letting the rich drink slide down his throat. John hides a satisfied smile and sneaks a quick sip of Mia's hot chocolate.

'Damn,' he says, accidentally drawing her attention back to him. He sets the mug down carefully, making sure the disembodied cup isn't visible to Sam.

Mia shoots him a look that is clearly asking why John is upset.

'What I wouldn't give for an actual sip of hot chocolate. Or a bite of something that doesn't taste like cardboard.'

'Poor baby,' Mia croons, with just a touch of sarcasm.

'Sorry?' Sam leans forward to catch her gaze and Mia snaps to attention.

'Nothing. Don't worry about it! I was just feeling bad pre-emptively for the Grinch. OK, so what do you need to know about this film before we start?' Mia presses a button on the remote and the intro music plays merrily. 'Well, actually, it's pretty self-explanatory. The biggest thing you need to understand is that in every Christmas film, the spirit of Christmas prevails over any and all obstacles and challenges. Once you accept that, you can accept the premise of any of them.'

'Got it.' Sam nods definitively and leans back against the sofa, draping one arm across the back. Mia sips from her mug as the film plays, and after a few minutes she relaxes back into the pillowy comfort of the sofa. Sam's arm is just a few inches above her, and John spends several minutes debating how he could move that arm down on to her shoulders. How will Mia react, though? Will she swat Sam away? Will this interference shatter the tenuous peace between them?

Sam is taking the Christmas film watching very seriously. He's giving the film his complete attention, as if he expects Mia to quiz him at the end, and knowing Mia, that does feel like a distinct possibility. Sam is barely moving a muscle, so any interference on John's part will be obvious. It will have to be Mia, then. A sudden burst of genius hits him. Watching for the perfect opportunity, he waits while Mia juggles the remote in one hand and the mug of cocoa in the other. Then John slides behind the sofa and lifts one corner just a few inches, toppling Mia in Sam's direction.

Trying to compensate without spilling her drink, Mia

drops the remote between them while she steadies herself. Once she's secured her sloshing mug, she looks around wildly for the remote.

'Oh, sorry,' she mumbles, reaching between them.

Sam, still engrossed in the film, does his crooked smile and says, 'No worries.'

Mia roots around in the blankets, looking for the remote. She's moving closer and closer to Sam, and when she's in the perfect location, John lifts the sofa again. Mia falls into Sam's side with an aggravated '*oomph*'.

Exactly as John had planned, Sam's arm curls around Mia reflexively.

'Oh, gosh, I'm so sorry.' Mia keeps looking but can't locate the remote in the mound of blankets. 'I just can't find the remote, but I guess it doesn't matter. I'll move back.'

He smiles down at her, now nestled in the crook of his arm. After a moment of careful deliberation, Sam ventures, 'I don't mind if you don't.' He licks his lips. 'The point of this was to be cosy and relaxed, wasn't it?'

Mia mumbles out an embarrassed, 'I guess so.' But she doesn't immediately move away. John takes her response as a good sign and decides this is his cue to leave. They seem to be working things out between them just fine. There's just one more tiny detail to adjust as he leaves. John heads for the doorway into the front room, but right before he leaves, he takes out the remote that he smuggled into his pocket and switches the film over to a much better selection.

15

MIA

Mia is still feeling vaguely mortified as she reclines on the sofa, comfortably curled into Sam's side. She's at war within herself. On the one hand, this is Sam, and she knows better than to let down her defences around him this significantly. On the other hand, he's been nothing but nice this entire week, and she's feeling rather cosy at the moment. The goal was to relax and spend a friendly afternoon together, and isn't that what they're doing?

Determined to get out of her head, Mia silences the objecting voice and resolves to enjoy the film. *The Grinch* is one of her favourites, after all. She's almost entirely relaxed when the image suddenly changes, Jude Law's face filling the screen.

'What the—' Mia blinks, trying to determine what's happened.

Now it's Cameron Diaz onscreen in a decidedly inviting cottage. Mia recognizes the film right away, but she's trying to figure out what just happened.

'Hey, isn't this that film with Kate Winslet? *The Holiday House* or something?' Sam frowns at the screen.

'It's just *The Holiday*,' Mia responds absently. Is the TV on the blink? Did she enter into another time dimension? How did they go from funny and quirky to atmospherically romantic? She could ask John, but he's nowhere in sight. 'Where did you go?' she mutters to herself.

'I don't think it was me,' Sam responds, still frowning at the screen. 'I wasn't even near the remote this time. But it's fine if you wanted to change it. Didn't you say this is your favourite Christmas film?'

'I didn't change it.' Mia is still distracted. He must be around here somewhere. What on earth would possess John to change the film?

'I really don't mind watching it,' Sam continues. 'I won't even accuse you of a bait and switch. I haven't seen this film in a really long time.'

'I didn't switch anything.'

Sam chuckles. 'Well, it certainly wasn't me . . .'

Mia finally focuses on the man at her side. 'I'm serious. I didn't change anything. It's so weird that it just changed like that! And where is—'

Sam sobers. 'See, I *told* you weird stuff like this keeps happening to me.'

'Well, yeah, but this wasn't the plan,' Mia responds, before she thinks better of it.

Sam cocks his head. 'Sorry, what plan?'

She shakes herself then, realizing what she almost revealed. 'Never mind. I swear I didn't change the film, but if you don't mind, I'd love to watch this one.' She pauses. 'Wait, I thought you said you didn't know of any Christmas films.'

'I said Christmas films weren't a thing in my house. I never said I hadn't seen this one.'

Mia tilts her head, considering him. 'You've seen *The Holiday*? My favourite Christmas film of all time?'

Sam smiles. It's that slow, crooked one that does funny things to her heart. 'Well, yeah, I know it's your favourite. I love the scene with Jude Law's girls in the tent.'

Mia blinks a few times, absorbing this information. Then she shoots Sam an all-out grin. 'I can't tell if that's a line or not, but I don't care. That's my favourite scene as well.' And with that, she gives herself permission to enjoy the afternoon and curls back into Sam's side.

They stay like that through most of the movie. As Mia sits there, watching devastatingly beautiful Kate Winslet and effervescent Cameron Diaz fall in love with different men, she can't help but wonder when it will be her turn. If she's being completely honest, she never felt that strongly about James. She wanted to, for sure, but deep down, in spite of the fact that James ticked many of her boxes, she always knew she only felt ambivalence towards him. Maybe that's why she didn't even fight the ghosting, in the end.

Sam laughs at a line in the film, and Mia's attention snaps back to him. She's been tucked against him for the better part of an hour, feeling every one of his breaths that lifts her head, listening to the rumble of laughter in his chest. Breathing in his spicy, woodsy cologne, she forgets about the past. She stops stressing about the future. She can simply *be* in this incredible moment, snuggled up against him and letting the cares of the world slip on by.

Mia sips at her cocoa. It's gone cold, but the sugary drink is still comforting. Sam's arm is slung around her shoulders, the sleeves of his cardigan pushed up from when he started the fire. His forearm is pleasingly tanned. He must still play enough tennis to maintain a bit of colour. His skin is sprinkled with – in Mia's opinion – just the right amount of dark hair. She's always admired his hands – with their long, strong fingers. If she closes her eyes, she can remember what those fingers felt like tracing their way across her hips and thighs. Goosebumps break out across her skin and she mentally shakes herself. Better to keep her eyes open. But if she does, she's confronted with the absolute marshmallow of a man who's perched beside her, wrapped in a blanket and crushing hot cocoa, cheerfully watching her favourite romantic Christmas film. Both the fantasy and the reality are bordering on irresistible.

Sam exhales, muscles shifting beneath her head. 'Sorry, love,' he says, gently disengaging her. 'I need to run to the bathroom.' Sam stands, and groans. 'Man, am I sore from all that shovelling. It's brutal on the back.' He laces his fingers over his head and stretches. Mia's gaze drops to where his shirt is riding up, showing off a band of tanned skin just above his waistband. The elastic of his boxers peeks out above the line of his trousers, and Mia bites her lower lip. She has an almost irresistible urge to explore those exposed inches. Would Sam stop her if she tried?

He leaves the room, and Mia flops back on to the sofa,

thoroughly miffed. Damn Sam and his mouthwatering physique. Damn her own weakness and the fact that she still finds him magnetically attractive after all these years. What happened to her stone cold resolve? Mia has the vague feeling she's letting someone down. Quite possibly herself, but then again, herself has been quite content for the last two hours, snuggled up against Sam's warm body.

Mia spends the rest of the time until Sam returns giving herself a pep talk. Perhaps the fact that she and John have been scheming against Sam is the whole reason she's enjoying herself now. Maybe it's been a really crappy week, and she has been *through* it, and what she deserves right now is to simply relax and not overthink things.

She takes another sip of the cocoa, grimacing when she hits a particularly watery bit. That story she spouted about the tradition of adding snow makes her giggle, and Sam walks back in just then.

'What's so funny?'

Well, she can't exactly tell him that she just invented the whole thing. But the fact of the matter is this. She's sitting here, sipping on melted snow, which was her cover story to let a ghost back into her family home so that she could continue to tease a guy who hasn't been in her life for the last six years. It's hilarious, is what it is.

'I must just have a case of the Christmas giggles.'

Sam chuckles. 'I haven't heard of those before. Are the Christmas giggles a thing?' He sits back down beside her, quite a bit closer than before. Mia resists the urge to melt into a puddle of happiness beside him.

'Oh, they're definitely a thing. You really have been

deprived when it comes to Christmas lore, haven't you? No snow in your cocoa, no film indoctrination, no fa-la-la-la-*ha-ha*-ing.' Mia snorts with laughter at her own nonsense.

Sam's smile is broad, and he leans towards her. 'Totally deprived,' he agrees. His eyes roam over her face, and then he reaches out, one hand gently cradling her jaw. Mia stills, watching him to see what he'll do next. 'You have popcorn in your hair.' He carefully raises his other hand and runs it through her hair, tugging gently on the strands. Mia's breath catches, and she desperately wishes her hands were free to respond instead of curled around her mug. Sam moves closer, and all the laughter fades from his expression. Instead, he is wholly and utterly focused on Mia.

He's going to kiss me, she thinks. She can still remember – with stunning accuracy – what it's like to kiss Sam Williams. The first time was after one of his tennis matches. Mia had congratulated Sam on his win, and he'd given her that smile that made her heart do silly things. And in this case, the silly thing had been to rise up on tiptoe and kiss Sam full on the lips. He'd been surprised, at first, and hadn't reacted. But then, just as she'd started to pull away, face flushing hot with embarrassment, Sam had reached out with those lightning fast reflexes and pulled her back against him. And then he'd kissed her hard. Like he meant it. Mia can still feel the firm press of his lips on hers. The hungry way he sucked on her lower lip. The gentle press of his tongue, asking permission to explore her mouth. Her stomach clenches as she imagines their tongues tangling together, as he pulls her in close, and—

Mia's hand jerks, tossing her mug from her grip and spilling cocoa every which way.

'Ack! Oh, man!' Sam exclaims, as he's doused in the contents of her mug.

'I'm so sorry.' Mia rushes to help him, grabbing the stack of nearby napkins and dabbing at his cocoa-spattered trousers.

'It's fine, it's not even hot,' Sam assures her, his own hands colliding with hers as he accepts some of the napkins and tries to address the mess.

'I should have been more careful—'

'There's some on you too—'

Sam is dabbing at her lap and Mia is pressing more dry napkins against Sam's chest, and suddenly they're completely intertwined, arms and legs and hands, and Sam's face is mere inches away from Mia's.

And this time, the whole world slows down. Mia is painfully, beautifully aware of every detail. One small movement will close the distance between them. They'll share a kiss, and suddenly, it's the only thing Mia wants. Craves. She needs to kiss Sam, to know if it's still that white hot, electric connection between them. Like there's never been with anyone else.

She's leaning in, a breath away from Sam, when it happens. Out of the corner of her eye, she sees a flash of argyle, and in that split second, realization dawns. Horrible, embarrassing realization. John has orchestrated this whole thing. The fire. The film. The closeness. She's misread all the signs. *Again.* Mia throws herself back, away from Sam. She stands on trembling legs, ignoring the bewildered expression on his face.

'I, ah, I can't sit here any longer. My foot has gone numb. And, I just remembered, I promised Aunt Gertie I'd help her with the paper chains.'

Sam's gaze flicks from the film back to her face. He's clearly confused. 'This is the big finale, though. When Cameron Diaz runs all the way back through the snow?'

'Yeah, I've seen it.' Mia tries to sound as disinterested as possible. Unruffled. How could she be so stupid? John's betrayed her and she almost missed it. 'Feel free to finish it without me.' And with that, she scoops up their empty mugs and flees the room, trying her best to ignore Sam's obvious confusion.

16

JOHN

After quite a lot of searching, John finally finds Mia tucked away in the sunroom with Aunt Gertie. This room is barely decorated for Christmas, since it's chock full of plants, but someone has strung twinkle lights from the glass roof and hung a few bows on the larger plants. The cactus, in particular, is a stunning specimen that is at least seventy-five years old. It's looking particularly festive with its oversized velvet bow tie.

The sunroom was always a favourite of John's. If he recalled correctly, Morris's father had added it on to the back of the house decades before even John had worked at Willowby. It was a marvel of its time, with mechanical windows that opened and closed for ventilation, and botanical samples shipped in from around the world. John remembered when some of these plants were just little seedlings. Now they towered over the sturdy wrought iron table where Mia and her Aunt Gertie sat.

'You know, your gran took quite an interest in botany

after Morris died. I used to spend hours out here with her. I don't remember the names of most of them, but Joan had named them all.' Aunt Gertie's hands tremble slightly as she reaches for another strip of paper. A long paper chain already runs across her blanket-covered lap.

'Tell me some of the names,' Mia encourages her, without looking up. She's working on her own garland, building a cheerful pattern of red, green and gold.

'Well, let's see.' Aunt Gertie sets down her stack of paper and looks around the room. 'That succulent back there is an aloe vera. Your gran called it Moses for some reason. I remember because I always thought it should have had a Hispanic name.'

Mia smiles faintly and unconsciously touches her earlobe.

'And then the tall one over there, the ficus? That one is Colin Marcus Ficus.'

'Quite a mouthful,' Mia quips. She looks over at a towering palm. 'What about that one?'

Aunt Gertie shakes her head. 'Can't remember. Maybe it didn't have a name.'

'It should be something punny,' Mia muses. 'Like Keanu Leaves.'

'Ha!' Aunt Gertie chortles, her whole body shaking. The chain falls off her lap and on to the floor. 'That's a good one! He's a looker, for sure.'

Mia sets aside her own chain and gets down on her knees to gather up Aunt Gertie's. John steps into the room and takes a seat on a nearby oversized pot. Mia sees him and snorts in annoyance. 'Thanks a lot, meddler.'

'What's that, dearie?' Aunt Gertie reaches for a new strip of paper.

'Oh, nothing, Auntie. I wasn't talking to you.'

'Hmm.' Aunt Gertie raises her eyebrows. 'Can't be too careful in this house, talking to yourself. You never know who might be listening.'

'Is that so,' Mia deadpans. She glares over at John and then turns back to Gertie. 'Are you saying this house is haunted?'

Aunt Gertie laughs. 'Well, of course it is! It's too old not to have a few extra tenants.'

'I see,' Mia drawls. 'And, would you say these . . . tenants . . . are mostly benevolent? Or would you characterize them as meddlesome, obnoxious persons of the past?'

'Now, wait a minute,' John objects.

Covertly, Mia raises a hand to silence him. Then she leans in towards Aunt Gertie, waiting for her response.

'Oh, definitely meddlesome. I never met a ghost who was content to mind their own business.'

John shakes his head, outraged, but Mia just nods sagely in an encouraging way. 'I agree with you. Go on . . .'

'Well, there's just too much that happens in this house that can't be explained any other way.'

'Yes. Exactly. Like strange things with the electrics.'

'I'm feeling very singled out here,' John interjects.

'Good. You should,' Mia says. Aunt Gertie looks at her strangely, and she hurries to ask, 'Good and bad happenings, you could say?'

Gertie laughs. 'Oh, very much so! For instance, we

got a pay per view channel for free for two whole years. Two years! Nary a bill ever arrived. You can't tell me that wasn't due to some well-meaning interference.'

'Ah, but it's not always well meaning, now, is it?' Mia says this completely seriously, without ever taking her gaze off Aunt Gertie. 'Sometimes it must be that these tenants have grown too big for their boots. They think it's OK to meddle in people's lives.'

'I wasn't meddling . . .' John defends.

'Absolutely. They can't help themselves. Poor dears. The temptation must be too strong for them.'

Mia nods along with Aunt Gertie. 'I can only imagine what a miserable existence it is for these poor souls. You really can't blame them for being obnoxious.'

'All that time alone isn't good for them.' Aunt Gertie's watch beeps and she looks down at it in surprise. 'Oh, dear me. It's time for my evening meds.' She sets aside the chain and straightens up in increments, shaking her head at how long it takes her. 'You know, my knees have never worked quite right since my surgeries. If you ask me, my doctor spent more time looking at my boobs than fixing my knees.'

'Aunt Gertie!' Mia guffaws.

Gertie shrugs. 'I'm just saying. He was a young thing, and I don't think he'd ever seen a pair of double Gs.' She pats the bosom in question. 'Well, I really do have to take those meds. Save my seat, dear.'

'Oh, I will,' Mia assures her.

Gertie shuffles off, still chuckling to herself. As soon as he's sure the old woman is out of earshot, John strides over to the table and moves to sit down.

'Don't you dare,' Mia threatens. 'I promised I would save her seat and I meant it.'

'You're mad,' John begins carefully.

'Very observant of you.' Mia states this with gusto, and then studiously ignores John.

'You can't be serious. You're just going to not talk to me?'

'You should be used to it,' Mia snaps.

'Mia,' John tries again. 'I just think there's something there. Between you and Sam. I was trying to help it along a little.'

'You were supposed to be on my side!' Mia nearly yells this. 'Make his life miserable. Make him think he's a little crazy. Not make things all swoony and romantic!'

'Was it so terrible?' John asks, staring at her straight on. Mia ignores the question, scowling at the chain she's making. 'Besides, you would only think it was romantic if there were already some feelings there. I'm not a magician. I can't fabricate something out of thin air.' He leans in. 'Admit it, you still care for Sam.'

'I'm not admitting anything. You'll use it against me. You were a gardener, not a priest or a lawyer. I have no assurance of confidentiality.'

John snickers, amused by her sarcasm. 'Point taken. And, I'll admit to some matchmaking tendencies. But, seriously, Mia. Sam—'

'Means nothing to me,' Mia states resolutely.

'That's *not* true! You still love him! Even after all these years. And if I'm not mistaken, he loves you back. Never stopped, I suspect.'

'I do *not* love him,' Mia objects. She's practically radiating with fury. 'In fact, I *hate* him.'

John shakes his head. 'There's a fine line between hate and love, Mia.'

'Hey, Mia, there you are.' Sam enters the room, startling both of them. John shoves up from the table, toppling his chair.

'Oh, woah! That was weird,' Sam says as he reaches down to set the chair back on its legs. 'Mia, are you OK?'

'Yeah.' Mia seems to flounder for a moment. 'Sorry, you startled me and my foot was on that other chair. Must have knocked it over.'

'I thought I heard shouting.' Sam looks around the room. 'Is it just you in here?'

'Sure is,' Mia quips, glaring in John's direction. Then she seems to realize how strange that must look and pulls her gaze back to Sam. John's struck once more by what an attractive man Sam is. He's changed clothes, opting for a worn pair of jeans with an open cardigan over a deep green button-down shirt.

Sam's gaze wanders around the room, taking in the plants, the lights and the mechanical windows overhead with open curiosity. The room is surprisingly cosy, with the panes all reflecting the light and the warmth of the plants. Sam's gaze softens as it returns to Mia, and John sighs. 'Sorry, I've never been in here. It's really beautiful. Adds a sort of exotic flair to the whole place.'

Mia folds her arms over her chest and nods, clearly uncomfortable.

'I'd love to curl up in a chair and work on my poems

all day,' Sam continues. 'Or even just read. This is kind of magical.'

'It has a whole different vibe during the daytime,' Mia responds reluctantly. 'Even when it's not sunny outside, it feels bright and open. I've always loved coming in here.' She draws in a deep breath and closes her eyes. 'Can't you just imagine ladies taking their tea in here, in fancy gowns, chattering about all the town gossip?'

Sam grins. 'I can. Or an intimate evening performance for a dinner party. I bet a string quartet would sound amazing in here. All the sounds echoing off the glass.' He steps around the table and squats down beside Mia. His voice softens into an intimate growl that makes John a little weak at the knees. 'Hey. I wanted to check on you. I wasn't sure what happened during the film.'

Mia lets out a nervous laugh. 'Oh, it was nothing. Just the usual clumsiness. Sorry about your trousers. I hope the stains come out. Chocolate can be such a challenge to get out of fibres. It's probably because it's an enzyme, which can be harder to remove than a grease stain. Or maybe I don't have that quite right. Anyway . . .' To John's immense surprise, Mia continues blabbering on about stains, her eyes flitting from Sam's face to the room and back again as a blush creeps up her throat. She can't quite seem to sit still either. Could it be that with John's declaration still ringing in her ears, and Sam looking at her so earnestly, Mia is reconsidering her stance on her love life?

'You missed the end of the film,' Sam says. 'Your favourite film.'

More nervous laughter. 'It's only my favourite *Christmas*

film. Not my favourite *film* film. It's not like I walked out during the lift scene of *Dirty Dancing*. Now, that would be alarming.' Mia puts on the most insincere, over-the-top smile, but her leg is bouncing a million miles a minute. 'I'm fine. Really! Just got a little flustered. It's been a long week. You don't need to read any more into it.'

Sam frowns. He doesn't seem to be buying the brush-off. But he stands back up and slides his hands into his pockets. 'It's just that I thought there was something going on between—'

Mia gives a quick shake of her head, and flashes him a smile that John thinks is a touch too fragile. 'It's just Christmas, you know? It messes with your mind that's all. No need to make mountains out of molehills.' Her voice is higher pitched than usual, but she soldiers on. 'I'll see you at dinner. I need to finish up this paper chain. I promised Aunt Gertie.'

Sam's eyebrows draw together, and he presses his lips into a straight line. After watching Mia for a long moment, he exhales slowly and nods. 'OK, Mia. I'll see you at dinner then.' His shoulders droop a bit as he leaves the room.

'Wow. You really took the wind out of that man's sails,' John says to Mia. But she's not listening. She's staring after Sam, vulnerability shining on her face. While she's distracted, John grabs the vacant chair and sits back down. 'And I'd love to hear more about how he doesn't have feelings for you.'

Mia worries her lip for a while before she directs her attention back to John. 'You really need to stop with the meddling. He doesn't have feelings for me. Other than a possibly mild annoyance at my existence.'

'How would you know?' John pushes back. Mia is so sure of herself, but from her own account, she and Sam never had much, if any, interaction after the swimming pool incident. 'It's not like you ever had a heart to heart with him. As far as you've told me, you never spoke to him again after that night.' John's eyes widen as he comes to a startling realization. He points an accusatory finger at Mia. '*You* ghosted *him*!'

'I did not!' she rears back, full of denial. 'I did not ghost him.' Mia looks off into the distance as she reviews her statement. 'I just blocked him and never spoke to him again.'

'Aha!' John throws his hands in the air. 'So, you admit it. That's exactly how you defined ghosting to me. Come to think of it, maybe this offensive term has its place.'

'You weren't there.' Mia's tone turns more sullen. 'It was horrible. I felt so betrayed. And he never even apologized.'

'Well, in fairness, you never gave him the chance. How was he supposed to reach you? By carrier pigeon?'

'Well, no,' Mia concedes. 'But, John, I really thought he liked me. I was certain of it. And then that night, standing beside the pool completely exposed . . .' She looks away, but not before John sees the sheen of tears in her eyes.

Well, that's horrible. He never meant to make the girl cry. And it *was* a legitimately traumatizing experience. To think a guy likes you, and you put your bravest self out there, and then find out it was all just a gag. Mia's resolution to hate Sam is entirely understandable, even if John can see that there's been quite a bit of thawing in Sam's general direction.

'You know,' he begins, 'I've always believed in second chances. Maybe everything has aligned on this trip; James ghosting you, Sam's presence, your ability to interact with me . . . so that you can reap the benefits of a second chance.' Something John was never given, since he passed away so soon after the whole debacle with Alastair at the Christmas party. Lord knows John has spent hours upon hours regretting the way he handled himself.

Would things have turned out differently for John had he made different choices? It is very possible. Probable, even. Maybe sharing some of his own regrets would motivate Mia to be a bit more courageous in her own love life. Then again, he really did overstep with the meddling during the film. Should he just lie to Mia and say he'll stay out of it? He'd be breaking his word, but is honour really a thing among ghosts?

'I don't care about second chances, John. I just want to enjoy my holiday, spend Christmas with my family and get Sam back a little for what he did to me.' She shoots John a dark look. 'Which is what you already agreed to do.'

'If that's what you really want . . .'

'It is.'

'All right then. I'll do my best to stop meddling.'

'Really?' Mia's face fills with relief. 'Thank you.' She lets her head fall back and closes her eyes, inhaling deeply. When she opens them, she looks at the paper chain in her lap as if just remembering its presence. 'Oh, I'd better get working on this before Aunt Gertie comes after me. She has no patience for slackers.'

Mia returns to looping the colourful strips of paper through each other, and after a while, she asks, 'So, you really can't eat anything?'

'I can eat it,' John replies morosely. 'I just can't taste it. Cruel and unusual punishment, if you ask me.' He looks at the cheerful garland strewn halfway across the room. 'You know, my mum made a garland just like this one year. Well, only with red and green paper, nothing as multicoloured as this. But I thought it was so beautiful.'

Mia curls another strip of paper and glues it in place. 'Did you put the garland on your tree?'

John shakes his head. 'We never had a tree. My mum was a single mother, and there was never a lot of money left for things that would just end up in the rubbish after a week. Practical and timeless were the words my mother lived by.'

'Was it just the two of you?' Mia asks.

John nods. 'Just me and Mum. But that year she must have thrown caution to the wind. I remember feeling so curious when she pulled the stack of paper out of her bag. "They were on special offer, John," she said. And then she sat with me the whole evening, making paper chains and telling me stories about my grandparents' farm where she grew up. They were from Scotland, and my mum had moved to London for university and then met my dad. He died shortly after I was born – some kind of cancer.'

'That's terrible,' Mia says. 'How sad for you both. Did

your mum ever consider moving back to Scotland to be closer to your grandparents?'

'They also both died when I was little,' John says. Try as he might, he can't really remember what his grandparents looked like. 'My mum was one of those late in life babies. They'd given up trying, and then my gran got the ultimate surprise when she got pregnant with my mum at fifty-five.' He rubs a palm across his cheek, thinking. 'You know, that's what has troubled me the most about my passing. I left my mum all alone. I have no idea what happened to her after I died.'

Mia makes a sound of dismay. 'How awful John. I'm so sorry.'

'I hate to think of her living out the last of her days on her own. I feel so guilty for abandoning her.'

Mia's tone becomes fierce. 'No, you can't think that. It wasn't something under your control. Truly!'

John smiles half-heartedly. It's sweet that Mia feels the need to absolve him in this regard. They sit quietly for a moment as Mia alternates colours in her chain, until she suddenly straightens up and bounces in her seat.

'John! We can google her! See if we can find any information about what happened to her after your accident.' She pulls out her phone. 'What was your mother's full name?'

'You can do that?' Hope courses through John, but it feels dangerous.

Mia nods emphatically. 'We can look to see if she's on any social media – I'll start there. But we can also search ancestry sites, things like that. The internet is chock full of personal information. My dad is always going on about what a violation of our privacy the internet is.'

'Susan Ann Hackett. She lives – or lived – in Birmingham. Born in 1936.'

'Oh. I'd forgotten about how old you actually are.' Mia hesitates. 'She's probably not on any social media then.' Still, she clicks through her apps and pulls up a search.

John waits patiently as Mia searches. After half an hour has gone by, Mia heaves a sigh and gives him a disappointed smile. 'I'm sorry. I'm not finding anything.'

'That's OK,' he hurries to assure her. He doesn't like how dejected she looks. 'It was a long shot anyway.' Mia's expression is resigned as she sets her phone down and picks up the paper chain again.

'I had another idea for Sam,' John says, trying to change the subject and lighten the mood. 'The man eats a banana in the morning right when he wakes up. He brings one up every night to his room and puts it on his desk. He must be chronically low in potassium or something. Here's what I'm thinking. I'm going to scratch messages into the peel. It won't be visible at night, but by morning, he'll see the message when he goes to eat it. I just need some ideas of what the messages could be.'

'Oooh! Yes. This is brilliant!' Mia sets aside the garland and props her chin in her hands. 'Let's see. They could say something sinister. "I know what you did." Or, vaguely threatening. Um, oh, I know! "You won't get away with this."'

John gapes at her. 'I was thinking something a little less dark. More along the lines of, "Your breath stinks" or something like that. We're messing with the hand-some lad, not trying to terrify him into an early grave.'

'Oh. You're probably right.' Mia thinks for a minute. 'But I would be more oddly specific. Something like, "Your socks are unquestionably hideous". That will fit on a banana, right?'

John bites his lip so as not to laugh out loud. 'You want me to write "unquestionably" on a banana? Do you know how small I'll have to write?'

'I believe in you!' Mia crows. And John has to admit, she seems pretty proud of her own brilliance.

17

MIA

24 December

It's Christmas Eve, finally. Of all the days before Christmas, this is by far Mia's favourite. There's an air of expectation surrounding the day. Plus, there's no need to get up early the next morning, now that they're all older and the allure of Father Christmas doesn't drag them from their beds before dawn.

She loves the family traditions on Christmas Eve too. Growing up, Penny always had them make gingerbread houses on Christmas Eve to keep them busy while they waited for the day to pass. Mia would sneak as many sweets as she could during the decorating, and Penny would pretend not to notice. And, best of all, there's the feast Mia will prepare for dinner. She's been planning this menu for months, and she's practically bursting at the seams to begin. The pork loin she's had brining since yesterday is a beast – nearly ten pounds – and it will take all day to cook.

Mia sets her outfit for dinner on the bed to air – an endlessly comfortable knitted pencil skirt and a silk blouse. The skirt is a thrifted Saint Laurent – a designer brand that she would never waste her money on at full price. The green blouse is one of her favourites simply because the brush of real silk against her skin always makes her feel incredibly elegant.

But for now, she pulls on a pair of leggings that make her bum look amazing. Normally she would opt for a shapeless t-shirt on top – easy to cook in and always a comfortable choice. For reasons she's not quite ready to explore, Mia pulls on a cute little cropped jumper instead. The powdery blue hue goes great with her rosy skin tone. She contorts her body to get a glimpse of the whole outfit in the tiny wall mirror, and lets out a satisfied sigh. She moves on to makeup. She will do most of a full face now, and just amp up the eyeliner and add some lipstick before dinner this evening.

'Hello, hello,' John calls out as Mia finishes the last swipe of mascara.

'I'm upstairs.'

'Decent, I hope,' John responds as he takes the stairs. His lanky frame appears in the doorway a moment later. He leans against the doorframe and rubs his hands together, blowing on them.

'Cold?' Mia asks as she pulls on her socks and stuffs her feet into her slippers.

'I wish. It just seems like a chilly morning, if that makes sense.' John gives her a rueful smile.

'I can understand that. How did the banana go?' Mia pads down the stairs and grabs one of the apples she brought to the cottage yesterday. 'Was Sam freaked out?'

Following her, John shakes his head. 'You have a bit of a sadistic streak, you know that?'

'Sure. Whatever. I'm a monster. Now, spill.'

'Well, I did scratch the words into the peel,' John begins. 'But he wasn't up yet this morning when I left the big house. I went for a walk to clear my head, and now I'm here.'

Mia rolls her lips together. 'Disappointing. Doesn't matter that much, though. I'm headed up to the big house. And when I see Sam, I'll just find a way to casually bring up bananas.'

'As one does,' John chuckles.

'Exactly.'

There's a sharp knock at the front door, and then it bursts open. Sam enters in a flurry of cold air and snow-flakes, his arms full of chopped wood. 'Morning, Mia.'

'Ah, good morning?' Mia's forehead wrinkles as she greets him. 'What are you doing down here?'

'It's colder today and I was worried about you down here in the cottage – thought you might be running low on wood. So, I thought I'd just bring some for you from the pile Charlie and I have been working on.' Sam says this last bit as he toes off his boots and heads for the back room, pulling up short when he sees the large stack of wood in the inglenook. 'Oh. You already have quite a lot.'

'Yep,' Mia muses, studying the man standing in front of her, with his half-tucked-in shirt peeking out of his coat and his windswept hair. Her eyes snag on the stubble sprinkled across his jawline. She finds she suddenly has an overwhelming urge to reach up and explore the texture, and quickly laces her fingers behind her to contain herself.

There's a moment of awkward silence. Sam shuffles his feet, glances around the room and then exhales. 'Well, I guess I can just leave these pieces with the rest, and then I'll get out of your hair.'

'Sounds like a plan.' Mia's cadence is wooden, and she silently berates herself for sounding so stilted. 'I mean, thanks. For . . . this.' She gestures vaguely at the pile in Sam's arms.

Sam sets the logs down by the hearth and straightens, brushing a few stray wood shavings off his coat. His eyes bounce around the cottage, taking in the homey touches. 'Wow, this place is really nice. I can see why you moved down here.'

Mia tilts her head, trying to work out why her stomach is feeling so unsettled. 'Yeah, it's really cosy. Mum is doing a great job fixing it up. My own bathroom is a big selling point too.'

'I'm sure,' Sam agrees. He doesn't seem to be paying much attention to the conversation, though, his eyes seemingly glued to the stripe of skin that's visible above her leggings. Unable to resist, Mia yawns widely, stretching her arms above her head and pulling her top further up as she does so. Sam swallows thickly as heat fills his gaze. Mia almost wants to laugh at how easy it is to bait him, until he takes a step towards her, his eyes burning as he looks into hers. Mia's stomach turns liquid and her breath catches, the confidence she'd had a few seconds before deserting her.

Desperate to break the sudden tension that's filled the cottage, Mia coughs and asks quietly, 'Shall we head back up to the house?' Sam's eyes seem to clear at her words, and Mia's breathing returns to normal as she continues, 'You're probably hungry for breakfast. Unless you've already eaten?'

'Just a banana.' Sam blinks a few times, and then after a pause, in which Mia does her best not to smirk, nods his head. 'Yes. Let's head up. After you.'

Mia spins around and locates her boots, silently berating herself for her moment of weakness as she bends down to tug them on. The laces have tangled, and it takes her a second to sort them out. When she straightens, Sam is waiting patiently with his boots on, one hand resting on the doorknob.

'Ladies first,' he says, turning the knob. But nothing happens, and a confused frown creases his face. The doorknob turns uselessly, while the wooden door stays resolutely shut. Sam rattles the knob. 'Well, this is weird.' He glances over his shoulder at Mia. 'Has this been happening much?'

She shakes her head. 'No, it's been fine. Let me try?' She edges up beside him, doing her best to ignore how great he smells and the heat of his body. It's harder than she expected, and she feels that same magnetic pull drawing her towards him. Her heartbeat picks up again and she feels a wave of heat rising to her cheeks. She's suddenly very thankful for the chilly draught coming from beneath the door. Shaking her head, Mia's hand closes over Sam's on the doorknob for a brief moment before he withdraws. Mia tries the knob several times, but it's clearly stuck. She stares at the ancient door, puzzled.

'I can call Charlie to come down with some tools,' Sam offers. 'He'll sort it out.' He pulls his phone from his pocket, but Mia shakes her head.

'There's no signal down here.'

Sam looks down at his phone with an adorably perplexed expression.

John could find a way to alert someone, she's sure of it. She glances around the room but can't see him anywhere. *Oh.* That sodding ghost.

'So, what, we're stuck down here until someone realizes we're missing?' Sam slides his phone back into his pocket and shifts restlessly. 'What if that takes hours?'

Hours they would have to spend just the two of them, locked in this cosy cottage. Alone. Though Mia knows she should be irritated by this, there's a hesitant thrill crawling up her spine, which she weakly tells herself has nothing to do with the man currently staring at the door in confusion. Sam resorts to pacing the kitchen. After a few trips, he comes to a stop. 'I could break a window,' he offers apologetically. 'That's the only other thing I can think of.'

The windows in the cottage are high, small and, most importantly, made with original wavy glass that would be a shame to break. Mia shakes her head. 'Let's not rush to property destruction. My mum will notice I haven't started cooking, or something. Hopefully, someone will find us before we need to start breaking things.'

There seems to be nothing else to do besides settle in. She tilts her head towards the front room. 'We might as well get comfortable while we wait.' Mia glances around the kitchen. 'I could make some tea . . .' she offers.

Sam gives her a rueful smile. 'Another set of hot drinks might not be the best idea. But sure, I don't mind sitting by the fire.'

He follows Mia into the front room, and once she's chosen a chair, he lowers himself into the other. Sam crosses his arms, then uncrosses them, awkwardly placing them on the chair arms after a somewhat lengthy deliberation. He begins to chew his lip as they both stare into the fire.

'Thanks again for bringing the wood down,' Mia ventures, desperate to break the silence. 'That was really thoughtful of you.'

Sam keeps his eyes on the fire and clears his throat. 'I'm not the monster you seem to think I am, Mia.'

'I don't think that,' she rushes to object. He turns to look at her, one eyebrow quirking up. The gaze he levels at her is full of . . . Mia can't quite tell *what* it is, but it makes her stomach flip and she can't work out if he knows the effect his look is having on her.

Sam's laugh is laced with unexpected sarcasm. 'No? I

could have sworn otherwise. You're constantly blowing hot and cold with me, Mia. I thought we were finally getting somewhere yesterday but now it feels like we're back to you either being spitting nails mad or trying to escape the conversation as quickly as possible. Even last night, you wouldn't talk to me.'

'Well, I can't exactly escape right this moment,' Mia says, with the startling realization that this was probably John's exact intent. She sighs, trying to mask the frustration in her voice as she says, 'What is it precisely that you're dying to talk about, Sam?'

He lets out another laugh. 'Anything? Everything? I want to hear anything you want to say. I want you to *talk* to me, Mia.' He says this with enough irritation that Mia can't help but take notice. She's never really seen Sam upset. Nothing ever seems to truly irritate him. But now, she can't help but wonder whether she might have the ability to irritate Sam Williams. Could *she* get under his skin? Mia chews on her lip, mulling this over.

After another awkward silence, Sam tries again. 'How about this? Why don't you tell me why you ran out of the room while we were watching the film? One moment I thought we were having a really nice time, but the next you were acting as if you just found out I have some awful contagious disease.'

Mia picks at a piece of fluff on her knee. There's definitely anger mounting in Sam's tone, and it's making her re-evaluate every assumption she'd ever made about his unflappable calm. 'I told you last night—'

Suddenly, Sam stands up from his chair, his eyes

burning as he looks at her. 'Spare me the lies, Mia. You actually have a tell, did you know that? There's a little wrinkle that shows up between your eyebrows when you're lying.' He shoves his fingers through his hair in agitation. 'Whatever you may think of me, I like to believe that I at least deserve to hear the truth. Or at the very least, a couple of sentences' worth of explanation.'

Oh, he's definitely angry. Too angry for it only to be about her awkwardness after the film last night. Mia *really* doesn't want to start digging up their past, not now. She's spent so long avoiding Sam, avoiding the emotional fall-out of the way things ended between them, and she's not sure she's ready to finally let it all surface. But as Sam's frustration radiates off him in this moment, Mia has the unsettling feeling that that's where this conversation is heading, whether she likes it or not. She pushes herself up to her feet, matching Sam's unflinching gaze with her own, accepting that she's going to have to be honest.

'It felt . . . weird, OK?' Her voice is hoarse as she fights to keep it steady, to force down the emotions rising within her. 'You're right, we were having a perfectly nice time together, all cosy and relaxed and laughing at one of my favourite films. It was all so . . . so easy. Which just felt so *wrong* after the last six years of—' She cuts herself off, suddenly embarrassed to finish the sentence.

'Just say it, Mia!' Sam's voice is raised, irritation pulsing beneath his words. 'It's not like I don't know! You cut me out of your entire life!'

'After the last six years of hating you!'

The words rush out of her, baited by his own anger, and

they both stand there in stunned silence as Mia's confession settles between them. Mia clenches her jaw together and forces down the tears that are threatening to surface. 'Is that what you wanted me to say? Are you happy now?' She's yelling and Sam's glaring at her. She can't escape it, can't escape him and the feelings that inundate her whenever she allows herself to be honest with him. 'It was a huge 180, and I didn't know how to process it.' She hurls this at him, heart pounding in her ears.

'You want to talk about a 180? You never even gave me a chance to explain myself!' Sam throws his hands up in frustration, eyes blazing. 'I thought—' Sam starts to say something and then catches himself. 'It doesn't matter.'

'I never did, did I?' Mia snaps, her own irritation rising to match his.

Sam's eyes widen, and after a moment he shakes his head in disbelief. He takes a step towards Mia and she stays put, the tangle of anger and shock overpowering any thought of retreating. Sam takes another step, and now he's standing right in front of her, pushing into her personal space. Her pulse turns thunderous.

'Is that really what you think? Mia, you blocked me on *everything*. You avoided me, used Lucy as a buffer, even forbade Charlie from talking about you with me. You were everything to me, Mia, and then overnight you completely removed yourself from my life. You were just *gone*.' His anger seems to be melting away as he speaks, leaving something behind that Mia can't quite identify. 'I've spent years wishing we could have one conversation, just one, so that I could explain myself, but I'd come to accept it was never going to happen.' His voice is choked with emotion now, and Mia studies his eyes intently as he goes on. 'And then, these past few days you're suddenly back in my life, and there have been moments where things have almost felt normal, where I've felt almost normal for the first time in years, but every time I think we might finally be at a place where I can explain, you pull away again. It's *killing* me, Mia. I haven't wanted to force you to talk about it and I can tell you don't want to, but I just need . . . I just have to know—' He stops, the words catching in his throat.

He moves slowly, giving Mia time to edge away if she wants. But she can't move, can't escape the onslaught of emotion playing across Sam's face. He reaches out, curling his hand around hers. When Mia doesn't immediately swat him away, he moves, sliding his hand over her wrist and up her forearm, sending a shudder throughout her body.

Sam makes a tiny, hoarse sound as he caresses Mia's skin, which immediately breaks out in goosebumps. Sam's eyes are on the path his hand is taking, and they're soft, like he's remembering previous times when his fingers danced across the contours of her body, making her writhe beneath him.

Sam traces his way back down to her palm and then he lifts her hand, bringing her fingers all the way up to his mouth. Mia's chest tightens and she can't breathe past the ache in her heart as Sam brushes his lips across her knuckles – warm breath skating over sensitive skin. Mia studies him, curiosity filling her as his words replay in her head. All these years, she'd convinced herself that Sam was just toying with her, but as he meets her eyes, there is unmistakable hurt and regret swimming in his brown gaze.

They're both quiet while Sam inches forward, their bodies now separated only by the space that their intertwined fingers hold. Mia doesn't know what to say or even think. All she can do is feel the sensory overload of Sam's body so close to hers, the heat radiating from him, his cinnamon and spice scent surrounding her. All of her anger and frustration dissipate as she holds his gaze, and her breath stutters as she waits for Sam to speak.

'Do you think,' Sam finally begins, 'do you think you could ever *not* hate me, Mia? Does that seem possible?'

A moment ago, Mia would have sworn it wasn't. She's been carrying this hurt around for so long, it's become a part of her. But standing here, feeling the weight of Sam's regret, she can feel her defences crumbling.

He hasn't moved back an inch. 'I wouldn't say this if that door wasn't stuck shut, but for once you can't run away from me.' Mia swallows hard, her body softening towards Sam in familiar ways that she never thought she'd experience again. 'Spending time with you yesterday was the highlight of my year.'

It's the perfect opportunity to take another shot at Sam, and even now there's a little voice in Mia's head, a mean, vindictive one, that is urging her on. But a much bigger part of her is holding its breath. Hoping for something different. Mia bites her lip for a long moment, and then gives a little shrug. 'I enjoyed it too.' Feeling like she can do better, she tries again. 'It felt like the old days. How I'd feel when we were hanging out at uni and I thought you liked me. Before everything.'

'I did like you,' Sam admits quickly, his voice low. There's a heat beneath his words, something charged and urgent, and Mia feels her body respond instinctively, desire skittering down her spine. But she can't let herself get pulled in again like she did last night. She shakes her head slightly to try to clear it as doubt fills her, warring with the desire pooling in her stomach. When you like someone, you don't treat them the way Sam treated her. He'd said he *loved* her back then, and she'd always thought it was just part of the game he was playing. But just now he told her she'd been everything to him, and the vulnerability in his eyes had been too sincere to be fake. Maybe she truly doesn't have that story entirely right. Sam had said he wanted to explain, but even now Mia isn't sure if she's ready to hear it. She just needs some more time. She turns her gaze to the window, watching the softly falling snow.

'I'm sorry I ran out on you yesterday. And then refused to talk to you. That was insensitive of me, and you deserved better.' She looks at him as she says this, hoping he can see the honesty in her face. His eyebrows rise in surprise and he seems at a loss for words, and Mia waits, eyes bouncing between him and the window.

'OK,' he says finally. 'Thank you.' He looks as though he wants to say something else, but Mia's not sure if she's strong enough to hear it in this moment. She drops his hand and steps back, breaking out of the bubble Sam has created around them. With a measure of distance between them, she feels like she can breathe again.

Out of the corner of her eye, she sees a flurry of movement outside the window, and she turns to see John sauntering by with a mischievous smile. He points towards the front of the house and mimes opening a door. Mia shakes her head. Apparently, the interfering ghost of Christmas present has decided she and Sam have done enough emotional work for now.

'Great.' Mia nods sharply. 'Glad to hear it. You know, I'm going to try that door again. I was just thinking that maybe if I jiggle it a little while I turn the knob, it will work.'

'It doesn't hurt to try.' Sam follows her back to the kitchen.

Knowing John has already undone whatever method he used to lock them in, Mia pretends to fuss with the knob, taking care to block Sam's view with her body. When she swings the door wide open, he smiles in relief. Perhaps all of this unplanned honesty was challenging for Sam as well.

'It would seem we are free to go,' Mia observes wryly. As they start back towards the big house, John is nowhere to be seen. Annoyed as she is with him, Mia grudgingly admits that she's somewhat grateful for the intrusion.

18

MIA

Despite the delayed start to dinner preparations, Mia's pork loin turned out amazing and her family have been effusive with their praise of the dinner she'd planned. Charlie and Sam have enthusiastically tackled the cleanup, and Penny has appointed herself cocktail wait-ress for the evening. Mia wanders into the living room to stand beside Martin's tree. Looking at the twinkling lights, she rubs her arm again, remembering the sensa-tion of Sam's hand snaking up it, sending shivers across her skin. Several times throughout dinner she caught herself rubbing the spot where Sam had kissed her knuckles, as though she could still feel the ghost of his lips there.

Her anger seems to have subsided significantly, as if she is actually on the path to forgiving Sam. She can't quite believe it, and yet, as she glances his way before taking a seat on the sofa, a flutter of hope dances inside her. Aunt Gertie is perched in a high back chair, patiently explaining the rules of their traditional game of Christmas Eve Fishbowl to Sam, who is listening intently.

'Let me see if I have this straight. There are four rounds to the game, and each one is different.'

'Yes, exactly!' She pats Sam on the leg. 'You're paying attention. The first round you can give as many verbal clues as you want.'

'That one's my favourite,' Martin chimes in. 'Although I'm always accused by my family of using words that are too highbrow.'

'Ah, and my favourite round is charades,' Penny adds. 'You know I was quite the starlet when I was at university.'

Charlie and Mia swap looks. Penny brings this up every Christmas, and is often personally offended when her team can't guess her clues.

'But between them is the one word clue round?' Sam clarifies.

'Yes.' Aunt Gertie nods emphatically. 'And then the last round, well, you'll see. It's the most entertaining. Mia, pass out the papers. Everyone needs to write down seven clues.'

There are a few minutes of quiet intensity, where the only sounds are pencils scratching across paper. Then the clues are folded and added to Penny's punch bowl, a pearlescent monstrosity inherited from Penny's Great-Aunt Ida that's too garish to use for any other event hosted at Willowby Manor.

'I pick Mia for my first choice,' Martin says gravely. Mia stifles a groan. Her father is notorious for giving way too much irrelevant information when it comes to the clues.

'Well, I simply have to have Aunt Gertie,' Penny muses. 'She's the secret weapon in the last round.'

'I'll take Sam,' Martin says, after a painfully long deliberation. Mia fidgets in her seat as Sam moves to the side of the room Martin has claimed for his team. Sam shoots Mia a look, and then – mercifully – sits on the floor nearer to Martin. To her immense relief, Mia's stomach settles down, but she can't seem to tear her eyes away from his square jawline and the chiselled outline of his shoulders under his shirt. Maybe it's best if she keeps some distance between them for now.

'I guess I'm on Mum's team, then. Which will be the winning team, obviously,' Charlie quips.

'Bold words,' Mia responds. 'I guess you're going first, then?'

"Course,' Charlie responds. He digs out a clue and opens it up to read it. His eyes crinkle and he bounces a little in place. 'All right, here we go.' Sucking in an enormous breath, Charlie begins at a rapid fire pace. 'OK, this is Dad's favourite book. Oh, too hard? OK, I'll narrow it down. Thriller, wait, no, horror genre, they made a film of it. There's an axe, and Jack Nicholson—'

'*The Shining*!' Aunt Gertie crows.

'Yes, *The Shining*! On to the next. Let's see, ah, OK. Holiday song, Elvis, perhaps? Involves Dad's favourite botany creation at this time of year – yes, a Christmas tree—'

'"Rocking Around the Tree"!' Penny claps in delight, but Charlie shakes his head.

'Not quite, Mum. Come on, what's the rest?'

'Oh, let me see, wait, don't rush me, I know it, oh!

"Rocking Around the Christmas Tree"!' Penny thrusts both arms in the air and shakes her fists, Rocky style.

Mia's swallowed up in helpless laughter at her mother's triumphant expression. Charlie leads his team to two more points in the time allotted, and then the game passes to Martin.

Martin and Sam huddle up, with Mia still giggling as she joins them. 'All right, folks.' Martin's tone is infinitely serious. 'This is no silly game. We have youth and beauty on our side. Our victory is a foregone matter.'

Sam's eyes widen as he meets Mia's gaze. 'Don't worry,' she finds herself assuring him. 'It's easy once you get into a flow.'

'That's what I'm worried about,' Sam mutters.

Martin takes his first clue. 'All right, here we go, into the fray. Brilliant! This one's a superhero, created by Stan Lee—'

'Like that narrows it down,' Charlie heckles.

'Yes, Stan Lee, and played by various actors over the years. Let me think of the first chap's name . . .'

Sam straightens. 'Oh, erm, Hawkeye, Thor, Ironman, Starlord, Black Widow—'

'Dad, just tell us what the suit looks like!' Mia begs.

'Right, there have been several iterations, and the latest is quite sophisticated, if you ask me.'

'Dad!' Mia is practically shouting, while Penny's team howls with laughter.

'Ah, well, let me see, the lad has an alliterated name. And is a photographer in—'

'Spiderman!'

'Yes! Brilliant, Sam. Very good. I knew you were a smart chap. OK, this next one is—' The timer buzzes dramatically, and Mia groans in disappointment. 'Not too bad. One point for us then.'

Mia shakes her head, but as soon as Aunt Gertie starts calling out clues, she forgets her disappointment and is caught up in the laughter again. After a lightning fast two minutes where Aunt Gertie racks up four points for her team, the bowl passes to Mia.

She stands in front of the Christmas tree, fishing out her first clue. Martin and Sam are watching her intently. 'Right, here we go.' She gives the nod for Charlie to start the timer. 'Mm. Like a piano, but older.'

'Harpsichord,' Sam yells out.

'Yes! OK, next. Merry Christmas but in Span—'

'Feliz Navidad!' Sam's leaning towards her, completely focused.

'Yes! Oh, food you eat on the second day of the week—'

'Tacos! Taco Tuesday!' Sam barks out the answer like a general.

'Lucy's and my favourite film—'

'Oh, ah, *Dirty Dancing*!' Martin rushes to answer.

'Yes! OK, another.' Mia fumbles frantically with the paper, one eye on the timer. 'Ah, water activity, you use an oar. Not surfing, but the same kind of—'

'Paddle boarding!' Martin and Sam yell out at the same time.

Mia does a little jig, thrilled at her success. 'Oh, and this one is when it's your day to be older, and you use your mouth to put out the fire and—'

'Blowing out birthday candles!' Sam pumps the air when Mia nods, flopping back in his seat when the timer buzzes. 'That was exhausting.'

'We got six points!' Mia excitedly tells her team. The grin Sam gives her is electrifying.

The turns continue at a dizzying rate, until the first round is finished and Penny's team is ahead by two points.

'Wait, before we begin the next round, I need to refresh my drink,' Aunt Gertie says. Penny is fanning herself, her face red from laughter. Charlie is tapping away at his phone, and Martin has excused himself for a bathroom trip.

'Would you like a refill?' Sam asks Mia, scooping up her glass.

Mia looks up at him, feeling warm and loose from all the laughter. 'Please. Cranberry martini with two shots of vermouth.'

'Your wish is my command, my lady,' Sam says, finishing with a silly bow. As he heads for the bar cart, he glances over his shoulder and catches Mia watching him. Sam shoots her a wink and she drops her gaze, trying to hide her smile. She hasn't seen this side of Sam since they were hanging out at uni.

Mia is still giggling when she looks over at the doorway that leads to the front hall. John is leaning there against the wall, watching her family with a broad smile. He catches her eye, but before Mia can decide if she should try to sneak out to speak to him, Charlie interrupts.

'I've sent Molly a video of us playing. She'll either think it's hilarious, or she'll never want to speak to me again.'

'My money's on the latter,' Martin chuckles as he returns to the room. 'All right. It seems to be my turn again. Mm, the one word round. Challenging, but we are up to the task. Aren't we, team?'

'Yes, sir!' Mia and Sam call out in unison. Sam hands Mia her drink and she sips from it, sighing in pleasure as the perfectly mixed cocktail glides down her throat.

'And, we're off then!'

The one word round is fast and furious, until Charlie and Penny get stuck on the single clue Aunt Gertie has given.

'Lift!' she says again, emphatically.

Charlie and Penny shout over each other, but none of their guesses are right. Sam leans back far enough to catch Mia's eye behind Charlie's back. *Dirty Dancing*,' he mouths, and Mia snickers, nodding vigorously.

'LIFT!' Aunt Gertie practically screeches, rising up on her toes.

'No, no! No body language! That's cheating, Aunt Gertie!' Mia scolds, and her great-aunt pouts. The timer goes off, and Aunt Gertie throws the clue back into the bowl, disgusted.

Mia takes another sip of her drink. From the corner of her eye, she can see that Sam is watching her again. He's been doing that all evening, starting with the wide-eyed, obvious admiration of her outfit that keeps making her heart flutter more than she cares to admit. She tugs at the hem of her skirt, feeling an all too familiar heat pooling in the pit of her stomach. It's probably just the alcohol in her system. It's definitely *not* the man sitting a few feet away from her, who can't seem to keep his eyes off her.

The game moves on fast and furious, and the lead swings back and forth between both teams, although Penny's team maintains a slight edge for most of the game. They navigate the third round with ridiculous hilarity, as Penny overdramatizes her clues and Martin gets predictably bogged down in unrelated details. When it's Mia's turn, she decides to take advantage of a certain manor resident to really sell her clue.

'OK, everyone ready? Here we go.' Her clue is *A Christmas Carol*, and Mia makes what she envisions is a scary ghost face, and bobs and weaves around her teammates.

'*Mr Popper's Penguins!*' Martin shouts out. 'Wait, was that one of the clues?'

'Well, you should know by now what the clues are,' Gertie scolds. Charlie holds up a finger and answers his phone, but even with his ear plugged, he can't hear the person on the other line. He hunches over, shouting into the device at his ear. Penny is laughing so hard that she drops her glass and it splatters across the floorboards.

'Oh, now I've done it. I'll get a cloth.'

Martin whips out a bar towel from – it would seem – thin air. 'Here you are, dear. It's to be expected. We never get through a game without some sort of spill.'

Mia has taken advantage of the pandemonium to covertly wave John over. 'I need you to help me levitate. When I pretend to jump, I need you to lift me and then set me down in a different spot.'

John frowns at her. 'That would be cheating,' he resists.

'Pssht. The rules don't say I can't have help. Especially from a ghost.'

Some of the pandemonium has died down. Mia squares her shoulders and announces, 'OK. Back to it! Here we go.' She flaps her arms around her body while Sam and Martin call out every bird species they know. Then she gives a subtle nod and John places his hands on her waist. His touch is cold and clammy, and Mia pushes away the strange feeling as she prepares to jump, leaping into the air. John lifts her in a smooth arc that is not too obviously high to be unnatural. Mia lets out unearthly howls, and moans, and fights back her own laughter at her teammates' befuddled faces as she does her best floaty walk around the Christmas tree.

'Zombie?' Martin guesses, clearly at a loss. 'No, that's not it. Maybe . . . sleepwalking?'

Sam jumps to his feet. 'A ghost! She's a ghost – the ghost of Christmas past! From *A Christmas Carol*!' His shout coincides with the buzzer as Mia nods. Sam gives an exuberant fist pump and then, unexpectedly, pulls Mia into a hug. At first, she stiffens in surprise. Sam is at once all hard muscle and gentle warmth. After a moment, she allows herself to relax into the confines of his body. Heat rises within her, turning her insides liquid as her focus is drawn to the way Sam's hand spreads along the small of her back. Before she can decide how she feels about it, he releases her and steps back, eyes shining. 'We're only down by two points!' he says with glee.

Teammate Sam is like an enthusiastic golden retriever.

It's adorable, and right now Mia can't remember why, exactly, she was ever so furious with him.

'All right. So, we've done these clues three times now. Everyone should be familiar with them. This is the round where we act them out once more, but with a puppet!' Gertie declares.

Everyone roars with laughter, but Sam just looks confused. 'Wait, what do we have to do?'

'It's the same as charades,' Mia explains. 'But you have to control someone else's body to act out the clues. Like a puppeteer.'

Sam's eyes widen. 'You can't be serious.'

'As a heart attack,' Martin responds. 'I'll go first. Charlie, come here. You'll be my puppet.'

Martin opens his clue and positions Charlie, giving the nod for the timer to begin. Then he begins marching Charlie around in a circle, bending Charlie's body in all sorts of ridiculous contortions.

'Oh, I've got it!' Mia calls out. ' "Rocking Around the Christmas Tree"!'

Martin cheers, releasing Charlie, who bends over wheezing with laughter. Penny is filming, laughing away behind her phone, and Aunt Gertie is nodding along beside her. Mia draws in a contented breath, soaking up the pleasantness of this evening. They move through several more iterations of the clues, until it's Sam's turn to be the puppeteer.

He glances at the folded piece of paper and his smile deepens. 'I need Mia's help for this one,' he declares. With only the slightest bit of hesitation, Mia steps in front of him and faces her family.

'Ready, go!' shouts Charlie.

Sam's hands are on her waist, sliding across her sides to take a firm grip just above her hips. Mia schools her expression. She is calm. Cool. *Unaffected.* But when Sam spins her towards him, all the noise in the background fades out. Mia studies the curve of his upper lip, so perfectly balanced with his full lower lip. Behind his clear framed glasses, the crinkles around his eyes have deepened, emphasizing the strong lines of his eyebrows. What a beautiful, stupidly handsome face. Sam shifts his hands slightly, and warmth spreads from Mia's hips upward and inward. She wants his hands to stay there, stroking, soothing, melting her from the outside in. Sam's head bobs slightly from side to side, as if he's keeping time to a beat. And suddenly, Mia knows. He's singing 'Time of My Life' in his head, and as he flexes his knees and tightens his grip, Mia holds her body tautly together, legs extended and arms flung wide. Exhilaration pumps through her as Sam lifts her up above his head like she weighs nothing, and spins in a slow, confident circle.

There's shouting, and cheering, and possibly a vague cry of defeat from Charlie. Mia doesn't pay attention to any of it. Instead, she soaks up the pure thrill of this moment, of Sam acting out her favourite scene from her favourite film, and lets the joy of this experience saturate her entire body. Then Sam lowers her down, his hands shifting once more to guide her carefully back to standing. The path his hands take leaves a trail of heat burning along her back. It's an out of body experience that leaves Mia reeling, but it's the look in Sam's eyes that threatens to flatten her, as though he might come undone. As though he's been drowning and she's just pulled him to safety. Like all his unfulfilled dreams have finally been granted.

'Ahem.' Mia steps back, stumbling a little because her eyes are still locked with Sam's. 'Ah, very nice. *Dirty Dancing*. If I'd known we were going to do that, I would have worn my ball gown.' Sam doesn't move. He doesn't even acknowledge that he's heard her. His chest rises and falls, and Mia has to turn away, because she can't bear the breadth of emotion flickering in Sam's eyes. It's too much.

And then Charlie smacks Sam on the shoulder, congratulating him for his team's win. Sam cracks a smile and hugs Charlie, clapping him on the back, thereby breaking eye contact and freeing Mia. She presses a hand to her stomach and heads towards the hall, pausing only to grab a thick scarf before plunging outside into the cold.

19

MIA

Mia rushes past John, barely aware of the fact that he's keeping pace with her as she hurries outdoors. The crisp winter air fills her lungs and stings her cheeks, and both sensations are enough to lend her a measure of calm. The snow crunches beneath her feet and she squints out into the darkness, trying to pull herself together.

'Fun time with your family?' John's eyes are dancing.

Mia shakes her head. 'Listen, ghost man. I don't particularly have space for your wisecracking at the moment.' She sucks in a breath. Up until this moment, she's been thankful for her family's presence preventing any uncomfortably intimate moments between her and Sam. But now that things are shifting between them, she suddenly wishes they didn't have a constant audience bearing witness to the minutiae of their interactions. If only she could find a few moments alone with Sam this evening. How would he respond if *she* initiated this time? She curses herself for not taking advantage of their time in the cottage earlier, for letting her emotions overrule her body.

John interrupts her train of thought. 'It was nice to see you so happy. You might even say it was a welcome change.'

Mia snorts. 'I'm glad my emotional state is so important to you.'

'I'm just saying. I think it's worth taking a chance. With Sam, I mean.'

'I know what you mean. You're about as subtle as a neon sign, John.' Mia kicks at a clump of snow. 'Sam is great. Always has been. But I'm just not convinced it's worth the risk to try and start something with him.' She's annoyed to find that her voice is trembling. 'I promised myself I would never fall for that schtick again. I'm smarter than that.'

'How's that been working out for you?' John's voice is gentler, all pretence of teasing dropped. It's not too much of a stretch to think he actually might care about her happiness. But then again, John is convinced helping Mia is his path to crossing over. What if that's the only reason he's pushing her towards Sam?

Mia sighs, shaking her head, disbelieving of how jaded she's become. For a moment she considers what life will be like if she continues on this path. Always doubting people's care for her. Shutting out anyone besides family who makes her feel, even the tiniest bit. The idea is terribly depressing. To be honest, that's not the kind of person she wants to be.

'That boy looks at you like you're his Mona Lisa, you

know. The masterpiece he's been looking for his whole life.'

Mia swallows hard, trying to rid herself of the sudden lump in her throat.

'It's a rare thing, for someone to see you and think you're beyond special. I should know. Trust me, Mia. Running from it will only get you a lifetime of regrets.'

'You seem like you're speaking from experience.'

John laughs. The sound has a bitter, hollow edge to it. 'Indeed.'

'Is this about that Alastair guy?' His head swivels around, meeting her gaze with wide-eyed surprise. 'You know, the redhead in the pictures.'

'I know who Alastair is,' John practically grinds out. 'It's not like he was easy to forget.'

'Do tell,' Mia says. Then she falls silent, waiting to see what John will say next. If he shares, it will be a welcome reprieve from her thoughts about Sam.

John leans down to pick up a stick that's been partially buried in the snow. He knocks it against the wall behind him to free it from the snow, then twirls it in his fingers.

'I'm not sure how to talk about this, Mia. You say things are different now. That's wonderful. But in my time, it wasn't – well, people weren't as understanding.'

Mia nods. She's had a suspicion about where this is going. 'I can imagine.'

John breaks off little pieces of the stick and tosses them one at a time into the yard. 'I never really felt like I fitted in when I was growing up. I liked school well enough, and sports weren't really my thing. My friends were all obsessed with how far they could get with the girls, and that just never appealed to me. It took me a while to realize that I was just wired differently. And I never felt like it was that big a deal. I've always resisted being defined by one thing, in any case. Well, at least until I became a ghost.

'No one would have accepted me being gay, anyway. Least of all my mum. She was always so supportive of me and I know she loved me, but she was ridiculously traditional. I think it would have been too much for her to accept. So, I focused instead on pursuing a career that I liked. When I started here, at Willowby Manor, I knew I'd found it. Working on this property filled me up in ways I didn't know were possible . . . it gave me a creative outlet I'd never had before.

'When Alastair came along, it took me by complete surprise. I was happy in my life. Truly. But he stirred up something in me. A longing, if you will, for more.' John flicks the last of the stick out into the yard and runs a hand through his perfectly coiffed hair. 'Alastair was larger than life. And I don't mean just physically, although that man could turn heads. But he just had this . . . passion. A zeal for life that I found almost irresistible. He didn't let anyone tell him who he could or couldn't be.

'We were in love, but I wanted everything to be kept secret. He wanted us to be together openly, always telling me that it would be a crying shame to let society dictate who we were allowed to love. He had no problem risking it all. Said there was no other way to live.'

John hesitates, looking out into the darkness as if

staring into his own past. 'But it wasn't the same for me. I saw what we would have been risking. What I might have to give up to be with him openly. And, honestly? The cost was high. I could have lost my job here. And if my mum ever found out . . . Alastair was asking me to be something I'm not. To be someone who doesn't weigh the consequences.'

'So, what happened?' Mia asks this gently, because she can see how much this walk down memory lane is hurting John.

'He showed up at the Willowby Christmas party. I must have mentioned when it was, and he thought he could force my hand by showing up and saying we were a couple. But I wasn't ready, and I was so mad that Alastair was trying to push me because he was tired of waiting. So . . .' John lets out a long exhale. 'I just pretended I didn't really know him. I made up some story about how we'd been in the same school growing up, but I was as surprised as anyone else that he had shown up to the party. Alastair stormed out, and I had to stay, because to go after him would have implied he meant something to me.'

'Did you work it out with him afterwards?'

John shakes his head slowly. 'I never saw him again.'

'That's so sad. I'm really sorry that happened to you. And to Alastair.' Mia shuffles in the snow, listening to it crunch beneath her boots. 'I guess I can kind of see now why you've been pushing so hard for me to give Sam another chance.'

'Exactly,' John says, his relief at being understood evident.

'And very interesting too. I thought ghosting was a twenty-first-century phenomenon. Turns out it's been around a lot longer.'

'Well, I'm not sure I would say I ghosted Alastair.'

'Really?' Mia tilts her head, studying the lanky man beside her. 'So, was he the one ignoring your efforts to reconnect after the party?'

'Well, no,' John reluctantly responds. 'I never actually tried to talk to him again. It was easier just to let things die between us.'

'Easier for you,' Mia says gently, not wanting to upset him.

'Well, of course! I was afraid, I think. Alastair was so hurt. I can still see the look in his eyes. It was clear he felt I'd betrayed him. When he stormed out of the party, I didn't know how to go after him without being obvious. So, I just stayed. And afterwards, well, I didn't know what to say. So, I didn't say . . . anything. I was going to let him cool off for a while. Let some time go by and then try to maybe explain my point of view to him. But then the accident happened. And I never got the chance to clear the air with him.' John sighs, shoving his hands deep into his pockets. 'It was a different world then. I'm not sure how things could have ended up differently.'

'Yeah, but this isn't about the world and whether or not it was accepting of your differences. This is about how you treated Alistair. You could have cleared things up in private. Even if you weren't ready to go public with your relationship.'

John hunches his shoulders, scowling out into the

darkness. 'I suppose that's true. I should have made more of an effort. Who knows how that would have turned out if I hadn't died. Although, to be fair, you could have talked to Sam after that night at the pool. And you didn't.'

'Because it would have hurt too much,' agrees Mia. 'So, I ghosted him instead.' Sadness settles over her like a blanket.

Despite everything, Mia knows, deep down, that she wouldn't have done anything differently at the time if she had the chance. She'd needed the distance from Sam to protect herself.

'I guess that's why it's called hindsight, isn't it?' Mia starts trudging towards the cottage, followed by John. She pulls up short at the door and turns to him while she pats her pocket, looking for her phone. The little light above the door illuminates him, displaying his sadness sharply.

'I've certainly had plenty of time to ruminate on my own mistakes.' John accompanies this statement with a hollow laugh.

'The fact of the matter is you could have done better with Alastair and I could have treated Sam better. At the very least, I could have heard him out.'

'Relationships can be the most challenging part of life,' John assures her. 'I hope you don't think I'm blaming you for how you acted.'

Mia knows this, but she still isn't sure what it all means for the future. She pushes against the melancholy she feels and turns back towards the house. 'I think I left my phone in the big house, John. I guess I'll see you in the morning.'

Mia lets herself back inside. The house is dark, with only a few lamps left on. The rest of the family must have already gone to bed while she and John were talking. She makes her way through the house, locating her phone and stopping in the kitchen to sneak one last jam tart from the batch she made today. As she enjoys the tart with its delicious, buttery pastry, Mia unlocks her phone and pulls up her contacts. A few quick taps bring up Sam's info. She could try again. Her thumb hovers over the screen. One tap, and he would be unblocked. Maybe John is right. Maybe Sam deserves a second chance. Or at least the chance to explain himself. She unblocks him quickly and pulls up her messages.

But she can't quite bring her fingers to type out the necessary words. Standing in the kitchen with sticky jam fingers and slightly damp hair, Mia has to admit that her courage has deserted her.

She sets her phone down on the counter, washes her hands and returns to the living room, thinking she just needs to loosen up a bit more. By the light of the still glowing Christmas tree, she mixes herself another martini.

Spending time with John this week has been incredibly illuminating. Mia hadn't really thought before now about what she might or might not regret in a few years' time. But she couldn't deny that allowing herself a smidge of emotional vulnerability might be worth it to see if there's something to be salvaged between her and Sam.

She sips her drink, resolving to invite Sam back down to the cottage. It's not that late. They can talk – maybe address some of the hurts of the past. Maybe, finally, give in to the tension that's been building between them all week. It is Christmas Eve, after all. And who doesn't want their own little Christmas miracle?

Mia types out her text before she can lose her nerve again. Reads it over, rereads it.

Will you come down to the cottage so we can talk?

She presses send.

20

MIA

25 December

The only acceptable tears on Christmas are the joyful ones. The ones that come with the sentimental gift, or when the carol singers hit just the right note.

The unacceptable kind are the ones that might be shed over a certain good-looking, glasses-wearing, tennis-playing, *heartless* excuse for a man. Which is why Mia is not crying. She didn't cry last night, when she finally gave up hoping Sam would come talk to her and went to bed. She didn't cry this morning when she woke up. And now, as she marches up the path towards the main house, she still does not cry. She even stays strong as she lets herself in and pulls out her phone, waiting for it to connect to Wi-Fi to check her messages one more time.

Unread.

The absolute nerve. The unabashed, bald-faced, hypo-critical nerve. After all of that emotional *bullshit* yesterday in the cottage, how could he not respond to her, not even *read* her message? Mia storms into the kitchen, in search of coffee, and contemplating murder.

Luckily, only Martin is seated at the counter. 'Hey, Mia bella, Happy Christmas! Coffee is fresh if you need some. I did the cinnamon roast, given it's Christmas.'

Mia grunts a response and snatches down a mug, the largest on the shelf. She just wants an excessive dose of sugared caffeine. She also wants all single, eligible men to be razed off the face of the earth, but she stopped believing she could get anything she wished for on Christmas years ago, and this Christmas is only reaffirming that fact. Mia leans against the counter and sips her coffee, eyes closed and anger raging.

'Christmas certainly is different from when you and Charlie were little,' Martin pipes up. 'Used to be I couldn't get a cup of coffee in before you were all dragging me in to open up presents. Now I can have two before anyone else even shows their face.' He leans back and looks up at the ceiling, chuckling. 'Do you remember the Christmas we got Charlie a make-your-own candle set? We had smoke rings on every ceiling in the house. I had to pay a painter a fortune to get all the ceilings redone.' Martin shakes his head.

Mia turns back to the pot and refills her cup, emptying the pot. The caffeine isn't working. She's still fuming.

He could have at least answered. Even a *no, thanks* would have been better than just being ignored. Or, at the very least, he could have read the text. There's no way he didn't see it. And she bets that if she asks him about it, he'll probably deny it. Maybe he'll make up something about being absorbed in his poetry, or some crap along those lines. She wouldn't put it past him.

She never should have listened to John. He's been trapped in limbo for thirty years. That hardly makes him an expert on romantic relationships. Especially after she found out how he handled everything with Alastair.

Aunt Gertie totters into the kitchen. 'Well, good morning! Merry Christmas, darlings.' Martin responds cheerily and Mia mumbles the expected response under her breath. Aunt Gertie gives her a long, appraising look, and then pats her on the arm. 'It will be all right, dearie. Next time, say no after the first two martinis.'

'I'm not hungover,' Mia protests.

'She's always been a lightweight,' Martin confirms. 'She gets that from her mother.'

'I'm just saying, there's no equating the World Cup with the Grand Slam. It can't even be compared in terms of audience,' Charlie objects as he walks into the kitchen.

'Well, how many people watch the World Cup?' Sam asks, following right behind him. They both make a bee-line for the coffee.

'Hey, who finished it off and didn't make more?' Charlie moans as he rifles through the cabinets for the grounds.

'Mia gets what from me?' Penny asks as she walks into the kitchen, fastening her pearl earring in her left ear. 'Please don't say Mia's poor vision. That's a Robinson trait through and through.'

'I can see just fine!' Mia exclaims. 'I don't even need

glasses!' Why has this morning turned into a full-on assault against her?

'Yes, but your night vision is abysmal.' Penny shakes her head. 'The Clarkes can see much better at night.'

Mia blinks a few times, unsure of how to even respond to this.

Sam perches himself in the breakfast nook, putting away a banana with impressive speed. Mia can think of half a dozen insults she could scratch into that peel – if only she'd thought of that last night. 'Ugh. I hate the smell of bananas in the morning,' she complains, glaring at Sam from her post beside the coffee pot.

'Mia, you're blocking the pot,' Charlie complains. 'Move over a bit.'

Mia takes one grudging step to the side, and then says, 'No one even cares about the Grand Slam any more. Tennis is just a social event for rich, entitled people. No self-respecting person watches tennis.'

Sam looks at her agog but doesn't respond, since his mouth is still full of banana.

Charlie scoffs. 'Whatever! You love tennis. I have half a dozen memes about Federer from you on my phone right now.' He whips out his phone and waggles it near Mia's face.

'Oh, shove off, Charlie. But what about you, Sam?' Mia seethes. 'Do you have proof of your ridiculous opinions on your phone too? Care to share?'

Sam pats his pocket, looking nonplussed. 'I think I forgot my phone upstairs.'

'I bet you did,' Mia snaps.

Charlie hip-checks her from his post next to her. 'What is your deal?'

'Watch it!' Mia objects, lifting her mug away from her body as the coffee sloshes. 'You're going to splash it on my clothes!' She's wearing her favourite Christmas jumper again, the beautiful cable knit one with the turtleneck and the rich reds and greens. Usually, it makes her feel incredibly comfortable and festive. But today, although she paired the jumper with dark green wide-legged trousers and deep red boots, she still feels like Scrooge. Even the vintage diamond studs she's wearing haven't been able to cheer her up. 'Speaking of which' – Mia gives her brother's attire a sarcastic once-over – 'it seems you've gone for the homeless look as usual.'

Charlie rolls his eyes. 'Oh, give it a rest, Mia. It's Christmas morning and I'm still in my pyjamas. I'll look perfectly presentable in a bit. Why don't you go align your chakras, or whatever it is you need to do to get out of this funk.'

'I agree,' Penny chimes in from her spot at the counter where she's arranging cinnamon rolls on a tray to warm in the oven. 'There's no need for all this vitriol. Especially on Christmas Day. Charlie, I'm sure whatever you wear today will be wonderful. And Mia, you look very nice as well. That jumper looks fantastic on you. Although I do wish you would wear Grandma Joan's earrings one of these days. They always looked so lovely on you.'

'They don't go with my outfit,' Mia mumbles. She's never had the heart to tell her mum that one of Gran's earrings went missing.

'I think your outfit looks wonderful,' Sam pipes up from his spot in the breakfast nook.

'Yeah, well, I didn't actually ask you for your opinion, thank you,' Mia snaps at him. Sam's eyebrows draw together as he studies her.

Charlie barks out a laugh. 'There's the miserable Mia we all know and love. I wondered where she'd gone the last few days.'

Aunt Gertie clucks her tongue. Mia can't tell if the sound is meant to be sympathetic or critical. All she knows is she feels awful, and snapping at her family isn't making her feel any better. Besides, *Sam* is the one who she's pissed off with. Shame on him for ever thinking they could move beyond the past. Mia looks over at Sam, who's watching her warily. 'Why are you even still here? Why didn't you have the decency to decline Charlie's invitation so we could just celebrate Christmas in peace as a family?'

'Mia!' Her mother looks up, appalled. Penny grabs Mia by the elbow and tugs her from the room, muttering under her breath. Mia lets herself be dragged into the front room, as her mother hisses her displeasure the entire way. Penny stops in front of the tree and finally releases her. 'What is *wrong* with you? Speaking to Sam that way. Or any of us? I don't know what's got into you, but I simply won't have it. Not on Christmas Day. You're going to need to pull it together. Sam has been nothing but delightful to us all while he's been here. Helpful to your father, kind to Aunt Gertie. And so polite any time he's talked to me. He's been an absolute joy. He doesn't deserve this kind of treatment.'

'But, Mum—' Mia begins, but Penny shakes her head.

'Don't "but Mum" me. I'm serious. This grudge has gone on long enough. You're not going to ruin Christmas over it.'

Mia is horrified to find that she's losing the fight against her tears. After everything that's happened, and now her mother is telling her to just get over it? 'Mum, you *know* what he did to me.'

Penny's expression softens. 'Yes, darling, I do. And it was horrible. But it was years and years ago.' She pats Mia's cheek gently. 'Holding on to this pain is hurting you so much, it's doing you no good at all. It's time to let it go. Now. Go upstairs and pull yourself together. We'll wait for you before we open presents.'

Mortified, Mia escapes upstairs to her room and shakily sits down on the bed. She traces the watercolour flowers on her duvet cover with a finger while she sniffles. She won't cry over Sam. What is there even to cry over? An unread text? She's tougher than that. She can walk away from this with a lesson learned. But as her anger dissolves, it's replaced by a burning sense of shame as her embarrassment at Sam's snub rises. Despite her best efforts, a few tears trickle down her cheeks. She feels like she's constantly getting things wrong, taking risks and opening herself up when she shouldn't, and closing herself off to the people who truly care about her.

Swiping away the tears, Mia checks her makeup in the dresser mirror. A few steadying breaths and minor touch-ups and she's back in business. She needs to go back downstairs – no use making everyone wait for her. But before doing that, she slides the top drawer open and removes her grandmother's earring, holding it in the palm of her hand, the gems sparkling in the soft morning light. Standing there in her bedroom, Mia can practically smell her gran's lilac and rose perfume. It had always comforted her when she was younger. Grandma Joan was a strong, confident woman, who refused to let anyone diminish her light. Mia can be like that. She can be strong and independent, even if she has to be alone.

She pulls out her phone and opens the messaging app. Ignoring the unread text, she fires off a quick message to Lucy.

Merry Christmas to my ridiculously hot, impressively fit friend.

Then she sends another text to her book club thread wishing them all a Merry Christmas as well. Her coworkers all respond right away, sending along pictures of them with their families. The rush of well wishes makes Mia smile. Men may be completely impossible for her to work out, but her girls are in her corner. She won't die alone when she's old. She'll always have Lucy.

Her phone vibrates. Lucy's reply fills the screen. *Merry Christmas to my wonderfully skilled friend who is a culinary wizard!*

Mia smiles, thankful for Lucy's predictable cheerfulness. Her phone vibrates again.

Also, I have news! Look what Tim got me for Christmas!

A picture comes through – it's Lucy looking excitedly at the camera, left hand extended. A gorgeous and obscenely large diamond placed prominently on her ring finger.

I won't be able to wear it during yoga obviously. But I'm engaaaaaaggggeeeedd!!

Mia stares down at her phone, her vision of growing old with Lucy fizzling out like a spent sparkler. Lucy is getting married.

Oh my God, Lucy, congratulations!!! You're going to be such an absolute stunner of a bride. Tim is one lucky man.

Lucy responds with a text that is just garbled letters and exuberant emojis.

Drawing in a deep breath, Mia tucks her phone into her waistband and hurries down the stairs. So, Lucy is engaged. That means that when she marries, which will likely be next summer, Mia will be the only one of her friends who's still single. Here's Mia who can't even hold on to a guy past the first time they sleep together, while all her friends are moving on with their lives. Maybe she can take up another hobby? Something really time consuming like cross-stitch or learning to play violin, so she doesn't have time to think about how crushingly alone she is.

Mia's family – plus Sam – are gathered in the front room, waiting for her. John is still notably absent, and Mia makes a mental note to go searching for him at the first opportunity. He must have returned to the cottage and she missed him on her way up. Aunt Gertie is fussing with the record player in the corner, trying to coax the battered device into playing the record she's chosen.

'Ah, there you are, dear. All right, let's begin!' Penny claps her hands together to get everyone's attention. 'Sam, be a dear and play Santa, will you? Martin usually does it but his knee is bothering him. He can't be bending under that tree over and over.'

'Sure thing, Mrs Robinson.' Sam has to walk past Mia to reach the tree. As he does, he sends her a questioning look where he seems to be almost begging for an explanation for her resumed coldness. Yesterday's Mia might have given in and talked to him, but today's Mia knows better. She squares her shoulders and takes a seat beside her father on the sofa, angling her entire body towards him and effectively turning her back on Sam.

Martin reaches over to pat her thigh. 'You doing OK, bella?'

'Of course, Dad,' Mia responds, as brightly as she can. Her father sends her a worried look, but she simply continues smiling, even as Sam places a wrapped gift in her hands.

'Mia,' Sam says her name quietly, and there's a distinct question in his voice. A flutter rises in her stomach at his proximity, but she shoves it down. Does he really think he can just act like everything's fine? She waits in stoic silence until Sam moves away.

'All right, does everyone have something?' Penny gives a queenly nod. 'You may open them.'

There's a flurry of tearing paper and exclamations. Martin chuckles as he removes a silk tie from a sturdy box. 'Oh, you clever minx, you. When did you sneak back to the shops for this? I just pointed it out on Tuesday.'

Penny giggles and accepts Martin's kiss of thanks on her cheek.

Mia is immeasurably thankful for the distraction of Christmas morning. She may be an idiot for nearly falling for Sam's charms again, but sitting here with her family is so much better than trying to nurse her broken heart in solitude. Aunt Gertie waits impatiently as Mia unwraps her gift. Inside is a richly coloured scarf – clearly vintage and probably French. 'Aunt Gertie, this is beautiful.'

'I know how you love the vintage things, dearie.' Aunt Gertie nods, wreathed in smiles. 'I thought of you the moment I saw it.'

'It's perfect. Thank you so much.'

Sam moves into Mia's line of vision and the ache in her throat swells until she can't say anything else. She shakes her head in confusion. How is it possible that she is still so bad at reading this man?

'My goodness!' Penny exclaims, withdrawing two bottles of white wine from a neatly wrapped box. 'My favourite Chablis!'

'That's from me and Molly,' Charlie offers with a smile. 'And thanks, Dad, for the hat. It'll keep my ears warm when I'm waiting for the bus.'

'That's exactly what I thought,' Martin says.

'I told you lot I don't need anything for Christmas any more,' Aunt Gertie objects good-naturedly. 'But I do appreciate a new electric blanket for these old bones.' She nods at Penny, who returns her smile brilliantly.

Sam patiently continues passing out presents until there's a massive pile of paper on the floor and the space beneath the tree is bare. Mia manages to avoid speaking to him in any way, taking her presents from him with a frosty nod of acknowledgement each time he approaches. By the last time he approaches her, Sam has the air of a dejected puppy. He sets the present at her feet and then clears his throat. 'Ah, I'm going to go call my family and wish them a Merry Christmas.' Mia's lips twist in a satisfied smile. At least she won't have to deal with him for the next few minutes. Sam pauses in front of Penny on his way out. 'Thank you so much for the gift of being with your family while mine are away.'

'Well, of course.' Penny reaches up to pat him on the shoulder. 'We're so glad you could be with us, Sam.' As he heads to the stairwell, Penny grabs her face with her palms. 'Oh dear, I've forgotten the cinnamon rolls!'

'I'll grab them, Mum,' Charlie offers. He stands and yanks Mia up from her spot. Her presents tumble to the floor around her – a marble rolling pin, a pound of her favourite coffee from Charlie (and Molly, allegedly) and several vintage editions of books from her father. 'And Mia will help me with the rest of the breakfast stuff, won't you?'

'Sure?' Mia lets herself be pulled along. Charlie clearly has something on his mind, and in her experience there's no reasoning with him until he's said his piece. He doesn't say anything until they reach the kitchen. Charlie clads his hands in oven mitts and pulls the perfectly toasted cinnamon buns from the oven. 'Want me to cut the fruit?'

'Yeah, I'm crap at cutting equal-sized pieces,' Charlie responds.

'It's because you rush it.' Mia grabs a knife from the drawer.

'Are you ready to tell me why you're in such a foul mood?' Charlie asks.

'What do you mean?' Mia says innocently as she thrusts the knife through the grapefruit she's picked up with surprising vigour.

'Don't play dumb with me. You couldn't be more obvious. Things were finally improving between you and Sam. And now today you've returned to being the ice queen.'

'I didn't realize you paid this much attention to my life,' Mia retorts.

'You're my sister.' Charlie lets this statement stand on its own, as if it needs no further explanation.

'When's Molly coming up?' Mia asks, setting aside the grapefruit halves as she moves on to slicing a melon.

'She'll be here this afternoon. But don't try to change the subject.' Charlie sighs, and runs his hand through his hair. 'Mia, you're my sister,' he repeats. 'And Sam is my best friend. Two of the people I care most about in this world. I really hoped you two could work this out, especially if you spent some actual time around each other.'

'So that's why you invited him here? Even though you knew how I felt about him?'

'Look, I know as your brother I'm supposed to be firmly in your camp. And believe me, Mia, I am. But this entire time, you've refused to look at that night through any lens other than your own. It's frankly maddening.'

'I'm sorry that my suffering has caused you so much

unrest.' Mia's tone couldn't be more sarcastic, and Charlie rolls his eyes.

'Don't pull the drama queen act. Why don't you try having this conversation like an actual grown-up?'

'Sure thing, Charlie. Just as soon as you stop inviting the person I hate most in the world to join our family for Christmas!' Mia arranges the melon slices on a plate with shaking hands. After the disaster that was this morning, she can't believe that Charlie's now giving her a hard time too.

She wipes her hands on a towel, and rests her palms on the cool stone counter. To her surprise, Charlie comes up and wraps her in a hug. 'Hey. I'll always be on your side. You know that, right?'

Mia pulls away until she's facing him. 'I know. But this has been really hard, Charlie.'

Her brother studies her carefully. 'But you've also been happy, do you know that? Happier these last few days than I've seen you in years.' He sighs, releasing her and stepping back. 'You never even gave him a chance to explain. After that night, Sam was so devastated and he wanted to talk to you, but you'd blocked him on everything. And then you recruited Lucy to keep him away from you at uni . . . what was he supposed to do?'

'He humiliated me, Charlie.'

'I know. And I also know it was an accident.' Mia makes a face, and Charlie shakes his head. 'Truly. You need to hear his side of the story. Do you know how many times Sam asked me if you were OK? Begged me to arrange things so he could talk to you and apologize in person?

I never did it because I thought I was supposed to be in your court. I was trying to do the right thing – which I thought meant being the protective older brother. I told him to leave you alone or I'd make him regret it. But now I'm wondering if that was the right call. Maybe I should have helped him have an opportunity to talk to you. It could have saved you both a lot of heartache over the last few years.'

Mia takes a minute to process everything Charlie has just told her. It's unsettling, to say the least. 'Charlie, I had no idea.'

'I know. I know you didn't. And that's what I'm trying to say. Sam's not the evil genius you think he is, Mia. He made a mistake years ago, and he's been torn up about it ever since. I swear to you, I'm not trying to hurt you. You have to believe that, OK? I think it would do you both a world of good to talk it out. Let him explain his side of the story, and then go ahead and tell him again how much of an idiot he is, if it will make you feel better. Heck, I'll go toss him face first in the snow when you're finished, if that's what you want. But give the man a chance to clear his conscience. And hopefully help alleviate some of your own hurt as well.' Charlie gives her a brilliant smile. 'After all, it's Christmas! What better time to make nice with someone. The story practically writes itself.' Charlie glances down at his phone. 'Whoops, I need to get going! I'm going to pick up Molly from the coach station.' He tucks his phone in his pocket and checks for his keys, then pauses and looks at Mia straight on. 'Hey, are you all right? Are we good?'

Mia raises her chin. 'We're good. I'm not making any promises that I'll talk to Sam, but I'll think about what you said. I promise.'

Charlie considers this, then nods. 'Good enough. Well, I've got to run. Make sure Mum doesn't start lunch without us, OK? We'll be back in time.'

'I'll hold her off. If need be, I'll mistime the Yorkshire puddings so that you have a buffer. But don't dawdle, Charlie. I'm dying to meet Molly.'

'Sure you are,' Charlie scoffs. 'I know you all think I made her up. But she's actually the loveliest girl. I think I'm gonna marry this one, Mia Tia. She's incredible. You'll see.' He kisses the top of her head and then rushes out to the hall, grabbing his heavy overcoat on his way out the door. Mia takes a moment to collect herself and then picks up the pan of cinnamon rolls and heads into the front room, mulling over her conversation with Charlie. It's unlike him to be so direct and serious, and she can't shake the feeling that there's truth in what he said. She never gave Sam the chance to explain himself. And she doubts that hearing him out could be any worse than what she's already suffered at the man's hands.

21

JOHN

John places another log on the fire and then returns to the comfortable wingback chair by the bay window. He's not sure when exactly he started thinking of this chair as 'his' chair, but as he settles in and opens his book, he acknowledges that he's definitely taken ownership of this particular piece of furniture. It was inevitable, he supposes. Everyone wants to feel like they belong, in some way or another, even disembodied ghostly beings.

He's just flipped a page when the log on the fire cracks, startling him. At the same time as the crackling fire, there's a clatter in the kitchen that piques his curiosity, and he sets aside the book to go and investigate.

'Oh, there you are.' Mia stamps her feet clean of snow and then unzips the red leather boots she's wearing. 'I've been looking for you all morning.'

'Well, it wasn't much of a search,' John responds, chuckling. 'I've been down here this whole time. Let's just hope no one ever actually goes missing. You'd never stand a chance at finding them.'

'Yes, well, we've been very busy with all the festivities.' Mia groans as she flexes her toes. 'These boots are so adorable, but they're killing my feet. Also, can I just say that you picked quite the time to return to your quiet, non-meddlesome ways. My family has been scolding me all morning. I could have used a good distraction to divert them.'

'Do tell,' John says, pulling out a chair at the rustic table and sitting down.

'Well, that's all there is to tell. They disapprove of me and everything I stand for.'

John laughs. 'I hardly think that can be true.'

Mia takes a seat beside him and crosses one leg over her other knee. As she kneads her sore feet, she seems to decide to unburden herself. 'Mum says I'm being horrid to Sam, and she doesn't understand it and why can't I just let the past be in the past.' She digs into the arch of her foot and sighs in relief. 'And Charlie thinks I never heard Sam out way back when, and that wasn't fair either. He knows how hurt I was so I don't get why he's throwing it in my face now.'

'What about your Aunt Gertie?'

'You know what? She actually didn't yell at me this morning. And she bought me the most thoughtful gift. A vintage silk scarf.' Mia straightens up. 'Speaking of which, I was going to grab my sunglasses when I came down here for my slippers. With all the snow reflecting the sun, I almost ended up blind on the way down here.'

She dashes up the stairs and the floor creaks above John's head as she walks back and forth. Then there's a thundering back down the stairs until Mia sits down again, setting her belongings on the tabletop. 'I'm going to need to switch to slippers or my feet won't make it through cooking,' she explains.

'These really are completely ridiculous,' John observes, looking at the garish slippers.

'I know. That's why I love them. Tacky as an American hugging the Queen.'

John tilts his head back and laughs, long and loud. He feels lighter today than he's felt in ages. 'I didn't realize how healing it would be to talk about how I treated Alastair. Thanks for listening to me last night.'

'Of course. I'm not the monster my family seems to think I am, even if I can't stand Sam.'

A curious statement, given how much she seemed to have thawed towards Sam yesterday.

'You're not a monster, Mia,' John assures her. 'At least not a terribly awful one.' He's teasing her, and it earns him the smallest of smiles. 'So the present giving and receiving went well?' he asks. 'Did you play Santa or did Charlie get assigned to that task this year?'

Mia sighs. 'Mum had Sam do it.' She massages her feet again, grimacing all the while.

Momentarily distracted from her foot ministrations, Mia picks up her sunglasses and slides them on to her head like a headband, pulling her hair out of her face. John admires the stylish glasses, and then does a double-take.

'Wait a minute. Can I see those?' He gestures to the sunglasses.

'Sure.' Mia pulls them off and hands them over.

'Well, isn't that fascinating. I used to own a pair just like these,' John gushes, turning them in his hands. 'These are Robert La Roche, aren't they?'

'Yeah.' Mia smiles wide. 'They were one of my best vintage scores. The seller gave me a discount because the owner carved his initials into them. Which to be honest, I considered a selling point. See?' She takes them back from John and shows him the letters inscribed on the inside of one arm. 'JHH. Isn't that awesome?'

John goes very quiet. What are the odds? He looks again at the glasses. Exactly the same style he wore years ago. 'You know what, Mia? I think those glasses might just be mine.'

Mia is silent, too stunned to say anything at first. After a beat she asks, 'But how did they end up at the market?'

John runs a finger over the frame while he considers her question. 'They packed up my things from the cottage a few weeks after I died. Boxed them up and loaded them on a van – I always assumed they shipped everything to my mother over in Birmingham. Maybe she eventually donated them to a charity shop, or sold them on consignment?'

Mia nods vigorously, her mood finally lifting. 'I bet you're right! How cool is this?' Then she startles, and sits up straighter in her chair. 'I can't believe I forgot to tell you! I had another idea of how to find out what happened to your mum.' She taps her phone and pulls up a photo album. 'Here, I saved the pictures to my phone.' Turning the screen, she shows John the picture.

John stares at the image for a long moment. It's undeniably his mother. Her face is much more wrinkled, her deep-set eyes cloudier than he remembered, and instead of the sensible, straight bob she had throughout his entire childhood, she now wears her iron grey hair in a close-cropped pixie cut. He wouldn't say it flatters her, but it seems appropriate for her age. 'That's my mum,' he says in wonder.

'Oh, amazing! I was so hopeful.' Mia swipes her finger across the screen and another picture shows up, this time of his mum in lavender trousers, standing beside a man with a cane in a dated suit. 'I couldn't find a Susan Hackett anywhere. But then I searched up retirement communities in Birmingham. There are quite a few, and most of them have a website of some sort. They all do these events for the residents – poker tournaments, jigsaw puzzle competitions, that kind of thing. Maybe it was just dumb luck, but I came across some pictures of a few weddings at these retirement homes. And I got to thinking, what if your mum got remarried after you died? It took some digging, but I combed through the county records and found a Susan Ann Hackett who married a Terence Crawford ten years ago. When I googled Susan Ann Crawford, I found these pictures.' Mia looks up at John. 'You two have the same eyes.'

'I can't believe you managed to find her.' John looks at the photo again, still in awe. His throat feels suspiciously scratchy. 'She looks so happy. Thank you, Mia. You have no idea how much this means to me.'

'It took a bit of digging,' Mia repeats. 'And a fair bit of luck. Just like I was lucky when I found your sunglasses at the flea market.'

'I paid fifty-five pounds for them, back then. They were the height of fashion, you know.' John's thrilled to know his mum is taken care of, and he's still grappling with the reality that Mia owns something that belonged to him when he was alive. Such a strange turn of events, but then again, it brings him a measure of comfort to think that all of those hours Mia has spent sifting through vintage wares has paid off in such a tangible way.

'Well, I only paid twenty-nine pounds. But hey, if they're yours . . . that's really cool. Do you think this is why I was able to see you? Because I own something now that literally belonged to you before? Did that somehow create a sort of psychic link between us or something?'

'Could be. It's definitely more plausible than some of the other options I've been considering.'

Mia leans forward, intrigued. 'OK, spill.'

John leans back in the chair, still fiddling with the sunglasses. 'Well, there's the secret blood relative angle, but that's a pretty uncomfortable connection. Let's hope it's not that one. Erm, we could have both been born on the same day with the same celestial conditions, kind of a planetary alignment sort of thing. Oh, and then there's my personal favourite – I could be simply a complete hallucination.' John waggles his eyebrows at Mia, making her giggle. 'And of course, we can't forget the possibility that everyone *can* actually see me, but they're all just ignoring me.' He feels remarkably heroic as he observes how Mia's mood is improving the longer she spends with him. Now, if he can just get her talking about whatever happened regarding Sam . . . but he'll need to be clever about it.

'Well, besides Aunt Gertie, of course. You know, I can never tell if she can actually see you or not when you're in the room.'

'Neither can I,' John responds wryly.

'This is fascinating.' Mia gives a delighted wriggle. 'Well, if these sunglasses are actually yours, I want to see you wear them!'

John slides them on his head and lifts his chin, striking a pose. 'What do you think?'

'Oh, extremely posh. I can see why you picked them, back in the day. They flatter your face shape.'

Pleased by her compliments, John takes off the glasses and folds them gently. 'Better not wear them, though. Can you imagine if I forget I'm wearing them, and people see a pair of sunglasses just floating around?'

'Admittedly, that would be pretty hilarious. But wait, what do the Hs stand for?' Mia asks. 'John Hackett, of course, but what's your middle name?'

'John Horatio Hackett,' John responds with a touch of embarrassment. 'Horatio was my great-grandfather's name, and I've always liked sharing that connection with my family history. But it definitely earned me more than my fair share of bullying when I was younger. Horatio Mustachio is what all the girls called me, which frankly was ridiculous, because I definitely didn't have any facial hair at eight years old.'

'That's a super cool name,' Mia assures him. 'Very distinguished.'

'Thanks. But what about your other presents? Aunt Gertie gave you a scarf. What else did you get?'

'Mm, books from Dad. A rolling pin from Mum. Some nice coffee to take back home from Charlie. And Molly, supposedly? Lovely gifts all round.'

'And from Sam? What did he give you?'

Mia frowns. 'Nothing. Why?'

John is surprised to hear this. Surely Sam didn't get cold feet. John's been trying to give the family space to celebrate without him looking on, but maybe this warrants a trip up to the big house to investigate the status of that present he saw Sam wrapping for Mia.

'I wasn't expecting to get anything from him. It's not like I got him a gift. I didn't know he was going to be here! Besides, the man can't even answer a text like a gentleman would. I'd be shocked to find out he has a gift for me.'

'Wait, what do you mean, he can't answer texts? When did you text him?'

'Last night,' Mia admits dejectedly. 'After all that talk from you about giving him another chance, I decided to invite him down to the cottage to see me. We could have talked, or . . . you know . . . done other things. But he didn't come. Didn't even read the text.'

John raises his eyebrows, touched that Mia listened to him. 'Well, the message probably never went through!

You've mentioned time and again there's no signal down here.'

Mia shakes her head. 'No, I sent it before I came down from the big house. It was definitely delivered. Sam just didn't bother to respond. Just swiped it away, unread.'

Oh, how hurtful. For Mia to take a little step towards vulnerability, and be met with this. 'I can go up with you to the big house. Do some ghostly eavesdropping and see if I can figure out what happened.'

Mia sniffs and waves a hand. 'It's fine. I'd rather just drop it. It's too much trouble to unearth all of this again.'

John tilts his head, studying her. 'You know, I'm starting to think you were really spot on the other day. When you said how similar you and I are? We'd both prefer to just suffer alone than have the hard emotional conversations. We were both so sure of our decision to cut the other person off – and yet it has caused us both so much anguish.' John leans back in his chair, ignoring the telltale creak of stressed wood. 'Imagine what might have happened if I'd been man enough to talk to Alastair. There are so many possibilities, and I missed out on them all. Just like you're missing out on what could be between you and Sam. I think you need to actually talk to Sam and hear him out. Ask him about the text, and about the whole debacle years ago.'

'Easy for you to say,' Mia pouts. 'You don't have to have any hard conversations.'

John snorts. 'Yeah, I've just been stuck in limbo for thirty years instead. It's been a real picnic.'

This makes Mia laugh. 'You may have a point there.'

She lets out a long sigh. 'Fine. I'll find Sam and see how he withstands interrogation. I have to get back up there anyway. I need to start prepping lunch; I've got mounds of vegetables to chop before Charlie gets back.'

John groans. 'Stop. Please stop. I can't stomach hearing another word about food I can't taste.'

'Sorry. Would it make you feel better if I promise to burn everything a little?' Mia offers.

'Ack! No! Don't ruin them on my account!'

'Fine. No burnt Christmas lunch. You know, you're very opinionated for someone who prefers not to even open a door for himself.' Mia stands and forces her feet back into the cute boots. 'Ouch. Ouch! OK, it's only a few steps up to the house. I will survive. And John, I hope, if you ever get to cross over to the afterlife, it's filled with creamy mac 'n' cheese, perfectly seasoned venison stew and luscious panna cotta. You deserve it after all this suffering through Aunt Gertie's biscuits.'

John chuckles. 'Thanks, Mia. I'll see you later. Have a nice time with your family.'

'Are you not coming up now?'

He shakes his head. 'Your family deserves their privacy today. Although you'll have to let me know if our suspicions about Molly are real.'

Mia giggles as she gathers up her fluffy slippers from the table. She waves goodbye over her shoulder and heads out into the snow, pulling the door shut behind her. John moves to the window to make sure she returns safely to the big house, and then sits back down in the wingback. If he's not mistaken, Mia was listening when he urged her to hear Sam out. And Sam seems like a decent chap – hopefully he has a solid explanation for what happened, or at the very least a sincere apology. John's certain he hasn't been misreading the chemistry between those two. He barely wants to let himself think about it, but he still can't shake the feeling that if Mia can find her true love at last, then maybe, just maybe, he'll finally be able to pass over.

A thrill of excitement shivers through John. It's immediately followed by a touch of melancholy. Passing over also means no more chats with Mia. He'll miss that, for sure. She's a singular girl, and he's enjoyed every minute he's had with her this year.

22

MIA

'Halllooo? Where are you all?' Charlie's voice echoes through the house, and Mia spins away from the counter in excitement.

Clattering out of the kitchen, she follows the sound of her brother's voice. He's in the front room, by the tree, speaking animatedly to their mum and dad and Aunt Gertie about how terrible the roads were after this latest snow. His arm is wrapped around the person beside him, a petite redhead.

'Hey, there you are!' Charlie squeezes his arm around the girl at his side and turns her to face Mia. 'This is my sister Mia.'

'Pleased to meet you,' the redhead says. 'I'm Molly.'

Mia's thoughts race as she tries to orient herself to what's going on. 'Molly? Oh, Molly! You're real?' Mia says, laughing, and her family joins in.

'See?' Charlie says to his girlfriend. 'I told you they all

thought I made you up.' He swaps a conspiratorial look with Molly, who giggles.

'You're telling me they couldn't believe someone as wonderful as you hadn't been snatched up in a heartbeat?' Molly wrinkles her nose. 'That can't be.'

'Aww.' Charlie reddens, and beams down at Molly, who is looking up at him with pure adoration in her striking blue eyes.

Something tugs at Mia's heartstrings as she watches her brother interact with Molly. The gentle touches, the shared smile. The obvious attraction that underscores every interaction. Understanding blooms over her as Charlie leans down to give Molly a quick kiss. The way they're looking at each other just feels right. It feels wholesome and pure and . . . full of love. Mia wants that more than she can say and she has to wonder if this is why she's been so tied up in knots about Sam.

Charlie releases Molly from his embrace and she laughs again, her nose wrinkling adorably. 'I'm sorry I couldn't make it up before now. My mum was quite unwell for a few days so I was looking after her, then it was my brother's birthday and then, wouldn't you know it, my dad's car broke down on the ride to the station!' She shakes her head, her smooth hair floating around her face. 'It's just been one thing after another.'

Mia gapes at Charlie. 'It was all true? We thought you were just making up excuses.'

They all share another laugh before Mia excuses herself – she's only halfway through Christmas lunch prep, and can't let her meticulous schedule be thrown off by more than a few minutes.

The turkey is coming along splendidly, and Mia tosses the potatoes into the boiling water before returning to her spot at the counter where she was peeling vegetables. Her hands fly as she works to bring all the components together on time and her mood continues to pick up as she preps the roast potatoes, tipping them into the roasting dish before adding salt and rosemary and brushes them with more butter. A small tingle of excitement flutters in her at the thought of Sam joining them for lunch – maybe he'll even be impressed with the feast she's pulling off.

While the turkey rests, Mia whisks together a rich gravy using the juices left in the pan. The Robinsons aren't fans of Christmas pudding, so yesterday she'd made an orange zest and olive oil cake, and she pulls that out as well to serve after lunch.

Half an hour or so later, all the components of lunch are nearly ready when Penny breezes into the kitchen, still on a high from the fun of Christmas morning. 'Mmm, smells amazing, as always, darling! We're so lucky to have you cooking for us. Do you think there will be enough for some leftover plates later? Dot and Earl are going to stop by at some point this afternoon to say goodbye one more time before their flight tomorrow.' Penny leans in with a sly grin. 'If you ask me, Dot's feeling a bit anxious about the move.'

'I'm sure we'll have more than enough for leftovers, but I can always do some more veg if needs be. And surely Dot knows that they can always move back home if it doesn't work out?'

'That's the thing,' Penny continues. 'Dot's son and daughter-in-law are taking over their house. They've told Dot and Earl they'll always have a place with them, but living with your children is entirely different from having your own home. I'm sure it will all work out, though. Dot has always been a worrywart. 'How are you, dear? You seem better than this morning. You were really out of sorts.'

'My feet were pinching,' Mia jokes, wiggling her slippers to catch her mother's attention. 'Put me in a bad mood. I'm better now.'

Penny snorts in disbelief. 'I'm sure that's all it was.' She leans on the counter, staring pointedly at Mia. 'And things will be easier now.'

'I hope so.' Mia carefully slices the turkey and sets the meat on a platter. 'Everything is just about ready, Mum. Shall I call everyone, or will you?'

'I've got it.' Penny goes to the stairs and calls out that lunch is ready, then returns. 'I'm so excited to eat in the sunroom. It will be so lovely with all the plants and natural light. Let me help you bring everything out there.'

Mia loads up her arms with Mum's juniper Christmas plates, some red cloth napkins and cutlery. Sam enters the room with a smile, which falters slightly when he sees Mia.

'How can I help?'

Seeing Sam so wary of her tugs at something on her

insides. She knows she was hard on him this morning, and it's not like it wasn't deserved. But seeing him so uncertain and dejected doesn't feel good either. Why can't things just be simple between them? It's so frustrating for Mia and she can't seem to make head or tail of it all. She takes a moment to collect herself and then says, 'Mum wants to do lunch in the sunroom. You can carry that dish of potatoes for me.'

'Sure thing,' Sam replies, scooping up the dish. Mia is tempted to tease him about dropping it like he dropped the ornaments, but she refrains for Penny's sake.

They walk together in silence, but Mia can feel the weight of Sam's furtive looks. She feels the pressure to say something, but everything she thinks of could come across as trite or – worse – mean. So, she opts for silence, and they reach the sunroom in the nick of time, before she caves under the pressure and spouts off something ridiculously sarcastic.

Once they reach the sunroom, Sam sets the dish on the table with a sigh of relief. 'These smell so amazing.' He takes a step back. 'I'm worried I'm going to lose all sense of self-control and just snarf them all up before anyone else gets here.'

Mia can't hold back the laughter that bubbles up at the mental image of Sam 'snarfing' the entire dish of roast potatoes. Sam looks relieved when she laughs, some of the tension easing from his posture. Penny walks in behind them and gives them both a delighted smile.

'Well, isn't this nice. See? I knew the two of you could get along.'

'Mum.' Mia shakes her head, and Penny lifts her hands, the picture of innocence.

'I'm just saying.'

'Oh wow, Mia,' Molly gushes as she and Charlie enter the room. 'Charlie told me you were a good cook but he significantly undersold your abilities. This looks incredible.'

'Thanks,' Mia says, ducking her head.

'I'm starved. Are we ready to eat?' Martin calls out as he guides Aunt Gertie to a spot at the festively decorated table. The dishes Mia has prepared fill the table, the shimmering Christmas crackers are tucked into every nook and cranny, and the flowers Molly brought for Penny are sitting in a place of honour in the middle.

'Yes, absolutely,' Penny says, flicking on the string lights and waving everyone to sit down. They pile succulent turkey, potatoes, Yorkshire puddings, a variety of vegetables, stuffing and cranberry sauce on to their plates, with a generous pour of gravy on top, and then dive in. Everyone is hungry, so the first few minutes are quiet, with only the occasional clatter of knives and forks hitting the dishes. Then Martin lets out a long sigh and leans back in his chair, wiping his lips with the crimson linen napkin. 'Mia, you've outdone yourself. Absolutely splendid.'

'Agreed,' Penny chimes in. 'Mia, if you ever decide to open up a restaurant, I have to insist that those honey-roasted carrots are on the menu.'

'I've always loved a good potato dish,' Aunt Gertie agrees. 'And the crisp vegetables are so wonderful too.

Except for the sprouts, they've never been for me. I always thought they taste like my father's socks used to smell.'

This sets off a round of laughter, until Martin finally flutters his napkin like a white flag and coughs a few times to clear his throat. 'Do we think it's time for dessert yet?'

'I don't know how you've still got room, Martin!' Penny chides, before exclaiming, 'Oh no! We were all so excited to eat Mia's veritable feast that we forgot to do the crackers!'

'That's OK, Mum, we can do them now before I go and get the cake,' Mia says cheerfully.

'I'm not wearing the silly hat,' Charlie declares. 'Especially if it's yellow. It's not my colour.'

'Aw, you have to!' Mia frowns at her brother, who just folds his arms resolutely.

'Martin, pull with me,' Aunt Gertie says, holding up one of the crackers. Mia's dad grabs the opposite end, and they pull together. Aunt Gertie crows in triumph when she wins.

'Read the joke to us!' Penny exclaims, while holding up a cracker towards Mia. Mia deliberately pulls gently enough to ensure her mum wins, and Penny's delighted giggle makes her smile. Penny has always been the sorest loser when it comes to crackers.

'Why are Christmas trees bad at sewing?' Aunt Gertie reads, squinting at the tiny paper in front of her.

'Oh, let me take a crack at it,' Sam pipes up. 'Because they put pins in the presents.'

Molly shakes her head. 'I don't think that's it. It needs to be punnier.'

'Because they keep dropping their needles!' Aunt Gertie calls out, and everyone groans in unison.

'That's terrible,' Penny says. 'Ooh, look! I got a little stretchy toy! So cute.' She hums merrily while unfolding her paper crown and setting it on her head. The green decoration hangs cheerily on her carefully coiffed hair.

'Bet all the prizes are junk from China again,' Martin grumbles good-naturedly.

Molly and Charlie share a cracker, and Molly wins, much to her delight. She empties the contents on to the table and picks up the crown first. 'Ah, a pink one.' Looking at Charlie, she gives him a sweet smile. 'I'd really love to see you wearing this. Would you mind?'

Charlie is already smiling at Molly and he reaches out to take the crown, much to Mia's surprise. As her brother sets the silly hat on his head, Mia glances over at Sam, who's watching the couple. He's clearly enjoying the banter and light-hearted objections. His smile is a tad wistful, and Mia wonders if he's missing his own family. Then Sam looks at her, and she is lost in the emotions swimming across his expression. In that moment, she doesn't care about the hurt he caused her all those years ago, or that he ignored her text last night. She only wishes they could have a clean slate to begin again.

Martin jostles Sam, breaking the moment. 'Sam, pull one with me.' Sam gives Mia a rueful smile and turns towards her father, but Martin manages to drop the cracker before Sam can grab it. As he goes in search of it on the floor, Aunt Gertie and Charlie pull a cracker on the other side of the table.

'Who is the preferred Christmas ghost?' Molly calls out, studying her tiny paper. Charlie spins a top on the table beside her, and the toy balances precariously along the edge.

Aunt Gertie raises her hand like a little schoolgirl. 'Oooh, I know this one! The Ghost of Christmas Presents!'

This sets the whole table into a round of laughter, and Mia has to wipe her eyes once they calm down again.

'Well, is that everyone, then?' Martin asks, looking around the table. 'Everyone had a chance to pull a cracker?'

'Mia and Sam haven't,' Penny calls out, wiggling her eyebrows.

'Well, come on, then!'

Sam extends his cracker towards Mia, and she copies his motions with her own. They each take a firm grip on the other's cracker, and the rest of the table counts down.

'Three . . . two . . . one!'

There's a simultaneous pop, and Mia leans backwards, surprised to find that she's holding both crackers with the middles intact. She looks up at Sam, who doesn't seem bothered in the least. He grins at her, that crooked one that makes all the noise and laughter around them fade away. Longing threads through her. What would it be like to have Sam look at her like that for the rest of her life? To spend every Christmas with him, just like this – surrounded by family and enjoying the jolly banter and silly hats and terrible jokes?

'Well, you have to wear both hats then, Mia,' Penny declares.

Grateful for the reprieve from her newest revelations, Mia unfolds both crowns – a yellow one and a blue one – and places them on her head. They're a little large, and her family giggles as one drops over her eyes. Mia pushes the crown back up and adopts her most royal of demeanours. Then she reaches for the jokes. Clearing her throat, she calls out, 'What did the rosemary say to the thyme?'

'Aw, that's the perfect joke for you!' Charlie replies, chuckling. 'How did they know?'

'Well, tell us!' Penny urges, and Mia flips the paper over to read the answer.

'Season's greetings!'

'The perfect one to end on,' Martin declares. He signals the others to help him clear the table. When Mia tries to pitch in, he waves her off. 'No, no, you did all the work of feeding everyone. Us old folks will clear the table, and Charlie and I will do the washing-up.'

'What about me?' Sam asks. 'I don't think I fall in the category of old folks, but I certainly didn't make this feast.'

'You stay here and make sure Mia takes it easy,' Penny says, reaching up to adjust her crown, which has got even more askew. 'Otherwise she'll try to sneak back in the kitchen and help.' Penny herds the others out of the room, everyone's arms full of dishes and leftovers. As they make their way down the hall, Mia can still hear them chattering to each other.

She listens until they've moved out of earshot, and

then returns her attention to the man sitting across from her. 'That was wonderful. I haven't laughed so hard in ages.' She reaches up to remove the paper crowns and folds them carefully, setting them on the table in front of her. 'Thank you for going along with my family's nonsense.'

Sam leans towards her, resting his elbows on the edge of the table. 'It was my pleasure.' He hesitates for a moment and looks as though he's having some kind of internal battle, and Mia leans back in her chair, doing her best to wait while he figures it out. 'Ah, I've been trying to decide when is the best time to give this to you. I had thought this morning with all the others, but then you were so upset with me. I thought you might throw it away without opening it. Anyway, I – I brought this for you.'

Sam draws a small, neatly wrapped gift from the pocket of his cardigan and slides it across the table until it rests in front of Mia. The paper is a cheery red foil with silver glitter dusted across it, and he's even tied a ribbon around it.

'Why did you get me a present?'

Sam looks troubled. 'Just open it, Mia, and you'll understand.'

Mia carefully pulls the ribbon loose, and then slits the tape holding the paper together. This reveals a black cardboard box, and when she lifts the lid, she gasps. 'Gran's earring!' She lifts the piece from its velvet bed. 'How did you know – wait, did you have this replicated somehow? Or did you just take the one from my room – is this some sort of joke?'

'Not at all,' Sam hurries to assure her. 'I found it recently.'

Mia shakes her head. 'I've combed every jewellery store and flea vendor in London. There's nothing even close to a replica.'

'It's not a replica,' Sam explains. 'It's the one you lost.'

'How is that possible? I lost it the night that I met you at the swimming—' Mia looks up at him, anger filling her all over again. 'Did you hold on to this for *years*? How could you keep this from me? When you *knew* how much it meant to me?'

Sam holds up his hands in self-defence. 'I swear to you I didn't know I had it. I told you when I arrived here, I've just moved flats. I found it while I was unpacking a few weeks ago.' He bites his lip. 'That's partly why I accepted Charlie's invitation up here, I wanted to return it to you in person.' Sam drags a hand through his hair, looking off into the distance for a long moment. Then his gaze snaps back to her and she feels the force of it, like a physical blow. 'It was tangled in the hem of the shirt I gave you by the pool. I hadn't worn it since that night, but something made me hold on to it. It's just been stuffed in the back of my drawer until I threw it into a box to move. When I took it out at the new place, the earring fell on the floor.' Sam looks at her earnestly. 'I'm so sorry, Mia. I know how much those earrings meant to you. How they were a piece of your gran. I promise if I'd found it sooner, I would have returned it right away.'

Mia turns the earring over in her palm. The amber stone sparkles in the light, nestled against the sapphires and emeralds. Miraculously, each of the fragile gold strands are still intact as well. What a gift, to receive her gran's earrings all over again. Her heart swells with emotion, and as she meets Sam's gaze once more, the last of her defences topple.

Maybe she's had it all wrong after all.

23

MIA

Mia shakes her head. 'I don't understand you, Sam Williams. Sometimes you are so wonderful. But others you are a royal jerk.'

Sam nods. 'I'm so sorry about what happened all those years ago, Mia.'

Not feeling quite brave enough yet to unearth the past, Mia focuses on the present. 'I mean that's all well and good, but that's not the only time you've hurt me.' At his confused look, she goes on, 'You *ghosted* me, Sam. At *Christmas*.'

Sam is clearly perplexed. 'What are you talking about?'

'The text I sent last night? You never even read it.'

'What text?' He looks completely at a loss. 'From you?'

Mia could double down on her anger. Insist that he should know and wait for him to figure it out. But her conversations with John and Charlie are replaying in her head, and so instead she pulls out her phone, unlocking it and opening the messaging app. 'Here. Look. I messaged you last night.'

Sam looks at her screen, clearly confused. He checks his own phone, and then looks back at hers. He shakes his head. 'I never got this.'

Mia snatches her phone back. 'I sent it at 11.41 p.m. See? I even waited up here at the big house to make sure it went through, because reception down in the cottage is so rubbish.'

Sam stares at the screen, as if, by boring a hole through it, he will find the answers he's looking for. He takes the phone from Mia's hand and taps on something. Then his face clears and a smile replaces the scowl.

He turns the screen so Mia can see that he was looking at his contact details. 'This is the number you sent it to?'

'Obviously.'

'That's not my number any more, Mia.' He makes a gentle tsking sound, picking up his own phone and typing something out. A moment later her phone vibrates and she opens the text.

This is my number now.

She sinks back in her chair, disbelief filling her. 'It can't be that simple.'

'Like I said,' Sam continues gently, 'I was laid off and had to find a new job. The old one provided the flat, my car *and my phone*. So, I had to get a new one, but the idiot techs at the phone shop screwed up the number porting process and I lost my old number.' He looks quite annoyed. 'I'd had that number since school, and I lost all my message history. Nearly lost all my contacts too, but luckily, they were able to restore those.'

'I would have been so stressed.'

Sam laughs. 'Believe me, I was unbelievably stressed. Nearly screamed my head off while I was at the store, but don't worry. I wrote a scathing poem about it that night from my sofa.'

'Sure showed them,' Mia says, trying to ignore the embarrassment blooming in her chest at her overreaction.

'Indeed.'

They sit together in the sunroom for a few minutes, neither feeling the need to fill the silence. Mia traces circles in the air with her foot, trying to work up the courage to ask the question she really wants to ask.

Eventually, Sam looks over at her, and asks, 'It's heavy, isn't it?'

'What is?'

'The elephant in the room,' he says, with a bit of a self-deprecating chuckle. 'Kind of stinks too.'

This makes Mia laugh, the perfect corny joke to rid her of the lingering tension. She takes a breath, pulls back her shoulders and says, 'Speaking of elephants. It's been brought to my attention recently that I may have never given you a chance to give your version of the events from years ago.' She spins her foot a little faster, then forces herself to stop. 'So, this is me, asking if you'd like to talk about what happened back then.'

'I would like to,' Sam says. 'I would like that very much.'

Mia folds her hands in her lap and forces a pleasant expression on her face.

'Let me start by saying that back then, I was an idiotic semi-adult who was stunningly bad at communication.

What can I say?' Sam asks ruefully. 'They say the human brain doesn't finish maturing until age twenty-five. Maybe that was the issue.'

Mia makes a face, but laughs a little despite herself. Her stomach is jumping around like she's on a rollercoaster, and now that she's worked through most of her anger, she's genuinely curious to hear what Sam has to say.

'When I invited you to the swimming pool that night, I didn't think to mention that I'd invited the other guys. And believe it or not, the reason it didn't occur to me to tell you was because I'd invited them to cover up my *own* insecurity.' He nods when he sees her incredulous look. 'Mia, you were the most gorgeous girl I'd ever met. I'd been trying to work up the courage to ask you out properly for months. For reasons I did not, and still cannot understand, you decided to give me the time of day. And after that night in my room, I knew I had to man up. So, then I was really trying to work up the nerve to ask you out on a date, but I thought going swimming would be a good icebreaker. You and me, spending time together, but with the buffer of the other guys there so there wouldn't be too much pressure. And . . . well, I was a competitive athlete obsessed with being the best. It didn't hurt that all the other guys would know you were there because I invited you. The ultimate win, if you will.' Sam drops his head into his hands. 'God, talking about this is so embarrassing. I wish I had done *so* many things differently.'

'Me too,' Mia whispers. Sam gives her a sympathetic look and then soldiers on.

'I was nervous all afternoon, driving Charlie crazy while I paced back and forth for hours. I remember he told me to go on a run to "burn off that nervous energy". It didn't work. I could have run a marathon, and I would have still been nervous to spend the evening with you.' He takes a breath. 'Then it was finally time to head to the pool. You're going to think I'm so dumb, but on my way over, I was completely wrapped up in my head and thinking about what perfect things I'd say to you so that you'd swoon in my arms like the love interest in one of those old, bodice ripper romance novels. I walked into the pool area and then I got even more excited because I knew the guys were all running late, and I would have a few minutes alone with you. I was so nervous as I walked in. And then there you were. Already in the water. Stripped down, skin all damp and glowing and looking like a damn siren. Mia, before that night, I thought I was interested in you. But that night? I fell. Hard.'

His words are coming faster now, and Mia finds that she's wrapped up in this version of the events, in a perspective she never could have imagined.

'At first, I couldn't believe what I was seeing. Yes, I mean, you were naked, and that was incredible. Obviously. I'm a guy – and you are put together like a total dream. But, Mia, you were so much more than I'd ever imagined. Even now, when I close my eyes, and focus, I can feel the power of you that night, how bold and confident you were. Let me tell you, I was lost, in the best possible way. In all the years I'd known you, I'd never seen you so sure of yourself, and it was so damn sexy.'

He enunciates the last three words with such force that Mia feels the heat rising in her cheeks, overwhelmed at the thought that she could make Sam feel that way. He takes a breath, and forces himself to continue. 'But then I remembered that the guys were coming, and I had this impending crisis. Suddenly I was so mad at myself for wussing out and inviting them in the first place. I wanted you all to myself. I wanted to stay in that perfect, beautiful moment, where you were open to me – to the idea of us – for ever.'

Sam looks down at his hands, and his expression twists. 'But then you were so angry, and at first, I thought you were angry because the other guys might see you. So, I tried to shield you, and I tried to explain, but you were so mad. Understandably, obviously, in hindsight. After that, everything that came out of my mouth was just utter rubbish. You thought I was blaming you, and then when I realized you thought I'd set you up, just to humiliate you . . .' Sam makes an aggravated sound and shakes his head. 'I never would have done that to you on purpose. *Never.* If you're going to believe me about anything, believe that. Seeing you that night – how upset you were – it absolutely crushed me. And then, while I just stood there completely frozen, unable to think of what to say or do, you were just gone. Disappeared into the night, and I was so embarrassed I couldn't bring myself to go after you.' Sam looks straight at Mia. 'I should have. I should have gone straight to your room and done whatever it took to give you my apology. Washed my mouth out with soap. Crawled over broken glass. Anything – *anything* – to keep you from thinking any part of how that night played out was your fault. I've rehearsed that night in my mind so many times and wished I could change it.

'I begged Charlie over and over to let me talk to you. He was like a brick wall. Just totally iced me out where you were concerned. I wanted to write you a letter, but I was afraid I would bungle the words again. It had to be in person. Like now. So you could see for yourself that I meant it. That it wasn't just pretty words and it wasn't cheap.' Sam heaves another sigh. 'Mia, hurting you that night is the single biggest regret of my life.' He stares off into the distance for a minute, then clears his throat and continues. 'Anyway. Over the years, I had tried to move on. Tried to date other girls, but none of them were you. It never went anywhere. Then I moved, and found the earring. Charlie called me the same day and we were chatting about holiday plans, and I was so down about my family being gone so I told him how I couldn't get the time off work to go with them. The idea of being alone for Christmas made me feel sick.'

'So, when Charlie invited you up here, it probably seemed like all the stars were aligning,' Mia murmurs.

'It was a chance to right some of my very worst wrongs,' Sam says simply. 'I had to take it.'

'It's kind of unbelievable, really,' Mia says as she mulls over everything Sam has just divulged. 'If I hadn't been so thorough at ghosting you, we could have cleared this up years ago.'

Sam makes a face. 'That's true.'

'It's going to take me a little while to rewrite the

narrative on this particular story,' Mia says. 'I've believed my version of what happened for a really long time.'

Sam nods vigorously. 'I understand. Really, I do. I didn't tell you any of this to put any kind of pressure on you. I just wanted you to know that none of what happened that night was your fault.'

But much of what had happened since then was on her, Mia realizes. It's ironic how she was so inflexible with John about how he should have had the courage to have a simple conversation and yet the same approach would have spared both her and Sam so much heartache. Sam is picking at a loose thread on his socks. One foot boasts sausage dogs reading books, and the other has dragons eating ice cream sundaes. They're utterly absurd, but Mia finds that there's something a bit endearing about Sam's awful sock choices. Almost like it's a bit of his more flamboyant personality leaking out around the edges of a carefully collected persona.

Sam gives her his full attention when she starts speaking again. 'I will say this, though. I'm hard pressed to believe that anyone actually treats you like a serious professional when you wear ridiculous socks like that.'

Sam laughs, throwing his head back and rocking his chair on to its back legs. The move exposes the length of his neck, and his throat muscles work as he chuckles, captivating Mia's attention. That sensation creeps over her again, the one where her hands want to roam and explore, to reacquaint themselves with every inch of him. He looks back at Mia, sensing the shift in her mood. She drinks in his face, the sharp edge of his jawline dusted with stubble and his deep brown eyes that seem to darken as he looks at her with renewed interest. His hand reaches up to cup her jaw as his face moves closer, and there's a question implicit in the look he levels at her.

Heat starts building in her stomach, pulsing through her as her want builds. She gives a tiny nod, and he moves in, closing the space and crushing his lips to hers. Mia leans her body forward, hungry for more of him as he wraps his arms around her waist, pulling her on to his lap so she's straddling him. Sam's hands, confident and firm, run up her back, one pressing her to him tightly and the other cupping the back of her head. He uses his tongue to coax her lips apart, and a groan escapes her as his mouth moves lower, kissing and sucking at her neck.

'Oh, Sam, fuck.' Mia can barely get the words out as her breath hitches when he nips a particularly sensitive spot.

'Mia, you have no idea how badly I've needed to kiss you like this,' he mutters into her neck, his voice a low growl that makes Mia's breath go ragged.

He shifts her on his lap, pulling her closer into him, and she feels beneath his trousers that he's completely hard for her. The thought turns her insides to liquid, and she realizes that she needs more of him, all of him, in this moment. Needs to be made his again, after all this time.

'Sam . . .' she murmurs.

As if reading her mind, he nods and says gruffly, 'Do you think we can make it upstairs without anyone noticing?'

Mia can't help but giggle at the ridiculousness of it

all, the two of them being reduced to sneaking around like horny teenagers, as she stands and takes Sam's hand, leading him down the hallway and past the open kitchen door as quietly as possible. Thankfully, the rest of the Robinsons seem to be too distracted with clearing up to notice Mia and Sam sneaking past, and the two of them hurry the last few feet to the stairs before taking them two at a time, desperate to reach Mia's room as soon as possible now they're in the clear.

Mia enters first, and as soon as Sam closes the door behind him, he spins her round, Mia's back colliding with the closed door. Sam leans into her until his lips are inches from hers, and his mouth quirks in that crooked smile that sends her mind spinning.

'Have you missed me, Mia?' he whispers as he dips his head, brushing his lips across the pulse in her neck. For a moment, sound can't escape her throat, her breathing too shallow to allow her to form the words, too turned on to think of anything except the heat building in her core. 'Well, Mia?' Sam prompts.

'Yes, fuck, yes,' she gasps out, and with a satisfied smirk Sam closes the gap once more, his mouth sweet and firm against hers as the heat in her veins rises. Goosebumps break out over Mia's skin as one hand caresses her thigh, while the other becomes tangled in her hair at the nape of her neck.

Mia hasn't let herself think about this, about how perfectly the two of them fit together. She had convinced herself that she could live without him, but now she's here with Sam's lips on hers she thinks she might not survive if she has to go the rest of her life without feeling him this close again. Mia's desire builds as he deepens the kiss, and she lets herself become lost in the sensation of his body pressed to hers, the need burning through both of them, pulling them together.

Sam's gaze is gentle on Mia's face, filled with a renewed tenderness as he lies facing her, their legs tangled and chests rising and falling in unison. He reaches up one hand and brushes a stray strand of hair from her forehead before pressing a kiss to her temple. Basking in the sweetness of the release she found with Sam, Mia finds emotion blooming in her chest, warm and bright and strangely familiar. Something she hasn't felt this clearly or keenly since they were both at uni, before everything fell apart between them. Mia realizes that it feels as though she can actually breathe again, as though her senses have reawakened after years of hibernation.

'Mia, I—' Sam begins, his voice quiet and thick with emotion.

'I know,' Mia replies, studying Sam's face intently, trying to memorise every detail. And then, with a small smile she adds, 'I guess you could take that as an apology accepted.'

Sam's eyes grow wide for a second and then they're both laughing, full belly laughs at the relief of it all, the joy that they're finally back here, in each other's arms.

As their laughter gradually subsides, Mia can't quite believe the about-turn she's done. She's spent years hating Sam, but when she searches herself for any residual anger, she finds none. After all those years of resentment, she's finally managed to cross over into something new, something healthier and happier for both of them. She can't deny that she's even a tiny bit proud of herself, for allowing herself to be vulnerable and brave again despite what happened the last time. As she lies next to Sam, there's a confidence burning through her that she hasn't felt since that night at the pool, and she only realizes now how much she's missed it.

They stay in comfortable silence for a few minutes more, until a clatter from downstairs breaks the tranquillity that's surrounded them. As though suddenly snapping back to reality, Mia jolts up, hastily looking around for her clothes.

'Oh my God, Sam, my family! We have to get downstairs! They'll have noticed we're gone by now and I don't think I can face my mum given what we've just done,' she garbles, flustered at the thought of her family working out what they snuck away to do.

'Hey, Mia, it's OK,' Sam reassures her gently, his fingers entwining with hers. 'Just take a second, it'll all be fine.' Her heartbeat instantly slows as he brushes his thumb against her knuckles. 'They don't need to know about us if you aren't ready for that yet.'

Us. The word catches something in her chest, and her eyes return to his face. He's looking at her with such sincerity, so much care underpinning his words, that she realizes in a rush that she's being ridiculous. She doesn't care if her family know that she and Sam have resolved things and that they're back on track after so long apart.

In fact, she *wants* them to know. Penny will be beside herself that Mia's finally come to her senses, Aunt Gertie will probably commend Mia's sexual boldness, Charlie will just be relieved that there's no more animosity forcing him to choose sides, and Martin? No doubt he'll just be happy that Mia's happy. The joy in her chest swells as a smile washes over her face at the thought.

'No, I'm ready,' she says simply. 'I want them to know. I want the whole world to know!' she says with a laugh bubbling up inside her. 'Although, actually, maybe I don't want my mum to know we snuck away on Christmas Day to hook up . . . perhaps we should stagger our arrival downstairs so she can't put two and two together so easily.'

Sam chuckles, brushing a kiss to her knuckles before sitting up. 'Whatever you want, Mia.'

They both begin to get dressed, and Sam fishes something out of his trouser pocket, handing it to Mia once she's fully clothed. It's the box containing the missing earring. She stands in front of her dresser, pulling open the drawer to find the other one, to complete the pair. She examines her reflection as she threads the earrings through the holes in her earlobes. She looks different. Softer, somehow. After a moment, Mia realizes the difference. She looks . . . happy.

She turns to Sam, who's waiting by the door.

'Thank you for returning Gran's earring. Mum will be so pleased to see me wearing them.'

Sam nods, his eyes roving over Mia's face. 'You look beautiful,' he says simply, and Mia suddenly feels shy under his gaze, like she's thirteen and meeting him for the first time all over again, and she can't think of how to respond.

'I'll head down first, if that's OK? Maybe give it five minutes and then you can follow?'

Sam nods, and Mia slips out of the door quickly, the emotion still bursting in her chest. She's not sure when exactly this came about. Or how, exactly. Loving Sam has just snuck up on her. It has happened without Mia's consent, or even her knowledge. But now that she knows, her love for Sam fills her heart. Her lungs. Her very being. She also knows that John is going to be absolutely insufferable when he finds out.

As she heads down the stairs, Mia begins to wonder where John has got to. She had explicitly asked him to come up to the big house, hadn't she? Probably for the best that he hasn't made a surprise appearance in the last half an hour, but still. What's keeping him?

Mia can hear the burble of her family's chatter, and she follows it into the front room where she finds them all standing by the tree. Aunt Gertie hears her enter and turns with a mischievous grin stretching her cheeks, a knowing look twinkling in her eye. Of course she'd know. Mia smirks, raising a finger to her lips conspiratorially. Gertie gives her a small wink of agreement, just as Penny spins round.

'Oh, Mia, there you are! We were beginning to wonder where you'd got to. We haven't had dessert yet because we wanted to wait for—' She cuts herself off, staring intently at Mia's face.

'What is it?' Mia asks, suddenly self-conscious.

'You're wearing the earrings,' Penny says softly, and if Mia isn't mistaken there's a definite waver to her voice.

'Oh, yeah, I decided they're too pretty not to wear, even if they don't go perfectly with my outfit,' Mia responds with a smile, touched that the small gesture of wearing the earrings means so much to her mum.

Everyone's looking at her now, and Mia feels the need to break the silence. 'Has, uh, has anyone seen Sam?' she tries to say as casually as possible.

Gertie looks at her with a wise smile full of secrets, lifts a gnarled finger and points straight at Mia. Confused, Mia just stares at Aunt Gertie, wondering if her elderly aunt has lost her mind.

But then she feels the warmth of someone at her back, and she's wrapped in the scent of spicy evergreen.

She turns to see Sam standing beside her in the doorway. He shoves his hands into his pockets and hunches his shoulders, smiling sheepishly. 'Am I interrupting—' he begins and then stops, because Mia puts a hand on his arm. She knew he was coming downstairs after her, but she still feels a deep relief at the fact that he's there, beside her.

'Oh, look, everyone!' Aunt Gertie exclaims, toddling over to the window. 'Someone's made a snowman in the front garden!' Mia's parents and Charlie and Molly crowd around Aunt Gertie to see.

'It's so big,' Penny says in surprise. 'Who would have had the time to make that?'

'Is it wearing a sweater?' Molly asks. 'What's that pattern?'

'Argyle, if I'm not mistaken,' Martin responds.

Mia breathes a quiet thanks to John, who's provided her family with the perfect distraction. A feeling of peace creeps over her, and she looks up at Sam, whose shoulders are nearly bumping with hers in the narrow doorway.

And as she does, Mia can't quite remember how to breathe. Sam is looking at her so steadily, and the warmth of his gaze is filling her up. There's something softer in the look he levels at her now that the tension between them has eased.

'Merry Christmas, Mia,' Sam says, in a voice that promises only good things in her future.

'Merry Christmas, Sam.' He smiles at her then, that crooked one that makes every part of her stand up and take notice. Suddenly, it feels like the most natural thing in the world to follow up that simple statement with the words, 'I love you, Sam.'

She could have told him he'd won the lottery and his smile wouldn't have been as bright. Sam leans in until he's right beside Mia's ear and then doesn't move for a moment. Mia holds her breath and waits. She is so glad she did when Sam whispers, 'I love you too, Mia. Completely.'

She slides her arms around Sam's neck and pulls him into her embrace. He comes readily, as if he's been waiting a lifetime to be in her arms. Everything fades away as they stand there together, their breaths intertwining and heartbeats synchronizing.

Christmas has always been her favourite season, but Mia knows this particular one will always stand out in her mind. Something brushes against her hair, and at first, she thinks it's Sam's hands. But the sensation comes again, and it's familiarly insistent. She glances up towards the doorframe above her and is startled to see a sprig of mistletoe hanging just above her and Sam's heads. Strange, she could have sworn there wasn't any mistletoe up there before. But then the mistletoe vibrates insistently, and when she tilts her head, Mia can see a man's hand shoved through the moulding. The ring on his little finger is all too recognizable, and Mia has to swallow her laughter as she imagines how much discomfort John has undergone to orchestrate this event. Is he lying on the floor upstairs? Mia glances over at her family, but they're still absorbed in the mystery of the snowman.

Taking pity on John's indigestion, Mia brings a hand up and runs it along Sam's jawline, thrilling at the slight scrape of stubble against her fingers.

'Mmm,' she says contentedly, all other words leaving her head. Sam smiles down at her and he's still smiling when she finds his lips with hers.

This kiss is different. Before, their kisses had been full of burning passion, both Mia and Sam desperate for release and hungry for each other. But this time, it's more careful, more considered, as though they can communicate all the emotion they can't say with words through this one kiss. Sam kisses Mia like she's a work of art, and he is the artist. Like she's nothing more than ephemeral words and it is his job to capture them. He kisses her until she's simultaneously desperate for air, and despairing at the thought of him ever stopping.

When he finally releases her, Mia just about stops herself from letting out a tiny moan of protest. She could keep kissing Sam for days. Then it dawns on her that the room has fallen silent. Still tangled in Sam's embrace, Mia moves her head just enough to peer out at her family.

They're all beaming at her, seemingly delirious with joy. Charlie looks absolutely delighted, and he tips Molly's chin up to claim his own kiss. Penny is starry-eyed, and Mia can practically hear the wedding bells already ringing in her head, just as she'd expected. And Martin is looking at Mia with such warmth and love, evidently just pleased that his favourite daughter is finally happy. Aunt Gertie looks the most satisfied of them all, while Mia could have sworn she gave someone in the hall behind her a thumbs up.

Her family crowds around her, calling out their congratulations all on top of each other. Mia hugs them each in turn, and when she reaches Molly, she pats the redhead surreptitiously on the back, reassuring herself the girl is real. Molly giggles, drawing attention to her actions, and Charlie shakes his head.

'Admit it, Mia. Molly is real and you doubted me.'

'I admit to nothing,' Mia maintains. 'But Molly, I do have some stories to share about Charlie in school.' She laughs at Charlie's horrified face. 'And even if I don't share them, you never know what ghosts are creeping about Willowby Manor. They know all of our secrets.' Then she sneaks a glance behind her, but the hall is predictably empty and there is no mistletoe hanging in the doorway.

She shrugs her shoulders, and turns back to her family as she reaches a startling realization.

'Oh no, you know what this means, right?' Mia wails, even as she smiles over at Charlie and Molly. 'I have to make everyone beef Wellington now!'

Her family dissolves into laughter once more at her dramatics.

'Serves you right for doubting me,' Charlie insists, and Molly jabs him in the ribs with her elbow.

'I'll help you,' Sam promises. And suddenly, Mia can't think of anything else she'd rather do than cook for her family with the help of the man that she loves.

Epilogue

SAM

One year later

Stepping down off the train, Mia grips her bag more tightly and gets her bearings. Worcester station is predictably crowded for the week before Christmas.

'Here, love, let me get that for you.' Sam steps down beside her, scooping up her luggage and shooting her a smile. Mia instantly returns it with one of her own, and Sam has to work for a moment to catch his breath. When she smiles at him like that, it makes his stomach flip, and little tendrils of happiness dance their way up his spine. 'Have you spotted your brother yet?'

'No, not yet. But he promised to be here, and Molly wouldn't let him back out on a promise.' Mia threads her hand through the crook of Sam's elbow and smiles up at him, gaze straying to the newsboy cap he's wearing. Mia gave it to him on his birthday this summer, and Sam's taken to wearing it more often than not, since it makes her so happy. She says it gives him a jaunty air. If she likes it, he's certainly not going to argue. Sam gently tugs Mia along as he scans the crowd bustling past them for their ride.

'Oh, did you remember the wine for Mum?' Mia asks worriedly.

Sam bumps the messenger bag slung over his shoulder. 'I tucked it in here for safe keeping. Right next to the signed Don Bradman jersey for your dad.'

'They already love you, you know. You don't need to butter them up with gifts,' Mia teases him. Sam grins back at her and then turns slightly to shield Mia as a thick-necked man carrying a wide bag over his shoulder pushes by.

'Mia! Sam! Over here!'

Mia turns towards Charlie's voice, searching for her brother. 'Oh, there he is!' Sam and Mia navigate their way through the crowd of holiday revellers until they connect with Charlie and Molly.

'It's so good to see you!'

'Merry Christmas!'

'I love your jumper!'

'You cut your hair!'

While the girls talk rapid fire, Charlie claps Sam on the back. 'Glad you could make it again, Sam.'

'Well, it wasn't up to you this year,' Mia pauses in her conversation with Molly to assure him. She smiles up at Sam, her expression softening. 'There's no way we were spending Christmas apart.'

'No,' Sam agrees, pulling Mia in close and dropping a

kiss on the side of her head. 'We've spent way too much time apart already.'

Mia smiles up at him, her eyes sparkling, and Sam feels something inside of him settle. It doesn't seem like it will ever get old, this feeling of contentment he discovered when he and Mia finally worked things out.

'How's your mum doing?' Mia asks Molly, and the two girls fall back into a boisterous conversation as the two couples head through the station and out to the car park. Charlie directs them to his car, and they load up, everyone still talking a mile a minute.

Halfway to Willowby Manor, Mia interrupts the conversation long enough to comment, 'This is already so much better than my trip up here last year.'

'Ah, but it's a shame you didn't get to hear how Trudy's cats are doing,' Sam says, with an insincere tone of despair. Mia snickers, and then leans in closer to Sam, pointing out little landmarks along their way.

Penny and Martin are waiting in the drive as they arrive, waving excitedly. Everyone tumbles out from the car, and Sam is immediately wrapped up in one of Martin's bear hugs.

'Welcome, welcome! So glad you're here!' Penny ushers them inside, taking their coats and hanging them on the coat rack, which has already been decked out in its festive glory.

'Mum, everything looks so nice,' Mia comments as she slips out of her shoes. Sam fishes in the top of the suitcase and pulls out her slippers – the pair he had given her last week. He knew as soon as he saw the goggly-eyed snails with their pink shells that they were perfect for Mia. She slips them on with a delighted smile.

'Dad, your tree is spectacular,' Charlie observes. They all move into the front room to admire it. This year, Martin has covered it in sparkling white snowflakes, tiny furry-capped gnomes and pine cones galore. The entire tree seems to have been dipped in snow as well, and the effect is stunning. A veritable winter wonderland.

'Do you like it? I spent all year collecting the pine cones. And the tree is flocked – isn't that unbelievable? I don't know how they do it, but it looks just like real snow.'

'Wait, is this tree . . . fake?' Sam clutches his heart as Martin laughs.

'Yes, it's one of those artificial ones. Turns out Penny was right, and I should have listened to her years ago. We had this sucker up in about thirty minutes. So much easier.'

'Compromise!' Penny sing-songs.

'It looks fantastic, Dad,' Mia praises. 'Your best one yet.'

'Now you can head upstairs and get settled in – oh, not you two.' Penny waves Sam and Mia back as Charlie and Molly head to the hall to retrieve their luggage. 'I figured the newlyweds would want to be in the cottage. You'll want your privacy, I imagine.' Penny waggles her eyebrows suggestively and Mia groans. 'And don't forget, the reception is Sunday evening.'

'How could we forget?' Mia asks, with just a touch of attitude. 'I'm cooking the entire menu.'

'Well, that's what you get for eloping and not including us in the wedding,' Penny returns primly. There's a moment where Sam worries the two of them might actually start arguing, until Penny's expression turns sunny once more. 'Oh, I'm only teasing. I'm so thrilled for the two of you. You know, last year I wasn't quite sure what would come from all my efforts, but here we are! And now that you're here, we get to celebrate in style! Oh, let me see the ring!'

Mia extends her hand with a shy smile, and her parents crowd around, exclaiming excitedly. After a moment Martin lifts his head and gives Sam an approving smile. 'Well done, son. You did a great job picking that out.'

'Of course he did,' Mia agrees, smiling up at him. It took Sam months of hunting to find it, but eventually he discovered the perfect ring: a gorgeous, vintage oval alexandrite surrounded by a crown of sparkling diamonds. As soon as he'd seen it, he knew it had been made for Mia. 'Mum, we'll just get settled in the cottage and then we'll come back up and get to work. I can make the biscuits to set out too.' She and Penny swap looks, and Mia leans into Sam, a touch of sadness colouring her expression. Two weeks after her one hundredth birthday, Aunt Gertie had finally passed away.

Sam hauls their luggage down to the cottage while Mia skips ahead, unlocking the door and stepping inside.

'Oh, someone's laid a fire already, how lovely. And they refinished all the woodwork – it looks so nice! Sam, will you just put the bags upstairs in the bedroom?'

'Of course,' he calls out, taking the steep stairs at the back of the kitchen with care. He's just manoeuvred the mammoth suitcase into place on the trunk at the foot of the bed when Mia comes in behind him.

'I'm going to go ahead and get changed,' Mia says, unzipping the bag and rummaging through it.

Sam crosses over to the dresser and looks down at the gleaming surface. 'Hey, what did you do with the note?'

'It should be taped to the back of the frame,' Mia replies absently as she slides off the clothes she wore on the train.

Sam lifts the picture frame from the dresser, smiling at the scene pictured there. 'John really was a good-looking guy, wasn't he?'

'He would be so happy to hear you say that,' Mia says, her voice muffled as she pulls her sweater over her head.

Turning the frame over, Sam removes the note that's written on thick cream paper. He unfolds it and reads it again – wonder spreading over him just like it did the first time Mia showed him the note last year.

Hullo, Mia! (And Sam, if I've done my job correctly!)
   If you're finding this note, hopefully it means that you couldn't find me (although we all know how terrible Mia is at finding misplaced things!). And if you can't find me, then maybe I've finally, finally passed over. Because, let me assure you, you both mean too much to me to ghost you! (Mia, did I use that right?)
   First of all, Sam, my deepest apologies for trying to drive you crazy. If I had any access to money, I'd reimburse you for the speaker you ruined. I hope I

didn't rattle you too terribly with the singing. I will say, though, the bananas and the pens were Mia's idea. Be mad at her if you want. Oh! And your missing socks are on the top of the wardrobe in your room.

Mia, I can't begin to tell you what it meant to me to have your company over the last week. It's been horribly lonely all these years, and I do feel like I missed out on many hilarious haunting opportunities during the decades I was stuck here. After seeing how much fun it was to mess with Sam (again, Sam, so sorry about that) I realized how much enjoyment I eschewed by trying to be an 'honourable ghost' all those years. Thanks for steering me in the right direction, Mia.

Sam, you had better take care of Mia, or I will send someone back from the other side to haunt you all over again. Just kidding! I know you think the world of her. I hope the two of you find so much joy and happiness together. Sorry I didn't get to say goodbye in person as it were, but I'm certain you'll find this note, and the glasses I left by the picture your mum found. Mia, they look better on you than they ever did on me. Sam, you keep your paws off them! You don't have the cheekbones to pull them off. But seriously, all my love.

Don't ever take each other for granted.

JHH

Sam folds the note and replaces it in its pocket at the back of the frame, setting the picture back down on the dresser. He can't help the smile that creeps over his face as he looks at John grinning back at him from the picture.

Meddlesome though he might have been, Sam has to give the man a lot of credit.

'Sam, will you zip me up?' Mia comes up beside him, turning so her back is to him. He tugs the zip up the smooth curve of her back, his thumbs brushing her soft skin. He can't stop himself from bending forward and placing a kiss at the base of her neck before he releases her. Mia turns around and sets her travel jewellery case on the dresser. 'Thank you.'

'My pleasure,' Sam says without hesitation. And he means it. There's nothing he wouldn't do for the girl – his *wife*! – standing at his side. He'll never get over the fact that Mia found the courage to let him back into her heart.

'We can't dawdle,' Mia is saying. 'Mum will start losing her mind. There's too much to do, and you know how she gets.' She flips open the case and places the large hoops she was wearing inside. Lifting her grandmother's earrings from one of the compartments, she carefully fastens them in her ears. 'How do I look?'

'Amazing,' Sam says. 'Incredible. Spectacularly wonderful.'

Mia giggles. 'You and your words.' She slides her arms around his neck and goes up on tiptoe, smiling at Sam. 'I love you, Sam.'

'And I love you, Mia,' Sam replies. 'I always will.'

Mia lifts up a little higher to kiss him and Sam's eyes slide closed. He soaks up this moment rich with the gift of Mia's love.

Hand in hand, they head downstairs and out of the

cottage. On the path up to the main house, Mia says, 'I miss Aunt Gertie. It seems weird not to have her here, toddling about.'

'Well, you promised to make her biscuits,' Sam reassures her. 'That would have made her very happy.' He looks up at the towering house and smiles. 'And something tells me that Aunt Gertie hasn't gone far. As she always said, this house is too old not to be haunted, and I'd bet Aunt Gertie has whipped all the other ghosts into shape.'

Mia snuggles into his side as they head towards the house. 'I bet you're right.'

Holly Whitmore grew up overseas, spending her school years in Europe and summers in the United States. She always dreamed of being a writer and now lives with her family on the Front Range in Colorado where she writes immersive stories about real people with real struggles who ultimately find their happily ever after. Holly also writes fantasy and romance books under the name J. L. Kodanko.

On a station platform, with nothing to read,
and a four-hour train journey stretching ahead of him...

That's where the story began for Penguin founder Allen Lane.
With only 'shabby reprints of shoddy novels' on offer,
he resolved to make better books for readers everywhere.

By the time his train pulled into London, the idea was formed.
He would bring the best writing, in stylish and affordable
formats, to everyone. His books would be sold in bookstores,
stationers and tobacconists, for no more than the price
of a ten-pack of cigarettes.

And on every book would be a Penguin, a bird with a certain
'dignified flippancy', and a friendly invitation to anyone who
wished to spend their time reading.

In 1935, the first ten Penguin paperbacks were published.
Just a year later, three million Penguins had made their
way onto our shelves.

Reading was changed forever.

—

A lot has changed since 1935, including Penguin, but in the
most important ways we're still the same. We still believe that
books and reading are for everyone. And we still believe that
whether you're seeking an afternoon's escape, a vigorous debate
or a soothing bedtime story, all possibilities open with a book.

Whoever you are, whatever you're looking for,
you can find it with Penguin.